A
Daughter's
Promise

RONE Award nominated author Lynette Rees is a former writing therapist, tutor and mentor. She has written in many genres and has seen a huge success in her self-published books. *The Workhouse Waif* hit the Amazon Kindle bestseller list and was No. 1 in 'Victorian Historical Romance'. It is the first in a series of orphan sagas, published by Quercus in the UK.

Also by Lynette Rees

The Matchgirl
The Cobbler's Wife
The Workhouse Waif

A Daughter's Promise

Lynette Rees

Quercus

First published in Great Britain in 2018 by Quercus
This paperback edition first published in Great Britain in 2020 by

Quercus Editions Ltd
Carmelite House
50 Victoria Embankment
London EC4Y 0DZ

An Hachette UK company

A CIP catalogue record for this book is available
from the British Library

PB ISBN 978 1 52940 387 9
EB ISBN 978 1 78747 290 7

10 9 8 7 6 5 4

Typeset by Jouve (UK), Milton Keynes

Printed and bound in Great Britain by Clays Ltd, Elcograf S.p.A.

MIX
Paper from
responsible sources
FSC® C104740
www.fsc.org

Papers used by Quercus are from well-managed forests and
other responsible sources.

There is nothing as strong and protective as a mother's love. I dedicate this book to my own dear mother who over the years has been the biggest fan and promoter of my books; she has the softest heart and the kindest soul. Thank you for your belief in me, Mam. I love you so much.

Chapter One

Whitechapel, London, 1888

There was a short series of sharp knocks on the front door of one of the houses in the middle of the long red-brick street. Cowering behind the curtains, Kathryn Flynn glanced at her younger brothers and sisters and said, 'Ssh, we have to pretend we're not in as we ain't got the rent money . . .'

Wide-eyed, they stared up at her, three-year-old Rosie tugging at her sister's skirts, her bottom lip trembling. Oh dear, was she about to cry? Scooping the little mite up into her arms, Kathryn hugged her tightly to her breast, planting a kiss on her forehead.

Another series of knocks almost rattled the door off its hinges, causing Kathryn's heart to pound with fear. They couldn't carry on like this for much longer, but if she opened the door she knew they would be flung out on to the pavement outside with all their belongings. Fergus O'Shay had been around to the house several times for the rent this week and his patience wouldn't hold out much longer.

She was expecting another series of knocks when she heard his voice outside. 'Any idea where the Flynn family are, Jimmy?' he asked gruffly.

'None whatsoever,' a familiar male voice answered. 'I ain't seen them, Mr O'Shay.'

The rent man let out a loud harrumph as if he didn't believe his ears. 'Well tell them if you see them, if they don't pay up by the end of the week I'm bringing in my men to turf them out of 'ere. I've given them enough chances as it is!' Then, raising his voice as if they were meant to hear him inside, he said, 'In fact, if they don't pay up it'll be all the better for me: I can get a new family in to replace 'em. There's plenty would love to live in that house!'

Then they heard departing footsteps as his hobnailed boots hit the pavement. Kathryn let out a long sigh of relief just as Rosie began to cry. 'Sssh, little one,' she soothed.

'Has the nasty man gone now, Kathryn?' her five-year-old brother, Damon, asked.

'Yes, he's gone now, kids. Go and wash yer hands and I'll make you some supper.' The children scurried through the room into the back scullery; Kathryn heard the sounds of them splashing around and arguing with each other as they pushed one another out of the way to try to get finished up and get eating as quickly as they could.

There was another knock at the door, causing Kathryn's

heart to feel as though it had ceased beating. Had O'Shay returned?

'Kathryn!' a male voice called out. 'It's me, Jimmy.'

'Oh, thank goodness. I thought it was the rent collector come back to throw us out,' she said, unbolting the heavy wooden front door.

Jimmy cocked her a grin, lowering his head as he entered the low-beamed room. His short dark-brown hair was tousled from where he'd recently removed his cap, which he was now clutching in his hand. His chocolate-brown eyes glittered as they usually did when he was pleased to see her. Kathryn had known him since she was a young girl, and it was only lately she'd realised how tall he'd become and how broad his shoulders were – he was no longer the young boy she'd known as her neighbour all these years and a friend of the family, but a young man. 'Are things really that bad, then?'

'I'm afraid they are, Jimmy. Ma's poorly upstairs and Mr Daley has laid me off from his slop workshop for a few days – he says he might have more work for me in a couple of weeks, but what do I do until then?'

Jimmy shook his head. 'That's awful, Kathryn. Is there anything I can do to help?'

She shrugged her shoulders. 'This is our mess. Only we can get ourselves out of it.'

Jimmy gazed deep into her eyes. 'I only wish there was some way I could help you all . . .'

'Thank you.' Her priority was her family. They'd fallen on

hard times since Pa had died. He'd been the sole breadwinner and once he was gone, taken with consumption, the responsibility had fallen on her shoulders as the eldest child. She turned to the kids. 'Hurry up, you lot!' Then, looking back at Jimmy, said, 'I'll think of something. I have got to get our 'eads above water somehow.'

Jimmy blinked. 'What's happened at the slop shop then?'

She drew in a breath and let it out again. 'It's the sweater. He informed Mr Daley last week that he's cutting our orders, reckons we're not working fast enough.'

'But you're already working long hours, sometimes up to fifteen hours a day as it is!' Jimmy said in astonishment.

'And the rest. I even did an eighteen-hour day last week to catch up on the orders. We have to pay for our own materials an' all. Mr Daley supplies them and we pay him.'

Jimmy's eyes narrowed to slits. 'You don't think he's pulling a fast one, do you?'

''Ow'd you mean?' She put her hands on her hips.

'Mr Daley, I mean. Is he overcharging you for the materials?'

Kathryn relaxed her pose. 'No, I don't think so. He's always charged the same, but the sweater says the slop shop 'ave dropped their prices, so there's more demand and while we need to work 'arder, we get paid less.'

Jimmy touched her shoulder lightly, then gave it a reassuring pat. 'It can't be easy for you, Kathryn. What's happened to your ma, anyhow?'

'A touch of bronchitis. 'Aven't even got enough money to pay a doctor to diagnose her, but I think that's what it is. Mr Daley's wife gave me a bottle of brown medicine for her, which is helping a little.'

Suddenly, the kids burst back into the room. 'Jimmy!' they shouted collectively, pleased to see him.

He bent down and scooped Rosie up into his arms. 'Great to see you, kids! I know I promised to tell you all about that time I saw that big ship come sailing into dock all the way from India . . .'

'Yes, tell us, Jimmy, tell us!' Damon and Shaun were enthralled by his every word as Jimmy explained what the ship looked like and all about those weather-beaten sailors who brought exotic treasures from distant shores. There were precious jewels in every colour of the rainbow and silks and satins so fine they were only fit for a princess or Queen Victoria herself! The children stood there with wide eyes and open mouths, spellbound by his tale, while only Kathryn guessed he was embellishing it just for them.

'When yer going to take us to Vicky Park again?' twelve-year-old Shaun asked, tugging on Jimmy's jacket.

'I want to sail a boat that looks like that big ship you spoke about,' said Damon. Last time they'd all gone there, Jimmy had whittled a boat of sorts out of a piece of fallen oak and sailed it on the lake, much to the delight of Shaun and Damon, though Mags, their older sister, had stood there looking thoroughly bored. At thirteen years of age, Mags was turning into quite the young lady, though she couldn't seem to see how she attracted glances from the opposite sex. She was fixated with her freckles, referring to them as ugly, but her red hair and hazel eyes were simply stunning. Kathryn had to constantly reassure her that there was nothing wrong with her.

'I wish I was as good-looking as you, Kathryn,' she'd often say.

Kathryn would always reply that she was lovely as she was and beauty came from within, but for some reason Mags didn't realise how beautiful she really was.

'Please, Jimmy?' Shaun asked again.

'Oh, Shaun, leave Jimmy alone, will you?' Kathryn snapped.

'It's all right, truly it is.' Jimmy turned to Shaun and the other kids. 'Yes, of course I'll take you, maybe on Saturday morning, if that's all right?' He looked at Kathryn.

'Yes, that's really kind of yer. I'm sorry I sounded so sharp, I'm just so tired – I was up 'alf the night finishing off stitching some waistcoats for the Daleys. It's the last lot of work from them.' She pointed to the pile, neatly folded in a wooden box in the corner of the room.

Jimmy picked one up and inspected it. 'They're right fancy, these are, gal. Such fine stitching an' all . . .'

Kathryn smiled. 'It were 'ard though. You try stitching by candlelight, it plays havoc with yer eyes.'

'You need to rest more, Kathryn,' Jimmy said gently.

'But what chance do I 'ave? I've got a lot on me plate as it is.'

Jimmy smiled. 'I'll send Dorrie over later. She can look after the kids and your ma – she won't mind. Meanwhile, I'm taking you out for some pie and mash. You look like you could do with feeding up, my gal!'

Kathryn nodded and smiled. She liked Jimmy's younger sister and was grateful for the help she often provided. As the kids scrambled to get seated at the old scuffed table, with its almost threadbare linen cloth, she went off to the scullery, returning with some bits of crusty bread dipped in dripping.

When the children saw it, they all groaned. Before Kathryn had a chance to say anything, Mags reprimanded, 'Be thankful for this little we have, kids. Some ain't so lucky as us.'

Kathryn patted her appreciatively on the shoulder as she sat at the table with the others. Kathryn rarely had time to join them and she didn't intend to now that Jimmy was going to take her out. She would keep some scraps of her meal for the kids as a treat for them. She hated people buying things for her, but Jimmy enjoyed helping out. He had regular work on a market stall and even if he was short of money himself, he often arrived with leftover vegetables that some in the West End would have turned their noses up at, but as he often said, 'Cook 'em with a bit of onion, some leftover scrag end o' lamb and yer'll 'ave a nice tasty soup that'll keep yer going fer days!'

While the children had their heads down eating, Jimmy slipped away to fetch Dorrie. They returned a quarter of an hour later; Dorrie's face was flushed pink from rushing, her brown knitted shawl pulled tightly around her shoulders. At sixteen years old she was turning into a fine-looking young girl, though small in stature for her age. She was sensible and that's what Kathryn liked about her. Her chestnut hair fell in ringlets on her shoulders and her face was peppered with a sprinkling of freckles.

The temperature had dipped. It was only September, but the nights were drawing in and coolness filled the air. At least for the time being, the family had a fire in the grate and some sort of food in their bellies. But for how much longer?

'Thanks for coming over, Dorrie.' Kathryn smiled.

'It's all right. I weren't doing anything anyway.' Dorrie removed her shawl and hung it on a peg behind the door; it wasn't the first time the girl had helped out. 'How's yer ma, Kathryn?'

'She's a little better, thanks. I was given a bottle of medicine for her. Can yer feed her a spoonful later? I'm keeping her well propped up with pillows to ease her breathing and if yer can take up some broth, I've left it in a tin mug in the kitchen with a spoon.'

Dorrie nodded. 'Of course I can, ducks.'

Reassured the family was in safe hands, Kathryn tied the ribbons of her bonnet and wrapped her shawl around her shoulders, ready to depart with Jimmy. At least she had a good friend she could talk to about her troubles. She pecked her siblings on the cheek to say goodnight and made her way outside.

*

Darkness was fading as they walked along the shady alleyways and courts. People spilled out on to the streets. Often in this area of Whitechapel there were several families holed up in one house, and that was if they were lucky. Many had to pay a penny a night, if they could afford it, to bed down at a doss house. The ones for a penny a night usually attracted the most undesirable of people. By the morning, some found their possessions had been stolen and sometimes the lodging-house owner was in on it as he got a share of the spoils.

Kathryn shivered. *There but for the grace of God, go I.* At least the Flynn family had a roof over their heads. For the time being, she reminded herself.

They turned down one alleyway and Kathryn felt something scamper past, close by, forcing her into Jimmy's path. He grabbed hold of her. 'Are you all right?'

She held her breath, feeling his heart beat beside hers as she was locked in his embrace. 'Something ran past me, dunno what it was, but it scared the living daylights out of me!' she yelped.

'It's probably a small dog or cat,' he reassured her, letting go.

Somehow she doubted that very much, but she always felt protected when he was around. It was more likely to have been a rodent of some kind, and she guessed he was only not saying as much so as not to scare her. This was a very dirty, rowdy area. As they reached the end of the alley, they turned on to another street that was better lit, the gas lamps reflecting a golden glow on to the people below, who were congregating outside a pub called The Horse and Harness. The smell of gin and beery fumes hit Kathryn full force, causing her to gag. Somewhere inside the pub someone was tinkling the ivories while a female voice sang beautifully, causing many shouts and cheers from the men.

A strong smell of cologne wafted towards Kathryn, and she turned to see a girl around the same age as herself, dressed in gaudy clothing. The neckline of her dress plunged far lower than was appropriate. Her face was heavily rouged from what Kathryn could make out from the street-light. The girl stared at Jimmy.

'Fancy a fumble, ducks?' she asked him in a cheeky manner, hoisting the skirts of her dress to reveal a red-frilled petticoat and slender ankles. He chuckled.

'Sorry, my dear.' He tipped his cap. 'I'm already in female company.'

''Ere I bet she won't show you a good time like I would!' she bellowed after them.

'What a bleedin' nerve!' Kathryn said, feeling most affronted. 'How can someone stoop so low?'

Jimmy's face took on a serious expression. 'It's necessity, Kathryn. Few choose to live like that, but they make a darn sight more money from prostituting themselves than sweating for some of the pigs around 'ere . . .'

'Like me, you mean?' She tossed back her dark curls as a shiver skittered down her spine as his words hit home.

'Not you in particular, love,' he said kindly, 'but people like yourself are paid so poorly. That girl, Sally . . .'

'Aw, so you know 'er, do you?'

'I do indeed. She's a good girl gorn bad. She used to work at the match factory in Bow, but she got laid off though for some trifling misdemeanour or other. She has a young baby to look after . . .' he said sadly.

Kathryn stopped mid-step, her hands flying to her mouth. When she'd digested what he said, she looked at him. 'Oh, that poor girl . . .'

'So don't look down on her. She told me she's doing a lot better for herself, and the young baby – at least he's got a roof over his head and food in his belly. She looks well-fed, doesn't she?'

'I suppose so. Is she happy at what she does though?'

'She told me she is. And no, I know what you're thinking . . . No, I ain't been with her even though she's offered it to me on a plate several times. This is just off her neck of the woods though, she usually 'angs around the Ten Bells pub on the corner of Commercial Street. Not sure why she's 'ere tonight.'

'I was just thinking, that's all. How much do you reckon Sally earns doing that – can't be much, can it?'

Jimmy chuckled. 'Put it this way, she probably earns far more in one night than you do working a seventeen- or eighteen-hour day at that sweatshop . . . She told me it's considerably eased the money problems at home. Don't like to see a young girl put herself in danger like that, but yer have to admit it might be better than the workhouse for her and the little 'un.'

Kathryn cleared her throat. 'Who cares for her baby when she's out on the street?'

'Her next-door neighbour – think she probably pays her something for her help, though.'

Kathryn nodded. Remembering the rat, she glanced this way and that at the mere thought of it coming anywhere near, but thankfully by the time they'd got to the other side of the alleyway, there was no encounter whatsoever. 'Yer look worried, gel,' Jimmy said. 'What's up?'

'It's this Whitechapel murderer business. It scares me 'alf to death, Jimmy . . .'

'Well by all accounts, he's only goes after bad gels, not good 'uns, so you've got nothing to worry about!' He chuckled.

'Please don't make light of it, Jimmy. No one knows who's going to be next after the murders of those two poor women.'

'Aye, I know, Kathryn. I'm sorry. I shouldn't have laughed. But sometimes if I don't laugh, I'll cry. It's me being silly, that's all.'

She shivered. 'The newspapers are calling it the "Autumn of Terror".'

Women and girls in the area didn't dare walk home alone at night, they were that petrified, even some of the working girls tried to stick together. And there was a vigilante group of men set up to track down the killer; they pledged they'd catch him at all costs.

Kathryn guessed maybe the competition at The Ten Bells was too much tonight, so the girl had come here to seek out a new patch. After all, she had to earn a living like everyone else in the East End. The thought gave her an idea, although she could barely contemplate it.

Chapter Two

The steamy atmosphere of the pie-and-mash shop hit them full force as they entered. The delicious smells wafting her way made Kathryn's stomach growl with hunger. It was pretty packed out with customers, but Jimmy spotted a recently vacated table in the corner. He guided her through with his hand placed on the small of her back as if she were a precious piece of porcelain.

They took their seats and immediately a short, portly, middle-aged woman with her salt-and-pepper hair drawn up into a bun arrived at their table. Her greasy mottled skin made Kathryn think she was someone with poor hygiene, and when she opened her mouth to speak, she noticed her teeth were rotten stumps.

'Whatcha both want? I've got meat and potato or chicken pies on the menu tonight with mashed potatoes and peas,' she said, acerbically.

Jimmy grinned and glanced at Kathryn.

'Meat and potato, please,' she said to the woman.

'I'll 'ave the same, and bring us a jug of ginger beer if you will. We're dining like kings and queens tonight!'

Within minutes, a tray containing two plates of steaming pie and mash appeared at the table, complete with a jug of ginger beer and two glasses.

'Thank you,' Kathryn said, before Jimmy had a chance to be clever again. The woman smiled, totally ignoring Jimmy, and went about her business of clearing up a nearby table.

'Thank you for this, Jimmy,' Kathryn enthused. 'Would you mind if I kept some back to take home for the kids?'

She watched as he chewed well and then swallowed. 'I do mind, indeed. Now eat what's on yer plate. I shall buy some to take back for the kids.'

She hadn't been expecting that; she would get a full belly herself and so would the kids tomorrow. 'I feel really bad you spending all your hard-earned money on us lot.' She poked her pie with her fork, not really getting stuck in.

'Don't be daft. You can pay me back some day – maybe you can make me something to wear like those toffs prance around about in!' he joked. 'Now come on, don't be maudlin, missus, eat up afore it gets cold!'

She did as she was told, savouring each meaty mouthful, unable to remember when she'd last eaten a meal so satisfying.

'So,' Jimmy said, filling up her glass with ginger beer, then topping up his own. 'What are you going to do about your situation if you won't accept any help from me? I could loan you the rent money and maybe by next week you'll get more work from Mr Daley . . .' He trailed off as if he realised that wouldn't be the case at all.

She chewed her bottom lip, then set down her knife and fork on her plate and took a sip from her glass, before resting it on the table in front of her. 'I honestly don't know. We've been living hand to mouth for weeks now, avoiding Mr O'Shay. To be fair, he did allow me some grace as I hadn't paid last week's rent, but now I've got that to pay along with this week's as well. What a mess I've got meself into!'

Jimmy shook his head, then looked into her eyes. 'Look, you don't want to be thrown out on to the street, not with your mother being so unwell. Please take the money from me, Kathryn . . .'

Quite unexpectedly, her eyes moistened with tears. 'I'm sorry, I can't.' She sniffed. 'I would never be able to pay you back – it would only add to the debt I already owe, can't you see that?' She looked at him through misted eyes.

He nodded. 'But if you and I were one, I would share the debt. What was mine would be yours.' He stretched out his arm and took her hand across the table, holding it to his lips as he caught her gaze and planted a kiss on it. She saw the love light in his eyes in that moment. 'Marry me, Kathryn,' he said with great conviction.

She held her breath; it should have been all she'd ever wanted. He was so handsome, but she'd known him forever and she couldn't put all her troubles on to him when he had troubles of his own to deal with. What if he was doing it out of pity for her? She knew he cared deeply, but she had to be sure about that. She shook her head vehemently. It wasn't what she wanted right now. Maybe in the future, but she didn't want to marry for the sake of it.

'Well, if that is the case,' he said, letting out a regretful sigh and releasing her hand, 'yer know I'll always be your friend. At least if you are thrown out, please come to my home – Dorrie and Nick wouldn't mind. Since our parents died, the 'ouse just ain't been the same. You and the girls could bunk in wiv me sister and the boys could sleep in wiv me and Nick, and your ma could 'ave the other bedroom till you all got sorted.'

Kathryn remembered her ma telling her that Jimmy's parents had died and that he'd struggled to bring up the kids on his own. She squeezed his hand. 'You're so very kind, Jimmy, but hopefully, it shan't come to that.'

He looked at her blankly as she carried on eating her food. She had an idea. *Pride comes before a fall*, a little voice spoke softly to her, but she chose to ignore it.

All was quiet outside The Horse and Harness on their way back home and there was no sign of Sally whatsoever. Kathryn guessed she must have gone home with someone or returned home herself if she couldn't find any work, and she hoped the poor girl wouldn't get accosted by someone. She realised that in that line of work girls often got roughed up by the men they picked up and some even lost their lives because of it.

'You're quiet,' Jimmy said, as he wrapped his arm around her and led her through the same alleyway where she'd earlier thought she'd encountered a rat.

'Aw, it's nothing at all. Just got a lot on my mind, that's all, thinking about where I can look for work . . .'

'As long as that's all it is,' he said, giving her hand a reassuring squeeze.

Jimmy left her at her front door and stooped to plant a kiss on her cheek, which was usual for him. He seemed none the worse for her turning down his proposal, but maybe he wasn't showing it.

'Thank you, Jimmy, you're a true friend,' she said, as she carried the bowl of pie and mash into the house. She'd warm it up tomorrow for the kids with some extra veg and gravy; it would make a right tasty meal for them. Ma wasn't up to eating big meals at the moment, so it would be broth for her again. Kathryn would have to return the bowl to the shop tomorrow.

She closed the door behind her. All was in darkness, so she used a taper from the mantelpiece to catch a flame from the fire in the grate to light a candle on the windowsill. After placing the bowl of food in the cool pantry, she sat back in an armchair by the fire, watching the flickering shadows on the wall as she thought about what she'd do next. She couldn't believe the train of her thoughts; it was what no decent girl should ever consider doing. She had a pretty dress upstairs that showed her off to her best advantage and a best bonnet with artificial roses on it too. If she pulled down the sleeves of her dress a little it would reveal her décolletage. She never wore any perfume, but when she'd earned some money she could buy some cheap cologne and maybe a little rouge as well. What would this do to her reputation, though? She'd be shop-soiled goods for the rest of her life and people would never see her in the same light again if they found out. And Jimmy? He'd be mortified.

No, I mustn't think this way. It's silly, she chided herself. *There are better ways to earn a living* . . . But for the time being she couldn't think of a single one where she could get paid right away. She'd already tried asking around local businesses in the area. Jobs were hard to come by as there were now so many immigrants in the area – the Jews from Eastern Europe and more Irish families. People were crowded enough as it was. She'd even seen a group of Jewish tailors meeting an agent in the street where he was assigning jobs to local sweatshops; a fight had broken out and fists had flown. The men spoke in a strange tongue that was alien to her ears.

As she took the candle in its holder and climbed the stone stairs to bed, she sighed deeply. What on earth was she supposed to do?

'Kathryn . . .' a weak voice tried to call out. *Ma!*

Quietly, so as not to wake the kids, Kathryn went to attend

to her mother. 'Are you all right, Ma?' She stood in the door-way, the light from the candle illuminating her mother's now gaunt and pale face.

'Yes, I feel a little better, thank you. Dorrie gave me my medicine and she brought me a bowl of broth – she slipped back home once the kids went to bed. This time I managed to eat all my food, so I feel I have a little more strength . . .'

'That's good, Ma.' Kathryn felt encouraged and she walked over to her mother's bed, sitting on the side of it.

''Ere darlin', this might solve our problems for a while. I 'eard O'Shay knocking again earlier and what he shouted in the street . . .' She pressed something small into the palm of Kathryn's hand.

Kathryn stared at her mother's gold ring, which was nestled in her open palm. A feeling of horror swept over her entire body. 'No, Ma!' She shook her head vehemently. 'Yer can't sell your wedding ring. It's all yer've left of Pa – I won't allow it.'

'Don't fret so, Kathryn,' her mother soothed. 'I was think-ing that maybe you could take it to the pawn shop. They'll keep it for a week and maybe in that time you can get some work and we'll buy it back from Mr Goldstein.'

Kathryn shook her head. 'No, Ma. What good would that do anyhow? I'd probably only earn enough to buy it back or pay the rent and then we'd have an awful decision to make.' Taking a deep breath, she prepared to tell the biggest lie of her life. 'There's no problem anyhow. When Jimmy took me to the pie-and-mash shop they said they needed someone to help out serving at the tables there, so I've got a few days' work at least.' She crossed the fingers of one hand behind her back and closed her eyes. *Oh Lord, forgive me for lying to yer, Ma! But I promise I will do everything in my power to keep our heads above water.* She vowed to pull them all out of poverty.

'That's wonderful news.' Her mother sounded pleased, making Kathryn feel as guilty as sin.

Opening her eyes, Kathryn asked. 'Now, can I get you anything, Ma?'

'Just pour me a glass of water from the jug, then I'm going back to sleep, now I can rest easy,' her mother said. Her face looked at peace. Rightly or wrongly, at least her ma now felt better about things. Kathryn poured the glass of water and helped her sit up to drink it, then settled her back down for the night. As soon as she became aware of her gentle snores, Kathryn sprang into action.

She quickly selected a pretty floral dress from the wardrobe, being careful not to disturb Mags and Rosie, as she shared a bedroom with them. Now where was her best bonnet? She fought to think. Ah, she remembered: it was under the bed in a box. She knelt down and pulled out the hat box and took it downstairs along with the dress, where she changed, pulling the sleeves down to show herself off to her best advantage. No decent woman she knew would even think of walking the streets alone at this time of the night, but needs must. Maybe she could just do it the once until the Daleys got more work for her.

The dress looked very nice on her as it skimmed her curves. She appeared more womanly, somehow. Kathryn pinned up her hair, which had earlier been loose on her shoulders, and wrapped her shawl around her to keep out the cold; it would also serve to hide her cleavage along the way. She stood in front of the over-the-mantel mirror and pinched her cheeks to redden them and moistened her lips with her tongue. She hardly recognised the harlot she saw in front of her. Quietly, she slipped out of the house, hoping she wouldn't encounter someone she knew. But what other option did she have if she wanted to keep a roof over all their heads?

Chapter Three

Kathryn's pulse pounded as she left the house, her mouth dry with apprehension. She glanced up and down the dimly lit street. A man and his friends were chatting on the doorstep a few doors down, a baby was crying somewhere in the distance and, further away, a dog barked. She hoped Ma and the kids wouldn't wake while she was on her mission.

With every step she took, she feared she was being followed as her footsteps echoed in the inky darkness, but when she turned, there was no one there. By the time she'd reached The Horse and Harness, she thought her heart would burst out of her chest. The old pub was a little quieter than it had been earlier, but she heard the odd laugh and shout from its interior. A man in a bowler hat, who looked a little smart for the area in a well-tailored jacket and trousers, stood outside. *Maybe he was some sort of foreman or manager,* she thought. Should she approach him? There was no sign of Sally or any other woman around right now.

The man, who she guessed was probably in his thirties, took in her form with his intense gaze.

'Fancy buying me a drink, sir?' The words tumbled out before she was even ready to say them. A new kind of boldness swept over her, stimulated by her need to improve the family finances.

He pushed back the brim of his bowler hat with a sweep of his hand and gazed curiously at her, studying her beneath the golden glow of the lamplight. 'Now aren't you a pretty young thing? I haven't seen you around here before. What's your name, miss?'

Thinking on her feet, as she didn't intend to give her real name, she replied, 'Miss Bella Cartwright, at your service.'

He chuckled. 'And what would *Miss Bella Cartwright* like to drink?' His blue eyes twinkled with mischief.

'I always drink gin!' she replied. 'With a little lemon, if yer don't mind.' It was a lie as she hadn't even tried alcohol before in her life, but it was the first drink that came to mind – Mrs Daley liked a tipple when she had finished her day's work.

'Come this way then, Miss Bella.' He took her by the arm and guided her inside.

Kathryn swallowed hard as she stepped over the threshold. Several men were stood around the bar drinking from pewter tankards, chatting away merrily, while in the corner two men were in company with a woman wearing a gaudy low-cut red dress. They appeared to be squabbling over which one was to have her. To Kathryn, the woman looked half-cut, as her eyelids lowered and she lay back in her seat, her head resting to one side. In another life this woman would have been quite the beauty. Her lustrous dark locks cascaded over her shoulders and a small beauty spot bloomed on her left cheek. But here, drunk in the pub, the life she led was obvious. As soon as the woman's violet eyes flicked open, she sat bolt upright on the wooden settle, appearing to sober up quickly. Her eyes narrowed as she bellowed, 'Who the hell is *she*?'

Kathryn's cheeks flamed with embarrassment as she glanced around to ensure there was no one there who might recognise her, but thankfully they all appeared to be strangers to her.

'Mind your own business, Jess,' the gentleman who was in Kathryn's company said. 'She's with me.' His words made Kathryn feel warm inside. Then to Kathryn he whispered, 'Jess is a little jealous of the beautiful competition in here tonight . . .'

The woman shot him a glance; they obviously knew one another quite well and Kathryn guessed it was because the man was a regular at the pub.

He led her to a quiet table at the back of the room. Kathryn's heart beat a tattoo, and he left to order the drinks at the bar, returning in no time with a tankard of beer for himself and a small glass of gin for her. 'I'm sorry, they had no lemon,' he said.

'That's all right. I've tried it neat before,' she lied. She waited until he'd seated himself and had begun supping his pint before she took a sip of the gin. It was dreadful – so strong and bitter! She'd never tasted anything so awful in all her life and to her horror she began to cough and splutter.

The stranger smiled as he drew in close to her. 'I'm guessing you've never tasted alcohol before, then? Now what's a pretty young girl like yourself doing in a place like this, accosting strange men?'

She smiled too and reckoned she'd better tell him the truth about how work at the slop shop had dried up. The whole sad tale came tumbling out and when she'd finished he nodded thoughtfully. 'Now I have an idea that might help you and it would involve working up West. That's where the nice gentlemen are with good manners. Mayfair or Knightsbridge . . .'

'B . . . but . . .' How on earth could she get up West of a night? She didn't have enough money for that.

He grabbed hold of her hand across the table. 'What's the matter? You look shocked.'

'I am – that thought had never even entered me 'ead, sir. I just wanted to make some quick money to get myself back on my feet and hopefully back to work in a normal manner.'

He chuckled, then let go of her hand. 'Look, if you do what I have lined up for you, you'll make plenty of money and more, and you won't ever want to return to sewing waist-coats and petticoats for a living ever again! And I can supply the transport and accommodation. I'll buy you some fancy new dresses, too. You won't want for anything.' He dipped his hand into his inside jacket pocket and extracted something she couldn't see, then pressed a shiny sovereign into the palm of her hand. 'Take that as a down payment,' he said. 'What do you say, *Miss Bella*?' He stressed her name as though he knew it wasn't her given name at all.

Staring at the coin in her hand, she nodded slowly, open-mouthed. How badly she needed that money: if she didn't take it, there'd be no food in the house for the rest of the week. She couldn't bear the thought of her brothers and sisters going starving. And although Ma barely ate enough these days to keep a bird alive, Kathryn knew she had to keep her mother's strength up. Slowly, Kathryn lifted her eyes to meet with the man's. 'But, aren't you very trusting, sir? I could run off with this and you'd never see me again.'

He smiled, his eyes glittering with amusement, then looked at her in earnest. 'For some reason, I do trust you. Look, this is a serious proposition. My work leads me to the West End for trading purposes. We could rent a room there. It would profit us both. All you'd have to do would be to act as a companion for wealthy clientele.'

A shiver skittered along Kathryn's spine. A room? 'But what would be in it for you, sir?' The thought of being given the opportunity to be anywhere near the West End sent a frisson of excitement coursing through her veins as she imagined all the finery and luxury before her very eyes, in contrast with the gloom and doom of the East End of the city.

For the first time she noticed a gleam in his eyes; she didn't know what it meant but maybe he was as excited by this as she was. 'It would be a money-making venture for us, my dear sweet Bella. There would be perks for us both . . .' Then he put his hand on her knee and patted it. Was he expecting more? What was it he really wanted from her? It seemed to her he wanted some sort of attractive female companionship. If she could provide that and be paid for the privilege, that was all right in her book.

She took another sip of gin; it was starting to warm her up and she was getting used to the taste.

'Come on, drink up. I'll buy you another,' her benefactor said heartily.

'But I don't even know your name, sir?'

'Just call me "Squire". That's all you need to know for now.'

She swallowed down the drink that was now burning the back of her throat. For a while at least, it was blotting out her troubles. 'Squire' was intriguing her, but he seemed guarded in some way, as if there was a big part of him she wasn't seeing right now.

Kathryn had no idea how long they'd been in the pub for, but she'd now had three or four drinks, and her eyelids were growing heavy.

Squire helped her to her feet. 'Now it's bedtime for you, young lady,' he said in a fatherly fashion. 'Come along, I'm taking you home. Now where did you say you lived?'

She explained the directions as best she could, slurring her words all the while.

'I know of the street.'

He held her close to his chest as he pushed his way out of the pub. She thought she heard whispers from all around, but maybe she imagined it. People were staring at them, their faces becoming one big blur. She knew they watched them together, but she no longer cared; she was just glad he was able to walk her home. For one, she was unsteady on her feet, and for another, who knew who she might encounter on her walk home alone?

Squire was a perfect gentleman until they got to the alleyway, where he pushed her up against a wall and began fervently kissing her neck. Her heartbeat hastened; he was handsome and she wondered for a moment if he was married.

'I don't want to despoil you, Kathryn,' he murmured. 'We'll get that large payment and then we'll be quids in. For the time being though, we can have a little fun, can't we?'

She giggled, knowing she had plenty of money to pay up for this week's rent and what was owed and even a little left over to purchase food. 'Yes,' she said. A heady feeling of desire coursed through her body as he closed the space between them and his lips hovered inches from her own.

Her breath came in short bursts as he kissed her firmly on the mouth, taking her by surprise. Not even Jimmy had ever kissed her like that. Her feelings were belying how she should behave when alone with a stranger, as strong emotions plundered her body, feelings she didn't even recognise as her own, which might carry her away. Remembering her reputation before she did something she shouldn't, breathlessly, she said, 'I think we should wait . . . I'm not that sort of girl.'

He drew away and kissed her forehead.

'You're right of course, my beautiful Bella,' he said, standing back from her. She could see the twinkle in his eyes from beneath the lamplight. He dipped into his pocket and handed her a shilling. 'To help you out further,' he said.

But now, for some reason, although she'd enjoyed his passionate kiss, she felt cheapened by the offer of the coin as the familiar phrase came to mind: *She was willing for a shilling!* She weighed up whether she ought to accept it, but the thought of Ma and the kids going starving soon wiped away any pride she might have had, so she took it from his grasp and placed it in her dress pocket. 'Thank you,' she said.

She should have felt glad, but now she felt nothing. A sort of numbness had overtaken her; it was as if she was in a daze.

'Come on, I'll walk you home,' he said, taking her by the hand. 'Can't allow a lady to be out on her own at this ungodly hour . . .'

They walked most of the way in silence, her hand in his making her feel protected and wanted. Kathryn couldn't believe she'd only set foot this way a few hours ago with another man, who now seemed so young and inexperienced about the ways of the world compared with Squire. He took her as far as the end of her street before heaving a long sigh.

'I'll be back,' he said finally. 'We could make money, me and you. I'll return in a couple of nights. Same pub. Look out for me. Meanwhile I'm going to see if I can rent out a room up West. Goodnight, my dearest Bella.' Then he swooped down to plant a final kiss on her lips.

Was this all a dream? It certainly seemed so. Maybe she'd never see the handsome stranger ever again. Kathryn smiled to herself as she walked away from him, feeling him watching her from the end of the street. She didn't turn around for fear he should realise how interested she was in him. She walked as far as the lane and then entered the house by the back door; it would be less likely anyone would hear her that way. So she slipped in through the scullery and then went to the living room where the small fire still remained in the grate, protected by a metal guard. Light was beginning to filter through the curtains; she glanced at the wooden mantel clock, which said ten minutes to five. Kathryn swallowed hard, disbelieving – she'd been out almost all night! Thankfully, it had still been dark when Squire had walked her home. She didn't want the neighbours to see her with a strange man – questions would be asked.

Stealthily, she climbed the stairs, stripped off her dress and bonnet, flinging them on the floor, and got into bed. In the corner of the room, Mags stirred and turned over, her bed springs creaking. She murmured something, but luckily it was in her sleep. Kathryn thought she'd never fall asleep herself, but before she knew it she was out like a light, and didn't even hear Mags and Rosie rise from their beds to get dressed for the day ahead a couple of hours later.

'Why Kathy still in bed?' she heard Rosie ask later. It was an unusual sight for them to see as she was normally up and around before they awoke, but she pretended to sleep on, in case questions were asked of her.

She peeped through one eye to see Mags drawing near to her, inhaling deeply. 'I don't know, she must be very tired, I suppose,' she replied to her younger sibling.

Kathryn realised Mags must have noticed the alcohol on her breath. How was she going to explain that?

By the time Kathryn had awakened and gone downstairs, her head ached and she felt slightly nauseous; she just wasn't used to drinking alcohol. Mags had the children seated around the table, eating meagre bowls of watery porridge. A surge of guilt coursed through Kathryn's veins; she felt bad she hadn't been up earlier to see to the family.

'Ma?' She looked at Mags through heavily hooded eyes.

'Don't fret, I've already seen to her and given her that medicine. She's drinking a cup of tea in bed.' Mags shook her head sadly as she sat down herself at the table. 'What are we going to do, Kathryn? There's no food left in the house and

Mr O'Shay will be back later. We'll be flung out on to the pavement outside for sure today.'

Kathryn smiled. 'Don't you worry about that, Mags. Pour us a cup of tea each, then we're going out!'

Mags blinked several times in disbelief. 'Pardon?'

'After I've had my tea, I want you to help me fill the old tin bath. You can get in first, then me, and then we're off to the shops. I have enough to pay the rent and to buy plenty of groceries for a few days.'

'But I don't understand?'

'Mrs Daley realised they'd been underpaying me this past few weeks, so she paid me yesterday.'

Mags narrowed her eyes with suspicion. 'But I didn't see anyone call here yesterday.'

'Ah, it was late last night. You were all in bed.'

Mags nodded slowly. 'Thinking about it, I thought I heard the door opening and closing last night, but I was too tired to rouse meself.' It seemed to make sense to her.

'Yes, so we'll be all right for the next week and O'Shay should be 'appy about it an' all!'

Mags smiled, but then a look of concern washed over her features. 'But 'ow come you're smelling of alcohol? Did Mrs Daley give you a bottle of gin, too?'

Kathryn chuckled. 'No, I just took some of Ma's medicine late last night, as I thought I had a sore throat coming on.' Kathryn hated lying to her sister, but for now there was little choice.

Mags seemed placated by Kathryn's answers. After they'd sorted the kids out and sent them to play in the street, they washed and changed their mother's bed clothes and Mags persuaded Kathryn to eat a little thin watery oatmeal. Then the girls were ready to bath.

'Keep a listen out for O'Shay; the money is on the mantelpiece. It should be ten shillings altogether as we owe two weeks' rent. So, we need ten shillings in change, understood?'

Mags nodded. She went over to the mantelpiece and took the sovereign in her hand, studying it. It wasn't often they saw one of those, well, not lately, at any rate. Mags was already dressed in one of her smarter frocks, her Titian hair well brushed, with a pretty green ribbon in it.

Kathryn had just begun to scrub herself in the lukewarm water in the tin bath when there was a sharp knock at the door. 'That'll be the rent man for sure!' she shouted to her sister.

But the voice at the door as Mags answered wasn't that of O'Shay, but another she recognised. Squire! What on earth was he doing here at her home? She hadn't been expecting this.

'Is Miss Bella in?' she heard him asking.

'No, sir. There's no one of that name here.'

Kathryn shouted to her sister, 'It's all right, Mags. Tell the gentleman I shan't be long and ask him to wait outside.'

'Miss Bella!' Squire shouted through the open door, and she thought she detected a note of merriment in his voice.

Then she heard her sister close the door behind him, and then approaching footsteps as she entered the scullery and looked down at her in the tin tub. 'Come on now, Kathryn, who is that man and why is he calling you "Miss Bella"?' She stood with hands on hips.

'He's just a gentleman I'm about to do some work with, that's all. He has a clothing business in the West End and he'd like me to help out there.'

Mags pursed her lips in annoyance, her eyes glittering with fury. 'Then it was 'im what gave you that money, weren't it? Tell me the truth!'

Kathryn nodded. 'Yes, it was him,' she answered, though she could never tell Mags the full truth of the situation.

'Well, you didn't have to lie to me about things!' Mags turned on her heel and stomped out of the room.

Kathryn had a lot of making up to do and decided she'd buy Mags a ha'penny sticky bun as a treat later, but now she concentrated on getting out of the tin bath and drying the soapy suds off her body. She quickly dressed and brushed her tresses, then, leaving her locks long and flowing, dashed outside to see Squire leaning up against the house, nonchalantly smoking a cigar. He looked well flash for the area, but seemed comfortable standing there, nevertheless.

He smiled broadly as she approached and then pushed back the brim of his bowler hat as if to get a good view of her. 'My, my, you look even lovelier with your hair loose like that, *Miss Bella*, and by daylight, too.'

Across the road, Kathryn noticed a lace curtain twitch as if she was being watched, but she didn't care; for all they knew he could be a sweater or a rent man or even the doctor calling to see her ma.

'Thank you.' She returned his smile. In daylight he looked even more handsome. 'But why did you decide to call at my home?'

'I've found a room,' he said excitedly, his eyes gleaming. 'I want to take you shopping for some new gowns. We can make ourselves a fortune up West!'

Kathryn swallowed hard. A little voice inside her head said, 'It's not too late to back out now,' but she ignored it when she thought of Ma and the kids and the looming gates and high walls of the Spike; that was the name attributed to the workhouse and feared by all. One neighbouring family had entered there last year and she hadn't seen them since. She didn't want that for her family.

'Yes, that sounds fine. But I need to go shopping in the market with me sister this morning – we're running short on supplies and the rent man is due to call and Ma is in bed sick and the young 'uns will be alone for a while . . .'

He chuckled, which annoyed her. How dare he laugh at her very dire situation! But then he said, with a note of seriousness, 'Look, I get the impression things are tough for you, *Miss Bella*, and for goodness' sake, please tell me your real name . . . I can take you to market and your sister can handle the kids and pay the rent man. Then we can drop the supplies off at your house and head up West. How does that sound?'

She nodded with tears in her eyes, her anger melting at his generosity. 'Thank you, Squire. And it's Kathryn. My name is Kathryn.'

'What a beautiful name.' He smiled as he stroked her cheek, making her feel all a-tremble inside.

She swallowed hard. 'Now, what is your real name, sir?'

He coughed and cleared his throat. 'It's Ronald, Ronald Arthur.' It seemed strange that he had such an ordinary name; it belied his appearance. But here was someone offering her the hand of hope; she couldn't bite the same hand that fed her.

'I'll be just a moment,' she said. 'I need to fetch the shopping baskets and ask Mags to keep an eye on the family and watch out for the rent man when I'm gone.' She turned, leaving him standing there.

When she explained to Mags, the girl wasn't very pleased at all. 'I thought *I* was to help you in the market today? You made me 'ave a bath for bugger all!' She stood with her hands on her hips, tossing back her red hair. She had a terrible temper on her. 'Yer all for yerself these days, Madam Bloomin' Bella!'

'Watch yer mouth!' Kathryn scolded. 'Look, this will be better for us all,' she explained. 'I don't like leaving Ma and the kids alone. What if O'Shay bursts into the house and throws them out into the street? We can't expect Rosie or the boys to pay him – they don't understand. And Ma is too weak to get out of bed.'

Mags nodded, as though she could see the sense of what her elder sister was saying. 'But how will you carry all that food on your own?'

'The gentleman will help me,' Kathryn said brusquely. Then, changing the subject, 'And you can empty that tin bath for me when I'm gone. Get the boys to help you to carry it.'

Mags gave her a filthy look and turned on her heel, but Kathryn knew she would do everything she asked of her; she was a good girl.

Chapter Four

Walking around the bustling market with its costermongers' carts and stalls containing all sorts of food, anything from bread and pastries to colourful fruit and vegetables, second-hand clothing, even home-made wooden toys, Kathryn felt protected by Squire. His eyes were focused on snagging a bargain too, haggling with the stall-holders and knocking down their prices. He had a lot of charm about him. The male stall-holders were trusting of him and the women taken in by his good looks and witty repartee.

Within half an hour, they had all they needed: two large bloomer loaves, a quarter of tea leaves, a hunk of cheese, a few fish ends and scrag ends of lamb, potatoes, carrots, onions, a bag of oatmeal and even a few sticky buns for the kids.

'There should be enough here to keep us going for a few days!' Kathryn announced as Squire handed over a shilling to yet another stall-holder. He had insisted on paying for it all, even though he had given her that money last night, but she only had one shilling on her person and O'Shay needed paying from that sovereign on the mantelpiece back home.

'How can you afford all of this?' She glanced at Squire, who had just dropped a bottle of ginger beer into one of the baskets.

Looking into her eyes, he tapped the side of his nose with his index finger and laughed. 'I told you, I conduct some business up West, trading, that sort of thing. That's all you need to know for now . . .'

She smarted inside: why wouldn't he tell her what he did for a living? Why did he need to be so mysterious? She couldn't complain though. Bills were being paid and now they'd have enough food in their bellies for a few days to come.

'Really?' She huffed out a breath.

'All right then, I do have contacts in the business world, but I've also recently had a big win. I like the occasional flutter now and again at my club. I enjoy having the odd wager on a game of poker.'

She blinked several times. 'I hadn't had you down as some sort of gambler!'

'Well, I am, my dear.' He flashed her a wolfish grin, and she wondered if that was how he made most of his money. He guided her by the arm towards a pub called The Market Tavern. 'Fancy a beverage?' he asked.

'Oh, I can't, I need to get home. Mags don't like me leaving her as it is.'

'We need to talk business and this is the best place, not out in the street where all and sundry can hear us, Kathryn.'

'I think I understand what you're saying . . .'

He smiled at her and whispered, 'I just thought you wouldn't want anyone to overhear your business.'

She swallowed, then nodded. 'All right, maybe a quick one, but then I really have to get back home.'

'At least you can leave your family at night when they're asleep,' he said, dropping his hand from hers and guiding her inside the tavern with an arm draped protectively around her shoulder. It was bustling as they entered, but he guided her to a table at the rear of the place.

He jostled his way through the throng to get to the bar, returning a couple of minutes later with a tankard of beer for himself and a glass of gin, this time with a slice of lemon in it, for her. She decided to sip it slowly after what had happened the previous night. Setting both baskets of groceries beneath the table, not wanting to risk them getting nabbed by some light-fingered passer-by, she settled herself back down on the wooden bench. Outside she could hear shouts from the market stalls: 'Come and get your fresh fish here!', 'Ripe strawberries going cheap!', 'Blooms for sale, five for a penny!'

He seated himself opposite her, then, taking a long swig of beer, patted the foam from his moustache with a silver-grey handkerchief from his top pocket. 'Now, what we'll do is get these groceries back to your house, then we'll take a carriage to an upmarket establishment I know where we can get you fitted for some gowns. Is that all right with you?'

She nodded, then took a sip of gin. It tasted more watered-down than last night's and in truth she was thankful for that.

'So you want me to work tonight?' she asked, blinking.

He shook his head vehemently. 'Good heavens, no. The gowns won't be ready for a few days anyhow. Best to keep your voice down if you don't want to be overheard,' he advised.

Her cheeks flushed and she looked around to see if anyone had overheard, but people seemed in deep conversation and the noise from the shouts and raucous laughter drowned out their conversation, even at this time of the day. 'I don't quite understand,' she said softly. 'Why do I need to keep quiet about your plans for me to be a mere companion for someone?'

His voice took on a serious tone. 'Walls have ears and it is no one's business but ours. After I've taken you for a fitting, I want you to view the rooms to see if you can add some feminine touches, to make it more appealing to your clientele.'

She swallowed hard. What had she got herself into? Things didn't appear how she first thought they were. There seemed to be something slightly sordid about it all. For the first time, she felt she wanted to back out, but how could she possibly do that? If she did run out on him, then how would she get any money? The Daleys had no more work for her at present and she wondered if they ever would offer her more. If he went to use the privy, maybe she could run off, but that would mean leaving the heavy baskets of groceries behind and now he knew where she lived.

The thought of the workhouse looming made her quash that very thought.

Why did she have to be so poor? Why did Pa have to die and leave them to fend for themselves? Life was so unfair. She took another sip of gin and, as it warmed her to the core, she realised she was about to set foot into a whole new world.

Squire helped Kathryn carry the food baskets back to her door and then left her there, promising he would return in two hours' time to take her to the ladies' outfitters. She was greeted by the kids, who rushed forwards, hugging her, as she entered. Rosie and Damon couldn't wait to see what she had in her baskets, and Squire had insisted on buying them a bag of Bentley's Chocolate Drops. Quickly, she hid them behind her back, but Shaun was too fast on his feet and grabbed them from her grasp.

'Now, you can have a couple each before dinner,' she announced, laughing at his antics, 'but then I have to get on with making us a fish stew.'

Damon wrinkled his nose. 'I don't want no fish stew, Kathy,' he announced. 'Me want somefing else, like chicken dinner.'

She ruffled his hair. 'Fish stew is good for yer. Yer'll enjoy it I promise.' But she remembered that the last time they had fish stew, Mags had made it and she'd cooked it to death, the house stinking for days afterwards. Thinking on her feet and remembering the cheese and potatoes she'd purchased, Kathryn said, 'I tell you what, I'll make us a fish pie instead, it's real tasty, me love.'

He nodded and ran off after Shaun to get a chocolate drop or two before he ate them all. Rosie stood there, clinging on to Kathryn's skirts. Kathryn glanced up to see where Mags was, wondering if the girl was still annoyed she hadn't taken her shopping as planned and that she'd lied to her. She heard a door open and close and then footsteps on the stairs as her sister paused on the bottom step. Kathryn's eyes were drawn to a small white enamel basin, covered by a muslin cloth, that Mags held in her hand. She looked at Kathryn with a vacant expression on her face. Any thoughts of her sister being annoyed were being wiped away by her concern for their mother.

Kathryn shuddered. She knew what that basin meant. Going over to where Mags stood, she asked, 'Has Ma been coughing up blood again?'

Mags shook her head. 'No, thankfully 'er phlegm is now clear.'

Relief flooded through Kathryn. 'Thank the Lord,' she said. 'I have a feeling this family's fortunes are about to change.'

Mags nodded and smiled. 'Ma's even asking to be fed. Did I hear you mention fish pie, Kathryn?'

'Yes. I am going to start it now. Can you help me?'

'I'll be there now. I'll just empty and clean out the bowl and take it up to Ma in case she needs it again.'

Kathryn nodded and smiled. 'Meanwhile, I'll make us a cuppa. I expect you could do with one yourself, and Ma too.'

Mags nodded. Kathryn realised poor Mags had gone without breakfast, like herself, for the sake of the kids. Everyone in the house was starving.

After a nice cup of tea and once the fish pie was in the oven, Kathryn explained that she would be going out later to meet up with Squire to view his premises. 'He's offered me a regular job as a seamstress,' she explained.

Mags sat there open-mouthed. 'But how are you going to get to work in time?' she asked. 'It's a fair stretch to the West End.'

'Whenever I work I'll be put up in accommodation. Much of the work will be during the evening and even at night time . . .' She hated lying to her sister, but needs must. If Mags had any questions, then she wasn't asking any, which might have been deliberate on her part. 'Just one thing, please don't tell Ma about my plans for the time being, I don't want her worrying about me.'

Mags nodded. 'No, I won't. No fear.'

'Did O'Shay call around while I was out?'

Mags shook her head. 'I'm glad 'e didn't an' all. I don't trust that man.' She wrinkled her nose in disgust.

'Me neither,' said Kathryn, lifting the lace curtain and gazing out on to the street. The trouble was, she had to go out again soon, so she hoped he'd call now, otherwise poor Mags would have to face him herself.

Later in the day, there was a sharp knock on the door, and there were no surprises for guessing who it might be. Kathryn went to answer to find O'Shay there with an angry look on his face. 'I came around here for the rent the other day and I know you were all pretending to be out!' he snarled.

Deciding it was best to keep her cool, Kathryn let out a long breath. 'I'm sorry about that, Mr O'Shay,' she said. 'Unfortunately, we weren't here and Ma could hardly answer the door in her condition, could she?'

'No, I suppose not!' he said. 'Now where's that money you owe me?'

She went to get it off the mantelpiece, then dropped the coins in his hand. Fortunately, she had been thinking on her feet and had previously got Squire to change the sovereign coin into shillings for her as she feared if she gave the coin to O'Shay expecting change, he'd refuse, claiming she owed it to him.

'Don't forget, the rent's going up soon and if you don't keep up with the payments then I'm well within me rights to rent this house out to someone else. There won't be any second chances for the Flynn family!'

'It shan't come to that, Mr O'Shay,' Kathryn said, trying to sound more confident than she felt inside.

He let out a loud harrumph and turned on his heel as if about to leave, but then he paused and asked, 'Seen that Jimmy one?'

'No.'

'Well, he owes rent for his place and all. Be warned, the lot of you!' He raised his fist as Kathryn closed the door in his face. It was going to be one of those days.

Gilmour and Co. was situated on a busy street in the West End of London. Squire had paid for them to take a hansom cab there. Kathryn, although a little worried about leaving Mags in sole charge of the household, was nevertheless excited by her impromptu and unexpected trip out.

The outside of the double-fronted store was impressive. There were two big glass windows, in between which a passageway led to a large wooden door, which bore the company's name in fancy gilt lettering.

She drew a breath and looked at Squire as if to ask, 'Should we really be here at all?'

But she needn't have worried because as soon as he entered the establishment, the staff were immediately on their feet running hither and thither and hovering around at his beck and call. It was patently obvious that Squire was well known to them there.

'And what can we do for you today, Mr Curtis-Browne?' a gentleman of advanced age asked. He wore a black suit, a grey and black pin-striped waistcoat and a silver-grey cravat. His movements were deft and meticulous, and his beard neatly trimmed. Although he was in service at the shop, Kathryn wondered if he was Mr Gilmour himself, until Squire explained quietly that he was just a humble tailor. And where had Squire's fancy name come from? He had omitted to give her that one – why wasn't he Ronald Arthur? And why had Squire told her originally that was his name? Why the need to deceive her? He obviously didn't want her to know his real identity and that disturbed her greatly.

'Good afternoon, Mr Forbes,' Squire greeted the man. 'I'm here today with my niece, who is visiting the area. She's looking for a whole new set of clothing that would be deemed suitable for a young lady in this fashionable and stylish neck of the woods.'

Forbes smiled. 'Then I shall send Mrs Harrington and her assistant to measure the young lady. You shall also be shown a book of material swatches to choose from.'

Squire nodded. 'Very well.'

'Meanwhile,' Forbes continued, 'I shall ask one of the staff to make you a pot of coffee while you both wait to be attended to.'

A pot of coffee while they waited? Kathryn had never known such service before.

When Forbes had departed, Squire took Kathryn by the arm and whispered in her ear, 'Whatever you do, don't speak too much. Just nod, shake your head, smile or whatever. Only say, "Yes", "No" and "Please" or "Thank you". I don't want this lot to realise you come from the poor end of London.'

Appalled that she had to hide her heritage, which she certainly was not ashamed of, Kathryn smarted inside. Who did Squire think he was, just because he had money?

Then he softened and leaned in closer to explain, 'Look, we want this to go smoothly and I really need these people to think you are my niece. If you talk in your normal voice you shall betray all that I am setting out to do here. The best thing you can do is just smile and nod and generally be agreeable to all that is asked of you, Kathryn.'

She nodded and then let out a long breath. How on earth was she expected to spend time in the company of a man without talking, though?

'I think you need to have elocution lessons soon,' he added. 'We'll make a real lady of you yet!'

Something that just occurred to Kathryn was what on earth was Squire, or whoever he was, doing in the East End that night when she'd first encountered him?

Seeing the worried frown on her face, he smiled. 'Please don't concern yourself, dear sweet Kathryn. Leave all the worrying to me.'

After they were taken to a little room with two gilt-edged, high-backed red velvet chairs and a low walnut table, a female assistant entered and placed a silver tray containing the coffee pot and cups on the table, then returned with a small plate of mini macaroons.

After Kathryn had taken several sips of the strong coffee, Mrs Harrington introduced herself. She was a middle-aged woman, well-preserved, who held herself beautifully, with good deportment. Her black silk dress, edged in lace, had a cameo brooch affixed at the collar and her salt-and-pepper hair was so tightly scooped back that none of it dared fall out of place.

She smiled broadly when she saw them. 'Mr Curtis-Browne, how good to see you again!'

What did this woman know about Squire?

After Squire and she made some pleasantries, Kathryn was led to a curtained cubicle by the assistant and a couple of minutes later, Mrs Harrington entered with a tape measure around her neck, clutching a small leather-bound notepad and a pencil.

She looked Kathryn up and down with her beady eyes. 'And who is this young lady?' she enquired, calling across to Squire as he stood outside the cubicle.

Remembering not to say too much, as instructed by Squire, Kathryn kept quiet. She could no longer see his face to gauge his response.

'This is Miss Bella Cartwright, my niece, who shall be staying with me and my wife. She's looking for a wardrobe of clothing befitting her stay in London.'

If Mrs Harrington didn't believe Squire's blatant lie, then she wasn't saying so. Instead she sniffed. 'Well, she'll have to have something more upmarket than she's got on at the moment, that's for sure.'

Why was the woman talking about her as if she wasn't even there but addressing Squire on the other side of the curtain? Kathryn bristled with indignation but fought inside to keep quiet.

Mrs Harrington continued to measure Kathryn up with her gaze, and then finally asked her what sort of clothing she'd like. Without waiting for Squire to reply, Kathryn answered, 'Something suitable for social events and pretty wear for the bedchamber.' For a moment, she worried she might have said totally the wrong thing. She popped her head outside the cubicle to check his response. Squire nodded and smiled as she met his eyes. Mrs Harrington sent her assistant off to bring back swatches of material and a large book containing sketches of various day and evening wear suitable for a young lady.

When Kathryn was fully dressed she returned to the waiting area. As they leafed through the designs, she took note of whether Squire approved or not when he nodded or shook his head behind Mrs Harrington's back. Finally, they chose three day dresses that were to be made of thick bombazine, three evening dresses made of pure silk, low-cut, and a selection of nightdresses and overgowns suitable for the bedroom. Mrs Harrington also suggested various corsets and underwear. Kathryn had never worn a corset in her life and as the woman laced up the stays she felt all hemmed in, but she had to admit when she tried a sample evening gown over it, it pulled her in in all the right places and emphasised her décolletage. Squire's eyes grew large when she swept out of the changing room into the waiting area to show him. The sample gown was the deepest of blue and it shimmered and shone like the ocean, making her feel beautiful and a touch mysterious.

Squire stood, then, walking towards her and taking her hands in his, said, 'You look beautiful, my dear.'

When Mrs Harrington left the changing room to sort out things with her assistant, Squire whispered in Kathryn's ear, 'I can't wait to see you in all this. You mean so much to me.'

Her heartbeat thudded beneath the bodice of the dress. Being alone together seemed to emphasise her feelings for him, and, as far as she was concerned, from the way he was looking at her with longing in his eyes, he felt the same way too.

Chapter Five

When Kathryn's fitting had finished, Squire thanked Mrs Harrington for her time and expertise.

'They'll be ready in a week's time, Mr Curtis-Browne,' she said, all the while looking down her nose at Kathryn. Ignoring her gratitude, she turned to face Squire. 'Shall I add the cost of the items to your usual account?'

Suddenly, Squire's face changed as his eyes widened with what Kathryn thought might have been fear and his cheeks flushed. He cleared his throat and said quite curtly, 'No, please do not use my usual account. Open one marked as "Miss Bella Cartwright", if you please.'

Kathryn didn't know if she was imagining things, but the woman's eyes had a strange gleam about them almost as though she had said that on purpose.

As they were preparing to leave, Kathryn noticed him hand Mrs Harrington a small, white, bulky envelope. 'For your time, madam,' he said.

Mrs Harrington sniffed as she took the offering, then she

smiled a smile that did not quite reach her eyes. 'Anything else I can help you with, let me know, Mr Curtis-Browne. Good day to you.' Ignoring Kathryn again, she turned sharply on her heel and left the fitting room.

'Who is she, Squire?' Kathryn longed to know after that strange exchange.

'No one you need worry about, my sweet. Now come along. We'll get a cab to visit the rooms I have lined up for you. They shall need decorating and furnishing. I reckon we could be up and running within a fortnight – you shall have all the gowns ready for wear by then and we can make the rooms look accommodating for gentlemen visitors.'

A shiver skittered along her spine as she wondered what was in store for her, and, swallowing down her fears, she took a deep breath and followed Squire out of the outfitter's and on to the pavement outside.

The entrance to the small apartment Squire had found for her was located down an alleyway just off a main shopping area in the West End. It had a shared toilet and communal bathroom at the bottom of the building, which would be a long walk downstairs for her, as she was on the top floor, but nevertheless it was very clean, without a hint of damp, and that was enough to please her. The people they passed on the landing on the way up to the rooms appeared to be young professional-looking people, well dressed and minding their own business.

Kathryn gazed in awe at the beautiful double-fronted bay windows that looked on to the High Street down below. There was a cast-iron fireplace with alcoves either side. Then a curtained area that led through to a bedroom. The flowered wallpaper was beginning to peel, but it was still beautiful, nevertheless.

'This is the room where you shall spend much of your time,' he said, brushing an index finger across his neat moustache.

She shivered in anticipation as he drew near, and he swept in for a kiss, almost knocking her off her feet. 'Oh, Kathryn,' he growled, 'I can't wait until we can be together. We just have to be patient until that special moment arrives. There will be a time and a place where the world will turn, just for us.' His breaths were short and intense.

As he drew away, she looked into his eyes and nodded. 'Very well.'

'Also I would like to spend the odd night here with you, if I may? Will it be permissible for you to stay here overnight sometimes?'

Her mouth was dry and she swallowed hard. 'Yes. I have thought of that, I shall tell my family I am working overnight for a West End tailoring shop.'

'Good girl,' he said, pulling her closer towards him. 'Now, meanwhile, there is something you can do for me that shall not wait a moment longer.' He drew the old drapes and she looked at him, unflinching. What did he want her to do?

Taking a deep breath, she closed her eyes. 'You'd better tell me what you want me to do . . .' she said in barely a whisper.

Her heart thudded madly as he drew near to her. Tracing the outline of her face with his finger, he planted a kiss on her lips. His kisses were so sweet she wanted to savour them forever, but then he drew away from her and turned to gaze out of the window with his hands behind his back. What was he thinking? She couldn't be sure.

Finally, she whispered, 'What's wrong?'

He turned towards her. 'I'm sorry, Kathryn. I can't . . . It wouldn't be fair.'

She couldn't believe how caring he was, that he didn't want to take her virginity there and then; many men would have, given the chance. 'I understand,' she said softly.

He hugged her towards him so that she could feel his heart beat in time with her own. Safe in his arms, she closed her eyes and savoured the moment.

Kathryn sat with the kids around the table eating the faggots and peas she had bought from a market stall on her way home.

'We haven't seen Jimmy in ages,' Shaun said finally when he laid down his spoon. The only time when they were all quiet was when they were eating. 'Why's that?'

'Yes, I was thinking that, too!' Mags stared at her sister.

How on earth was she going to explain things to them?

Mags knew about Squire, of course, but not what was going on behind the scenes.

'Aw, we just don't have the time to see one another these days. I'm busy working up West and he's busy, too.'

Shaun nodded, seeming placated for the time being, but Mags narrowed her eyes, then mumbled something under her breath.

'Pardon?' Kathryn asked.

'Nothing,' the girl replied, with a sullen expression on her face.

'No, go on, you might as well say whatever you've got on your mind!'

'You've changed so much, Kathryn. Once upon a time you were happy to be in Jimmy's company. Go on, admit it, you don't care for him anymore now that you've got airs and graces!'

'Don't be so silly,' she replied, and forced a smile. Her sister was growing up more than she cared to admit, and Mags was no one's fool. It was true; she had let her friendship with Jimmy drift.

'I reckon he must be heartbroken the way you've blown him out!' Mags folded her arms and jutted out her chin.

Kathryn shook her head. 'It's not what you think. Can you please clear the table for me as I have to go out?'

'Not again!' Mags said. 'That's all you do these days. I liked things better when we saw more of you.'

'You mean when I was dog-tired from working all those

hours and we hardly had a pot to bleedin' pee in!' Horrified at what she'd just said, Kathryn felt her face grow hot with embarrassment. 'I'm sorry, I didn't mean to use language like that.'

But it was too late. Mags had already risen from the table and busied herself clearing the dishes away. It was obvious she was in no mood to speak to her elder sister. Shaun sat there at the table, eyes wide in astonishment. He was old enough to understand, but had not been privy to all the things Mags knew about Kathryn. The other children seemed blissfully unaware of what had occurred, and for that she was extremely grateful.

It took just over a fortnight for her trousseau to be ready for wear and delivered to the apartment. Meanwhile, Squire brought decorators in to brush up the paintwork. Now fancy flowered wallpaper adorned the walls of the alcoves near the fireplace. He'd purchased a couple of comfortable armchairs, a chaise longue, even candlesticks for the mantelpiece, though he assured Kathryn they were only silver plate; he couldn't risk leaving the real thing there, lest they be stolen. He did assure her that the class of clientele she'd receive would be high, but he couldn't take the risk of leaving solid silver around the place.

Maroon velvet drapes swathed both large windows overlooking the High Street and lace curtains were installed inside those to maintain a level of privacy. Even though they were on the top floor, Squire said he didn't want to risk any clients being viewed through the window, for both her protection and theirs.

The bedroom, or boudoir, as he told her to call it, was dimly lit with an oil lamp and candles creating a warm glow. Lace drapes and silk damask curtains adorned the window, but the best thing of all was the four-poster bed he'd had installed, with its walnut posts at each corner and muslin drapes, silk sheets and fancy embroidered cushions. It was a spectacular sight.

As if picking up on her thoughts, Squire touched her cheek softly and kissed her lips. 'Do you like it?'

'I love it,' she said, with tears in her eyes. 'But I just wish this was our place as I know you care about me, really care . . .' She couldn't believe how kind and thoughtful he was to her; no one except Jimmy had treated her so well. But Jimmy was inexperienced compared to Squire. He was the typical lad next door. She couldn't imagine him creating something as special as this for her. Squire had lived and seen things she could only dream about.

'I wish it to be so too,' he said, gazing intensely into her eyes, breaking into her thoughts, as he brushed away her tears with the pad of his thumb, 'but I can't leave Mrs Curtis-Browne – it would break her heart and she doesn't deserve it.' He never really spoke about his wife and Kathryn yearned to know what the woman was like. Was she good-looking? Did she dress well? Did she have a portly frame or was she slim and petite? She didn't even know if Squire had any children.

Her bottom lip quivered as she realised how deep the feelings she was developing for this man were. He had a hold over her that she couldn't seem to break.

'Please don't cry, Kathryn,' he said, planting a kiss on her forehead. 'You must look on the bright side. I will be keeping myself just for you, so I will be all yours, my love. You are too precious to me.'

'Then, if that is the case, why do I have to be a companion to other men? When I'd much rather I were in your company alone?'

He smiled at her. 'It will only involve you accompanying the men to various social functions, usually because their wives cannot or do not wish to attend, then a little entertaining afterwards. All you'll need to do is make yourself beautiful, charm them and listen to what they have to say. Some of those men don't have the luxury of having a wife who will truly listen to them and put their needs first. And the ones who are unmarried are so lonely.'

'But I'd much rather just listen to you, Squire. Can't we just have our place together to talk?'

He shook his head. 'If only it were so. I have invested all my savings in this place and in you. If we do not earn them back, then I shall go bankrupt and you don't want that now, do you?' She shook her head. She would hate for that to happen. 'And you need the money to keep your family afloat, so it has to be done. Do you understand me, Kathryn?'

She nodded as she swallowed a lump in her throat.

His voice took on a serious tone. 'Tomorrow night I have arranged a meeting I will take you along to; it is at the house of a good friend of mine. There will be several gentlemen there of fine breeding, who you will spend some time with. How does that sound to you?'

She nodded. He did have her best interests at heart and maybe he also loved her in his own way. 'What will I need to do?' she asked.

There was a flicker of something in his eyes, but she couldn't detect what that something was. 'It will be nothing you can't handle. You'll just have to meet with some wealthy gentlemen who are nothing like the low-life men you'd find in the East End of the city. There are plenty who would pay good money to spend time with you.'

She looked at him and he quickly glanced away, then back at her again and smiled, though to her way of thinking, his smile didn't seem to reach his eyes as it usually did.

'And don't forget, after that meeting you and I can be together as much as possible. You'd like that, wouldn't you, Kathryn?'

She smiled back at him. He wanted her as much as she wanted him. She watched as he fumbled in his jacket pocket and brought out a small black velvet box. 'What's that?' she asked, wide-eyed with wonder.

'Open it and see,' he said, handing it to her.

Slowly, she lifted the lid and was astonished to see a solitaire diamond ring there, sparkling and shimmering in the light. She gasped. 'For me?'

'Who else?' He smiled. 'Put it on. We might not be married in name, but we know what we mean to one another. Go on. Try it on.' He took it from the box and slipped it over the fourth finger of her left hand. 'Now you're mine at last,' he said, as he claimed her lips. She had never been so happy in all her life.

When they finally pulled away from one another's embrace, she said, 'I'll have to wear the ring away from home. I cannot show people, as questions will be asked of me.'

'That's understandable. Just wear it when we are alone together. It's a token of my love.'

There, he'd said it: his love!

'Oh thank you so much, Squire!' She hugged him tightly, then gently he pushed her away.

'Come on, we're going out to celebrate,' he said. 'I know a nice little restaurant a couple of miles away where no one will recognise us.'

Kathryn dressed herself in a sea-green gown he'd bought her with a matching cape and frilled bonnet, feeling every inch a lady as he took her to dine. She also felt such a fraud, though, as Ma and the kids thought she was working a night shift at a tailoring business and here she was being wined and dined by a gentleman! If only they knew! Partly she felt excited by the deception, as it was like a private world just for her and Squire, but the better side of her found the deceit hard to live with.

The following evening, Squire drew a dress from the wardrobe and held it up in front of her. 'Wear this one,' he said.

It was a white silk dress that reminded her of a bridal gown, except that it was less elaborate – there were no lace edges or seed pearls to adorn it, but maybe that was the idea.

She took the dress from him and made to go to the bedroom to try it on, but stopped mid-step as he cleared his throat.

'Here will do,' he commanded. 'And do not wear any corsetry – I want you to look unfettered and uncomplicated, my dear.'

She frowned, feeling strange as he watched her disrobe, his eyes taking in her near-naked form as she trembled before him, but he made no move to draw near her. She slipped the white silk garment over her head and allowed it to fall as it skimmed over her curves like a second skin.

'Stunning!' he enthused. 'Now you really look the part!' He circled her, his warm breath blowing on her neck.

'What's the idea behind this?' She blinked several times.

'The idea, my dear, is for you to look as lovely as you are.'

He stepped forward, closing the space between them, and brought his hand to her head and unclipped her hair slide, allowing her hair to fall loose on her shoulders. 'Perfect,' he gasped in appreciation as he stood back to admire her.

'Now hurry along or we'll be late.' He held up a matching hooded white cape and draped it over her shoulders. She shivered beneath his touch as he placed both hands on her shoulders from behind and whispered, 'Beautiful . . . Now let's leave, shall we?'

She nodded and followed after him as he made his way to the door, wishing things didn't have to be this way, but one thought of Ma and the kids was enough to spur her on.

The drive to Squire's friend's house was quite a long journey as busy built-up streets and congested traffic gave way to green fields and trees. She strained her eyes to see if there were any buildings of any kind in the area, but there were none: no houses, no offices, no factories blowing out sooty fumes.

'Are we nearly there yet?' she asked, as the carriage bobbed along yet another country lane. It seemed an age since they'd left London and she feared it would grow dark by the time she got there.

'It won't be much longer,' he reassured her. He did look astonishingly handsome in a grey tailcoat, crisp white shirt and silver cravat. His black breeches showed off his muscular legs and his long leather boots made him look quite the gentleman. She shivered in anticipation of what was to come.

Would she like any of the gentlemen? And why were they all so keen to spend time with someone like her? Didn't they have wives and girlfriends? Men were such strange creatures.

She was feeling drowsy after the long ride, so as she laid her head against the window she found herself nodding off to sleep. It had been the early hours of the morning when they'd returned to the apartment following their night out.

Suddenly Squire was gently rousing her. 'Wake up, sleepy head. We're here.'

As they disembarked from the carriage, she noticed a hansom cab sweep past with another young woman like herself inside with an older gentleman. She guessed she was the daughter of whoever owned this house. Neither person looked in their direction, but they must have been aware they were there. A thought occurred to her: the young woman . . . maybe she was here for the same reason Kathryn was?

Dusk was falling as fingers of apricot and pink hues streaked the sky. It really was a glorious evening. She turned towards the house, and what an impressive house it was too – Georgian. She caught her breath at its splendour, never having seen such a large house in her life before, marvelling at its pillars and tall windows. Outside were a fountain and a small lake set into lush green lawns. Excitedly, she ran around looking at everything, in awe, with Squire in pursuit.

'Kathryn!' he called with an edge to his voice. 'Please, you can see that later. We have to go inside – I shouldn't want us to be late!'

Bringing herself back to the moment, the sharp tone of his voice making her realise they urgently needed to get inside, Kathryn reminded herself that this was a business transaction, after all. But how she would love to splash water from that fountain on her face, toss off her shoes, tuck her dress into her bloomers and run around having fun in that water, then visit those colourful flowerbeds, pick a handful of blooms and inhale their sweet perfume. It was such a shame as there was nothing like this back home, except at the park.

Sighing, she allowed him to take her by the arm and lead her into the house.

They were met by a butler, whose hooked nose was held high in the air as he led them further inside. She couldn't help feeling he was looking down on her.

'Come this way, sir, miss,' he sniffed. For a brief moment, Kathryn almost erupted into a fit of giggles, until she realised why she was here in the first place, then her heart started to pound. She shivered, but it was too late to back out now. Even if she ran away, she'd have no idea how to get back home, and she'd be letting Squire down after all he'd done for her. She reassured herself that all would be well: Squire would see to that.

Inside the entrance was a crystal chandelier suspended from the ceiling, emitting a prism of colours. Kathryn gazed in awe. She had never seen such opulence in all her life. Even the black and white floor tiles shone and sparkled to perfection. A large polished oak staircase with a high arched window behind it caught her attention, and she imagined herself as the lady of the house, gliding down those stairs. Oh, how the other half lived! But she could experience some of this lifestyle when she became a companion. Oh, there'd be fancy wining and dining and evenings out where she'd dress up to the nines and be escorted up and down elaborate staircases just like that one there. It would all be a far cry from the East End.

The butler led them down a long corridor and in the distance she heard the sounds of male voices and huge guffaws. What were they laughing at? The smell of acrid tobacco smoke wafted towards her.

Seeing her wrinkle up her nose in disgust, Squire chuckled. 'It's no worse than The Horse and Harness!'

'I know, but this smoke is much stronger,' she complained.

'That's because it's cigar smoke, not cigarette,' he said. 'You'll find a very different kind of clientele here.'

They stood waiting by the open door as Kathryn studied the scene before her. Several pot-bellied middle-aged men sat around a large table. From the discarded plates and empty glasses she deduced they'd just finished a hearty meal.

'I'm sorry, Mr Tamworth, the gentleman has brought the young lady a little early . . . The other young lady has only just departed. Are you ready to see them now?'

'Yes, but not in here. Jenks, take them to the drawing room and fetch us another decanter of port and another box of cigars, my good fellow.'

Jenks nodded. 'Very well, sir.' Then, turning towards Squire and Kathryn, he said, 'Please come this way.'

Kathryn drank in the house's grandeur again as they followed the butler. She glanced across at Squire, but he was looking ahead like a man on a mission. There were several gilt-framed paintings of various landscapes on the walls and pieces of china displayed on the shelves, even a marble bust or two.

'Squire, where are we off to?' she hissed.

He rubbed his chin with the palm of his hand. 'We're going to the drawing room, where it shall be more comfortable for us.'

Drawing room? What was a drawing room? They only had a living room at home, not even a parlour. It sounded very grand to her. But she just nodded and pretended she understood.

Jenks marched ahead of them with his nose in the air and showed them inside a resplendent room. There was a roaring fire inside the grate, some comfortable-looking high-backed leather chairs and wall-to-wall shelves of books, with portraits of noblemen looking down on them from the other walls. It all seemed a little posh to her, but what was she expecting from such a large house with landscaped lawns and a fountain? Such opulence wasn't what she was used to, but she could become accustomed to it if she became some rich man's companion. She imagined herself strolling down the hallway with servants in attendance to see to her every whim.

'Your cape, miss?' a young maid asked, breaking into her thoughts as she bobbed a curtsey. Kathryn's eyes widened; no one had ever curtsied to her before. It made her feel important. She nodded and allowed the young girl to remove her hooded cape, leaving her in just her silk dress, which clung to her slight form.

Kathryn wondered if she was supposed to sit or not, but Squire remained standing, so she followed suit. Another maid arrived carrying a silver tray with a thick-stemmed, bulbous glass on it for Squire, with what looked like a dark-red drink inside. Was it wine?

'Sorry, m'dear,' he whispered behind his hand. 'I told them not to give you anything to drink – we need to show what a lady you are. This glass of port is for me.' He nodded at the maid as he took the drink from the tray.

Puzzled, Kathryn said nothing as she watched Squire take a sip from the glass. As if realising she didn't understand he said, 'There are some ladies who like to pass themselves off as – how do I say this? – intact. And although I know you are intact, as it were, if I allowed you to drink alcohol these men might get the wrong impression about you. They might think you're one of *that* sort.'

She nodded, all the while wondering what was in store for her and what Squire meant by *intact*. Surely, they couldn't be the men she had seen earlier? Those were old and overweight. Maybe there would be other men, good-looking ones. Someone like Mr Darcy in the novel *Pride and Prejudice* would be nice.

They were kept waiting a few minutes longer, the only sounds being the ticking mantelpiece clock and the flickering flames from the fire. Then she heard muffled voices and footsteps as the men approached. She swallowed hard.

To her horror, they *were* the same men, except that they'd now been joined by two younger, eager-looking men, who were eyeing her up almost as if she were a piece of meat on the hook at Spitalfields Market.

'Gentlemen,' Squire announced, 'are you ready to begin?' He glanced at Kathryn and gave her a smile of reassurance, which comforted her. It was nice knowing he was on her side and wouldn't allow anything bad to happen to her.

A couple of the men nodded and Mr Tamworth signalled his approval. 'Please introduce the young lady to us, sir.'

Squire cleared his throat and, with a flourish of his hand, gestured towards Kathryn. 'This, gentlemen, is Miss Bella Cartwright . . .'

She smiled nervously at the men, who seemed to be panting in anticipation of what was to come.

He continued, 'The young lady is in the bloom of youth at the age of eighteen and is untouched.'

The men muttered amongst themselves.

'I have to say, she does have a young, nubile body. It's positively breathtaking,' one elderly man said, as he approached with his monocle in place over one eye, slightly shuffling along. Kathryn thought he looked old enough to be her grandfather, never mind her father. He drew up close to her and, moving his monocle back and forth as if trying to focus, he closed his other eye to inspect her. 'Yes, a fine filly in fine fettle too!' he said, pleased.

One of the younger men, who had blond hair, drew near to her, so close she could feel his breath on her face. 'Now, what do we have here?' He chuckled. He was very good-looking indeed and she prayed it would be him who would choose her, but then his dark-haired companion seemed to want in on the action.

'I'll tell you what, Brutus,' said the dark-haired one, 'how about we join forces? Think what fun we could have!'

'Oh, no, this pretty little one is all for me.' The blond man ran his hand down her cheek, until Squire slapped his hand away with his cane. There was something about the way he was looking at her with hard cold eyes that sent a shiver down her spine. Her instincts told her he was cruel-hearted.

She didn't much care for the young man's tone. Looking around, she realised there wasn't one man in this room she wanted to spend time with except Squire himself.

A large gentleman with fuzzy red hair and matching moustache pushed his way through the crowd and elbowed the two young men out of the way, before peering more closely at her.

Mr Tamworth asked, 'And I have your word she has never been broken in, Squire?'

Why were they all talking about her as if she wasn't even there? She felt like an 'it', not even a 'her'. Even more peculiar, why did they seem to favour a young woman who was untouched? What was it to them?

'My word is my bond,' Squire answered. He sounded truthful in his reply and she knew that at least she trusted his word, if no one else would.

Tamworth turned back to the men. 'On that table there, gentlemen, is a piece of paper each. I want you to write your bid there and place it in the envelope provided and then seal it. I have been assured by Mr Curtis-Browne that bids are to begin at fifteen pounds.'

Kathryn gasped. She hadn't realised that this was an auction and the exhibit on show was herself! But the thought of earning a lot of money just for giving one of them her company far outweighed the fear of what she would be about to do. In any case she would only be the prize for one of the men and not all. Of course she would have to share the spoils with Squire, she understood that, but at least she wouldn't be standing on the corner in Whitechapel touting for business or having a knee trembler up a stinking dark alley frequented by rats. Instead, she'd be taken out for the evening, escorting him to the finest establishments. People would think she was a lady of fine breeding in her fancy gowns. How exciting it would be.

She watched as they took turns to scribble down their bids, using fancy-looking fountain pens, dipping their nibs into bottles of black ink, the nibs making a scratching sound as they touched the paper. Indeed, how much *was* her worth to them? All she cared about was money to feed her family and get Ma well again. She trusted Squire implicitly and all would work out for the best. She could go through with this, she simply had to.

Finally, the last bid was written and sealed and Mr Tamworth instructed his butler to collect them all and place them in a black leather wallet, which he handed to Squire.

Squire smiled broadly. 'I shall be in touch by the weekend, sir. If we might have Miss Cartwright's cape, then we shall be on our way.'

'Not so fast.' Brutus stepped forward, a glint in his deep-brown eyes. 'I will match any bid you have there and more to bed this young lady here now this very night,' he said and grinned, much to the chagrin of the men in his company. 'But, gentlemen,' he protested, 'I'd be quite prepared to allow any of you to have her after I've finished with her.'

Inwardly, Kathryn's spirit crumpled. She looked at Squire with her eyes wide open with horror. That wasn't what he had promised at all. Surely, he would never let this happen to her? After all his reassurances?

I feel cheap and worthless, she thought. *A mere chit of a girl! Who are you to treat me this way?* She stuck her chin out in indignation and forced herself to hold back the tears which were threatening to spill down her cheeks, not wanting her fear and distress to show.

As if reading her mind, Squire stepped forward and whispered in her ear, 'Don't worry, I shan't allow such a thing.' He leaned in close to Mr Tamworth and said something in his ear. Tamworth nodded. Then a young maid arrived with Kathryn's cloak and they beat a hasty retreat out of the room. She could still hear the men's muffled voices and shouts as she skittered, along with Squire, down the passageway.

Once inside the carriage, Squire said, 'I'm sorry about what happened there, Kathryn.'

He settled back on the leather-cushioned upholstery and closed his eyes as if trying to mentally shut it all out.

She opened her mouth but nothing came out. 'I . . . I . . . just felt like a piece of meat in there, that Mr Brutus was 'orrible!'

He opened his eyes and nodded, then, patting the leather wallet said, 'Well, at least we have these bids.' Seeing the look on her face, he reached for her hand and, raising it to his lips, kissed the back of it. 'Kathryn, you do not have to do anything you don't want to. I can put a stop to this right now, if you like?'

She swallowed hard as a tear left her eye and travelled down her cheek. She reached into the pocket of her cloak for her handkerchief to wipe it away. But Squire beat her to it. He already had his large black silk handkerchief to hand and sat forward to pat her cheek dry.

He squeezed her hand. 'Like I said, you don't have to do anything you don't want to do. No harm will be done. I can give you some money until you get yourself a job, just to get you back on your feet as it were.'

She shook her head, vehemently. 'No, it has to be done.' She couldn't let Ma and the kids down. How would they survive?

He smiled. 'Very well, I shall choose your . . . companion. And if the winning gentleman is the one you dislike most intensely, I shall tear up his bid and choose another.'

She nodded, but she didn't even want to sit with the least objectionable of them all, anyhow. Simply because none of them were Squire. 'No, please, we'll carry on with the original plan.'

He nodded, but said no more for the rest of the journey.

Chapter Six

The following morning when Kathryn awoke, a shaft of early autumnal sunshine was showing through a chink in the bedroom curtains. She yawned and turned over in bed. There was no sound of Squire. All was quiet in the apartment – no creaking of the floorboards as he moved around, no doors opening and closing, no manly sniffs or coughs in the background. Where was he? She drew on her dressing gown and padded through to the living room. The floor beneath her feet was cold to the touch. A fire crackled in the grate, its flames dancing before her eyes, providing her with much-needed warmth on such a chilly morning. She was grateful for it too as she warmed her hands in front of it, watching her skin turn a pallid shade of mottled-white and pink. She turned, then noticed a hand-written note on the table propped up against the candle-holder, beside which was a basket of bread rolls, a jug of milk, some cheese and a small bunch of freesias with red, orange and white blooms in a small crystal vase. The note read:

Had to slip away on business, will pick you up from the end of your street at six o'clock sharp this evening. Meanwhile I've left you some cheese and rolls and a jug of milk for your breakfast. Squire. X

She reached out to touch the bread. The rolls were still warm and smelled heavenly. She guessed he must have purchased them from the bakehouse down the road. How thoughtful of him. She lifted the small bunch of freesias, inhaling their fresh fragrance. They brought back such memories for her. Ma had always loved these simple flowers and, when there was enough money at home, Pa would buy her a bunch from Mrs McCarthy's flower-stall at the market. He always said the lilac ones matched the colour of Ma's eyes. How she'd blush like a young girl whenever he told her that.

After breakfasting and saving some food for Ma and the kids, she washed, dressed herself in her day clothes, and went home with the food wrapped up in a sheet of newspaper in one hand and the bunch of freesias in the other.

Mags greeted her as she entered the house and the kids came running. Kathryn handed her the package. 'For you all, we had some left over from last night. Mr Bates is kind to us all. I've also brought these flowers for Ma. Put them in water when you get a chance, Mags; freesias are such delicate blooms.'

'How did your night shift go?' Mags asked, through narrowed eyes.

'Quite good last night,' Kathryn lied. 'We had a big order to work on.' Then, to change the subject, she asked, 'How's Ma?'

Mags shook her head and sighed. 'Not much better, I'm afraid . . .' There was a look in Mags's eyes that told Kathryn the girl was giving up hope their mother would ever be well again. She had to jolly her along; there was no good them all giving up.

Kathryn laid a hand gently on her sister's shoulder. 'Is she eating at least?'

Mags frowned. 'Not much, she's not. She managed a 'alf a round of toast and a cup of tea but has refused anything since.'

'Give some of that bread and cheese to the kids and keep some back for yerself and Ma, I'm going to pop in to see how she is.'

Mags nodded and as she opened the package out on to the table, the kids came rushing to see what she had for them, making such a racket with their whoops and chatter that Mags needed to shush them so as not to disturb Ma.

Kathryn removed her woollen shawl, tossing it over the armchair as she went to see her mother. She was in bed, fast asleep, and so Kathryn sat by the side of her bed and, taking her mother's pallid hand, held it to her face. It felt cold to the touch, so she went over to the wardrobe and found a couple of her mother's old shawls and draped them over the bed to keep the heat in. Her mother stirred and opened her eyes momentarily.

'Kathryn, it's you . . .' Her voice sounded a little croaky.

'Yes, it's me, Ma. Would you like a cup of tea to warm you up?'

Her mother smiled and nodded as Kathryn went to brew up. If ever she needed convincing she was doing the right thing, now she was sure. She couldn't let Ma and the kids down. If she didn't do something to earn some money fast, they'd all be out on their backsides, and what about Ma? If they had enough money they could get better medical care for her. Looking at Mags, she asked, 'Did Mr O'Shay come to collect this week's rent money?'

Mags nodded. 'He did an' all, but now he said he's thinking of putting the rent up and next time we're behind with it, there'll be no second chance for us.'

Kathryn slowly shook her head. They just couldn't win. 'I'm making Ma a cup of tea, would you like one?'

'Yes, please. At least we have the food you bought the other day, enough to keep us going, eh?'

Yes, but for how much longer?

Kathryn nodded. 'We'll be all right for a few days and at least we have a roof over our heads for the time being.'

Mags's face brightened up. 'By the way, Jimmy called to see you last night.'

Terror struck at Kathryn's heart. She'd deliberately avoided him these past few days, for fear he should find out what she was going to do. 'What did you tell him?'

'Just that you had a job on at the West End and it involved you working nights sometimes.'

Kathryn smiled and nodded. 'Good.'

'Why? Should I have told him something else, is it a secret?'

'Oh no. I didn't want him to worry, that's all, yer know how he takes on so. Right, I'll go and make us all a cup of tea and the kids can 'ave that bit of food I've brought them. Doubt Ma will eat any of it and I've had my share already, so there's even more for you, Mags.'

Mags shook her head. 'I'd rather Ma had her share, but yer right, she won't touch it. I'll make her some broth later. She can only seem to manage that and water or tea these days. She 'ardly eats enough to keep a bird alive.'

Kathryn knew that to be the truth. It was pitiful to see how thin their mother was becoming, her bones sticking out from beneath her clothing, and her dress hanging from her small, delicate frame. Her eyes were beginning to look large and her cheekbones sunken.

There was a sudden knock on the door and Kathryn's heart hammered beneath her blouse. Was that O'Shay? She couldn't risk the other kids answering as they'd be too frightened to stand up to him.

Tentatively, she opened the door, to be faced with Jimmy.

He smiled at her. 'Well, ain't yer going to invite me in, stranger?' he asked.

She swallowed. 'Yes, of course, come inside.'

He followed her into the small room as the kids stood there looking at him. Shaun looked as if he was about to say something, but Mags carefully ushered them away. 'Come on, you lot,' she said, as if she was herding a flock of sheep, 'let's go play hopscotch in the yard and leave this pair in peace. They look like they have lots to talk about!'

Kathryn nodded and smiled at Mags, grateful that she'd come to her rescue.

When they heard the back door close and the kids' voices fade away, Jimmy looked at her. 'What's going on, Kathryn? I haven't seen you in ages!'

'I've just been busy with my new job, that's all.'

'I called around last night to see you, but Mags said you weren't at home.'

'I know, she told me.'

'What is this new job anyhow that makes you work such strange hours?'

What on earth could she possibly tell Jimmy about her 'new job'? She certainly couldn't tell him the truth. He'd held a candle for her for years, and it would break his heart to think what she was getting up to. She cleared her throat. 'I'm working at sewing, up West,' she explained. 'My new job often involves working overnight.'

He nodded. 'Well, I think it's a shame that we've lost touch with each other.'

For a brief moment, she felt a pang of regret too that they

were no longer stepping out of an evening going over to the pie-and-mash shop or for a walk in Victoria Park. And if she could only turn back the clock, then maybe she would have accepted his marriage proposal, but now things had gone too far.

She was going to have to avoid him for the time being. She'd stop after she'd made enough money to treat her mother, she reassured herself. She could do that and no one else need ever know, it would get them over a difficult time.

'Me too,' she found herself saying, and she did mean it – but knew that cutting ties with Squire just so she could see Jimmy wasn't going to solve the family's finances or Ma's condition.

As if on cue, she heard her mother's cough from the bedroom and saw it as a sign she was doing the right thing in going along with Squire's plans for her.

Jimmy was quiet for a moment, then he said, 'So, how about coming out with me the next time you have a free evening?' Expectation was shining in his eyes.

She hesitated for a moment. 'I can't see that happening for a long time,' she said regretfully.

He took a deep breath and let it out again. 'Don't worry, Kathryn, I get the picture. I won't pester you no more . . .'

She was about to say something, but nothing came out when she opened her mouth.

'I'll see myself out,' he whispered, and she watched him walk away from her. Something inside her felt like yelling at him to come back, but something stronger was stopping her and that something was pride.

As Kathryn was getting ready for work, brushing her hair, she heard Ma coughing again in her room. Her coughs were becoming more laboured. Kathryn discarded her hairbrush and went to attend to her.

She entered Ma's room without knocking, to find her hunched-up over the bed with the small enamel bowl in front of her.

'Aw, Ma,' she said, drawing closer, 'you're not at all well today, are you?'

Her mother looked at her with wide eyes, her face sunken and her skin sallow. Slowly, she shook her head. It was as if all the fight had gone out of her weak, emaciated body.

Kathryn checked the medicine bottle by the side of the bed. There was only a little left in it. She unplugged the cork and poured a little on to the spoon. 'Here, take this,' she urged. 'I'll buy some more later. Where's Mags got to?'

Ma shook her head. 'I don't know,' she said weakly, 'I haven't seen her in a while . . .'

Kathryn pursed her lips. Her sister was supposed to be taking care of Ma while she got ready to leave? She took the spoon from Ma's lips, then Ma closed her eyes and her head flopped back on the pillow. It was hard to see her mother suffering like this. She needed medical treatment.

'I won't be a moment,' Kathryn said.

She went downstairs and called out her sister's name, but there was no answer. Then she checked the yard, but only the other kids were playing out there. 'Where's Mags gone?' she asked.

'No see Mags,' said Rosie, then she stuck her thumb in her mouth.

'Nor me.' Damon shook his head.

'Have you seen her, Shaun?'

'No,' he said, turning away to pick up the old ball they'd been playing with. 'One minute she was with us, then when I turned around, she'd gone. I thought she was in the house seeing to Ma or something.'

If her sister wasn't back soon, then Kathryn could hardly leave to go off with Squire. What should she do? She noticed her neighbour, Stanley Morgan, in his back yard shovelling up some coal into his coal hutch. Stan was a northerner who had settled in the East End years back, a good solid reliable sort.

'Anything wrong, lass?' he asked, his eyes full of concern.

'I'm due to leave the house, Stanley, but Mags hasn't returned, have you seen her?'

He removed his flat cap and scratched his head. 'No, I haven't, but I'll come and sit inside with your mother, if you like?'

Kathryn relaxed and smiled. 'Oh, would you? Thank you so much!' Ma had helped out when Stanley's wife had been at death's door. She knew they got along well with one another and had formed some sort of bond.

Just like you and Jimmy, a little voice inside her head reminded her.

'How is your ma now?' Stan asked, putting down his shovel and coming around through their back gate and into the yard.

'Not so good, to be honest with you.' She lowered her voice so the kids couldn't hear, then, laying a hand on his, said, 'She'll be pleased to see you, though.'

He smiled and nodded as if he understood all too well; after all, he'd been through it with his wife, too.

At precisely six o'clock, Squire arrived in a hansom cab to pick Kathryn up from the bottom of her street. By now Mags had returned, making excuses for her sudden disappearance, mumbling something about having had to call at a friend's house. Kathryn feared that maybe looking after their mother was proving too much for the girl. She'd had a lot on her shoulders lately.

Mags thought Kathryn was off to work the night shift again – which was a convenient excuse. Kathryn gave special instructions for her to keep a close eye on Ma while she was away. She promised as soon as she'd earned enough, they'd be getting Ma some medical treatment as she didn't seem to be improving. Before leaving, she'd ensured her mother had taken a little broth and the room was warmer than it had been that morning. She'd insisted that Mags must keep the fire going in that room, as the temperature was dropping outside. There was enough coal and chopped wood for a few days, but, hopefully, soon, they wouldn't have to worry any longer.

When they arrived back at the apartment, Squire took Kathryn by both hands and, looking deep into her eyes, said, 'I'm sorry to tell you, the man with the highest bid was Brutus. He has offered forty pounds . . .'

Kathryn gasped. That was a lot of money. It would be enough, after Squire had taken his share, to really do some good at home, but he was the man she feared most and after what he'd said about taking her virginity, she knew she should be wary of him. If that's what was to happen, then she'd be no better than those girls in the East End. But she trusted Squire, and, still, Brutus was a gentleman. And forty pounds was a huge sum of money. Although part of her wanted to tell Squire to tear up the bid and take the next one, she refused to do so.

'I must do this,' she assured Squire, with tears in her eyes.

He shook his head. 'If I could afford to pay you that sum myself I would, but I can't. I'm sorry and now I regret getting you involved.'

She shook her head, even though she could detect the genuine concern in his eyes. 'I need that money for Ma's medical treatment and for us to keep a roof over our heads.'

'Then I'll tell you what I shall do. As I cannot possibly

match that offer, you must keep all of it.' He touched her hand with such tenderness and as she looked at him she saw the love he had for her in his eyes. How selfless of him! She found herself falling in love with him just that little bit more in that moment.

'I can't allow you to do that,' she said breathlessly.

'You can, and you will. And you shall only have to suffer that man for the one night, anyhow, I promise.'

Just one night. Would she have to sleep with the man? She looked at Squire and he looked away. It was then that she knew why the sum was so high. He hugged her to his chest.

Realisation dawned on her about what she was going to do. Her feelings were so conflicted: on one hand she felt Squire really cared for her, but on the other, she was aware of the deceit he'd created.

She closed her eyes at the thought of it. For the time being she felt safe in his embrace. Looking up at him, she asked, 'When shall it be?'

'Tomorrow night. But tonight we have each other. Come and lie with me . . .' He kissed the top of her head and led her over to the bed. They both sat side by side as he allowed her to weep on his shoulder, while he held her tightly to him.

As she stared at her surroundings through a haze of tears, she took in the ornate four-poster and its fancy drapes and realised tomorrow night she would lie with another . . . That's what lack of money did for you; it turned you into a whore. And while she wept she realised that what had once been a dream of being a rich man's companion as she spent her time wining and dining in the best establishments and attending operas and stage productions by his side, as people turned their heads to look at her, was in reality fast fading away and turning into the nightmare of being a set-up scarlet woman who was no better than a nymph of the pave. Her Lothario would be able to walk away from her afterwards, feeling pleased with himself having taken his pound of flesh after ravishing her nubile body, while she'd feel morally ashamed for the rest of her life.

Chapter Seven

She'd thought of nothing else all day: of how one act of debauchery tonight was going to change her family fortunes and how she viewed herself forever. Squire had been kindness itself, bringing her a bowl of warming stew and fresh crusty bread from a nearby eatery, but she found it hard to digest the food. The disappointment overwhelmed her. She no longer felt the same person. How had he gone from being her Sir Galahad to someone she now felt she didn't really know, in one fell swoop? She now knew how Ma must feel each time they encouraged her to eat something, but images of her mother being well again and rosy-cheeked danced before her eyes, and spurred her on. She could never break her silent promise.

She bathed herself in the communal bathroom downstairs, realising the next time she used that bathroom she would be a different person.

'Don't worry, Kathryn. I shall stay in the living room just in case you need me . . .'

The thought alarmed her greatly: not just that he might be needed should things go wrong but the fact he would be there, knowing what was happening on the other side of the door.

'No,' she insisted, 'I want you gone when he arrives, you can come back in the morning. I've told them at home I am working on a big order so shall be late arriving home.'

'Very well.' His voice sounded dull, lacking the chirpy, happy quality that was usually there when he spoke to her. Was it her imagination or did he look sad today? He had a wistful look in his eyes she hadn't noticed before. It was almost as though a blanket of despair had enveloped him.

'What do you think I should wear?' She tried to keep her tone bright.

He coughed. 'I forgot to tell you, he has insisted you wear the white silk gown you had on the night of the auction.'

Surprised, she looked Squire in the eye. 'And why might that be, do you know?'

'He wants you to look the part of the maiden.'

She nodded. In some ways now she wished it was the old gent who had won the bid; the way he had shuffled along, he wouldn't have had much life in him. Maybe he'd have spent the whole evening inspecting her with his monocle and telling her about his wife. What was it her mother always said, 'A man wants his wife to be his angel of the home'?

Unfortunately, after tonight was over, and guessing what indeed might happen, she'd never be anyone's angel ever again.

*

Kathryn glanced out of the window down on to the street below. The last of the shoppers had all but gone home. The church bell chimed the hour of seven o'clock, but Brutus hadn't arrived as yet. She glanced nervously at Squire.

'Don't worry,' he reassured her, 'he's due to arrive at half past seven.'

By the time the bell had chimed the quarter hour, Kathryn's palms were perspiring profusely and her heart thudded heavily in her chest. Mouth dry, she reached out for a glass of water on the table and took a sip.

'Might I have a glass of brandy?' she asked.

Squire looked amused and smiled. 'Yes, you shall have whatever you like, my dear. But please, only a few sips to calm your nerves. We don't want Brutus smelling it on your breath.'

She nodded as she watched him walk over to the cabinet and take out a cut-crystal decanter and pour her a small glass, much smaller than the glass she and Squire had enjoyed the other evening before falling into a deep sleep.

Trembling, she took the glass from his outstretched hand, tentatively taking a sip of the amber fluid that warmed her up inside as their eyes met. Yes, in another time and place, maybe, they'd be together as one. She could see it in his eyes, his longing for her – or was it regret at having got her into this situation in the first place and having to give her up to someone else?

The mantel clock's ticking seemed to grow louder the later

it got. But they remained in silence; there was no need for words between them as their eyes said it all.

As the church bell chimed the half hour, she peeked through the lace curtain to see someone alight from a carriage down below. The young man looked up at the building and stepped towards it with purpose as Kathryn moved away from the window. He was here at last.

Kathryn was seated by the fireside drinking a cup of tea and staring into the flames. Things hadn't gone quite how she expected, much to her surprise and enormous relief. She heard a sudden noise as Squire burst in through the door and was at her side in a moment.

'My dearest Kathryn, I should never have allowed you to go through with it.' His voice was cracking with emotion as he knelt and wept into her lap.

Smiling, she held his head and forced him to look into her eyes. 'But you need not cry. All is well, I am still intact.'

His brows lifted. 'But how? I don't understand. Brutus was determined to have you and paid a high price for the privilege of doing so.'

'When it came down to it he couldn't manage the deed.'

Gazing at Squire's face she realised he didn't know whether to laugh or cry, but his relief appeared immense.

He blinked several times. 'But surely now he will want his money back?'

She held a little black velvet drawstring bag in her hand and dangled it over his head. 'This is full of bank notes and coins. I've never seen so much money in me life before.'

His eyes widened. 'But I don't understand, why would he pay you?'

'Don't you see? He's too embarrassed to tell anyone that he couldn't perform the act! He will seem a figure of fun otherwise. It was his excitement that caused 'is failure. So he's told me to pretend that he has taken me and not to tell anyone the truth of it, and for this amount of money I surely will not, well only yer!'

Squire threw back his head and laughed. It was like a huge weight had lifted from their shoulders. 'Then my darling Kathryn, someday you will be mine and we'll still have the money, too.'

Kathryn placed a finger to his lips, which he removed and began kissing her fervently. She was helpless to do anything else other than love him.

The following morning, Kathryn awoke and turned over in bed to find Squire by her side fast asleep, his gentle snores reassuring. She sat up in bed and smiled. He had remained by her side all night long without even taking any liberties, just kissing her and holding her close to his side. She had felt like Eve to his Adam, part of his rib. She lifted the little velvet bag from the chair where she'd left it the previous night. She couldn't take all that money even though he'd offered it; half belonged to him, but there would be more than enough to get a doctor for her mother. She needed to get home to check on Ma and the kids as she was leaving Mags with too much responsibility for her tender age, and she felt guilty about that. An idea was taking hold of what she could do next to get more money for the family's future. O'Shay was going to put the rent up soon but now she could afford to move them all out for a while to somewhere much better, where with luck they wouldn't be hassled by a rogue landlord and could live comfortably for some time to come.

When Kathryn arrived home she got Shaun to summon the local physician, Doctor Arnold Beck, to see Ma.

'Is there somewhere we can speak in private?' he asked, after giving her mother a full examination. His grey eyes were full of concern and he cleared his throat.

'Yes, Doctor.' Kathryn looked at her mother's drawn, pinched face. 'Ma, Mags will sit with you for a while, I'm just going to talk things over with Dr Beck.'

Ma nodded, then closed her eyes, her complexion a deathly shade of grey. Sometimes lately, either herself or Mags had entered the bedroom and wondered if she were still alive at all.

Kathryn led the doctor to the scullery as the kids were seated and on their best behaviour in the living room.

'I'm afraid your mother might only have weeks left to live,' he said gravely.

A sudden burst of pain hit Kathryn like a bolt of lightning. Of course she had realised that maybe this was a possibility, but wasn't there something that could be done to save Ma? Anything at all?

As if reading her mind, the doctor looked her in the eye. 'There's not a lot that can be done – unless you are wealthy, my dear.'

'What do you mean, Doctor?'

He drew near and in a hushed tone said, 'There is a convalescent home I know of near the seaside in Kent. I used to work there. It's had good results with pulmonary patients. They get them rested and well again by feeding them a diet rich in nutrients, and the sea air and sunshine do the patients good. In your mother's case the bronchopneumonia that's set in has been worsened by living in damp and, er . . .'

'Squalid conditions?' Kathryn finished his sentence for him.

He nodded and then carried on. 'It's badly affecting her health, I'm afraid. Living in this area too, with all the fumes from the factories and tanneries, doesn't help either. It all takes its toll on your mother's health.'

'How much money would be required to get Ma in that rest home for a few weeks?'

Doctor Beck placed the palms of his hands on Kathryn's shoulders as he looked into her eyes with concern. 'More than you could probably afford, dear. I'm afraid it would take more than just a few weeks, more like months, possibly a year to build your mother up to full health again, and that would take a lot of money for that sort of intensive care.'

In the room next door, Kathryn heard her mother's painful racking coughs. 'I understand, Doctor. But if I could get her booked in for a few weeks, then I'm sure I'll be able to raise the rest of the money.'

Doctor Beck nodded. 'Very well. I shall write to the physician who runs the home, but you will need around thirty pounds up front, Kathryn. I don't know how in your position you could afford that kind of money?' He quirked a brow.

Thirty pounds? Even though she felt rich with twenty pounds in her pocket, she realised it would not be enough. She chewed on her bottom lip and then said, 'I think I can raise the money, Doctor. My mother needs that help.'

Doctor Beck's eyes widened with surprise. 'Very well, then I shall make all the necessary arrangements.'

Even if her mother could only spend a few weeks at the convalescent home, it might be enough to bring her back to good health and hopefully, by then, they would all have moved out of the house and on to better accommodation where the walls weren't black with mould and running with moisture.

When the doctor had departed, Kathryn turned to see Mags stood behind her. 'Kathryn . . .' she began as she wiped away a tear.

'Come on now, Mags, we'll cope, you'll see. We always have.'

She hugged her sister to her, allowing her to weep on her shoulder.

When Mags had drawn away after patting her face dry with her handkerchief, she looked at Kathryn through glassy eyes. 'Can you get me a job working with you too? I could help out, maybe work during the day while you work during the night? That way we can both help Ma.'

Kathryn smiled at her sister, realising how much she cared and feeling a little guilty for previously being so hard on her, but she couldn't possibly set her up with a non-existent job. 'Don't you worry. It won't come to that as I know someone who will help us.'

Mags sniffed and narrowed her eyes. 'You're talking about that Squire sort again, ain't yer?'

Kathryn nodded, then took Mags's hand in her own. But there was no way she could possibly tell her the truth about her other life and she felt sad about the need to lie to her own dear sister.

'I'm not so sure that I want you to do this, Kathryn,' Squire said after she told him the plan for him to auction her again. She noticed his furrowed brow, realising his concern for her was genuine.

'But if there's no other way I can get that amount of money? It's only until Ma gets well again, then I can stop altogether.'

Taking both her hands in his, he said with tears in his eyes,

'Look, I'll give you my share of the money, would that be enough for you?'

She shook her head. 'No, sorry, it won't be. Ma is going to need months of care and the bills will all mount up.'

He stayed silent for a moment and she wondered what he was thinking.

Chapter Eight

Arrangements were made that evening for Dorrie to go around to Kathryn's family home to look after the kids for the next couple of days, while Mags accompanied Ma to the rest home in Kent. Squire insisted they both take his carriage. Realising it was all for the best, and the only way for Ma to get well again, she thanked him for his kindness.

'Think nothing of it, Kathryn. My driver will take care of their needs on the journey. It's the least I can do to enable your mother to make a full recovery, and we need to get you all moved out of that hovel.'

Kathryn felt her bottom lip quiver; it might be a hovel to someone like him who was used to the finer things in life, but to her it was still her home where her mother and father had brought them all up. She was about to say something but feared she'd cry, so kept silent as she watched the driver load a trunk of her mother's belongings on to the back of the carriage. Kindly, Squire had loaned them an old leather one he claimed he no longer used. Kathryn had bought Ma a second-hand dress from the dolly shop down the road, far better than anything she'd ever owned.

Squire and Kathryn watched as Ma, guided by Mags and well wrapped up in two shawls, walked unsteadily out on to the street. She stooped to kiss all the kids goodbye, then Kathryn and Squire helped her aboard the carriage. Kathryn covered her legs with a tartan rug to keep her warm for the journey.

'Now, I've made up a basket of food for you both, Ma,' she said, trying to keep the conversation bright and breezy for fear she should break down and cry. 'There's ham and egg sandwiches, an apple pie I cooked, and some ginger beer. Mags will give you your medicine on the way. The carriage driver, Mr Parsons, will stop any time you need to take a break.'

Ma looked at her eldest daughter with eyes as big as saucers. 'There's good to me you are, gal.'

'And don't you be worrying, we'll get you well again, no fear. The kids'll be well cared for.' Kathryn felt something being pressed into her hand. When she opened it she could have wept; it was her mother's wedding ring again. 'No, Ma, you keep it!' Her eyes were brimming with unshed tears.

'It keeps sliding off me finger, I've lost that much weight. Hang on to it for safe keeping then, if you don't want to pawn it.'

Kathryn held the ring up. 'Ma, I promise you, you'll never need to pawn this ring – I shall take good care of it.' She leaned over to give her mother a kiss on her sallow cheek.

Then clambering down from the carriage, she allowed Mags to board. Mags looked at her with apprehension in her eyes. 'I think Dorrie has something she wants to tell you. About Jimmy.'

'Oh?'

'Don't look at me, you threw him over. She wants to speak to you, not me!' she said in a haughty fashion. Kathryn marvelled at what a little madam her sister could be when she got on her high horse.

She waved her family goodbye. 'Have a safe journey both, see you soon . . . Mags, the carriage will bring you back tomorrow.'

Mags nodded. Even though she was almost fourteen years old, she was a very capable girl, however headstrong she could be at times.

'What's wrong?' Squire asked as she stepped back on to the pavement. 'You look a little flustered . . .'

Did it really show that she had concerns about her oldest friend? She hoped Jimmy was all right. She stood there waving until the carriage had all but disappeared down the road and, turning, realised she had to face up to things. 'Nothing that might concern you!' she said sharply as she made her way back to the house.

Dorrie was stood on the doorstep with the kids, who were still waving even though the carriage was almost out of sight.

Kathryn cleared her throat. 'Mags said you had something important to tell me about Jimmy?'

'Yes, we'd better speak inside . . .' It was obvious the girl didn't want to discuss such matters in front of all and sundry, and that included Squire too, so Kathryn asked him to wait outside.

'Jimmy's leaving home,' Dorrie said, biting on her lip as if to hold back tears as they stood inside the passageway.

Kathryn couldn't believe her ears. 'But why? How? He was happy here, weren't he?'

'He was an' all, once upon a time . . .'

The girl's tone stressed that she thought something, or someone, had made him unhappy, and you wouldn't need to be a mind reader to guess who that person was.

'Me? You think he's leaving because of me?' Kathryn blinked several times.

She nodded. 'He's been very discontent this past few weeks, said yer'd refused to marry him and refused his 'elp an' all.'

'It's true, Dorrie.' She laid her hand on the girl's shoulder. 'He did ask to marry me, but I'm not ready for marriage yet. I admit he got a bit annoyed with me recently as I haven't had much time for him, but all I'm guilty of is working up West. I'd never hurt yer Jimmy for the world.'

The girl's face relaxed. 'I know that, Kathryn. Our Jimmy's always thought highly of you and it ain't yer fault he's off to sea.'

'Off to sea! I thought you meant he's – just going somewhere out of the area to look for work, not setting sail some place overseas!'

She shrugged. 'All I know is he'll be gone for a long time, he told me not to worry and left me most of his savings. He reckoned he'd been saving up to marry you but yer don't want to know. He'll be calling around here afore he leaves, he said.'

Kathryn put her head in her hands and wept.

Shaun came up behind her and tugged on her sleeve. 'Jimmy's going? Are you sending him away, Kathryn?'

'I don't want Jimmy to leave us all behind,' Damon said, his bottom lip jutting out as if he was just about to burst out in tears.

She shook her head, though she might just as well have sent him away. Jimmy was the best friend she ever had, and it was only now she was realising it for the first time. Jimmy accepted her for who she was, just for being herself. 'But did you have any idea he was going to go away? Had he ever spoken about such things to yer, Dorrie?'

Dorrie shook her head, then sniffed. 'No, I can't believe he's going to leave us all like this.'

Kathryn laid a hand on the girl's shoulder. 'Look, if yer and your little brother need any help you're to come to me, right?'

Dorrie shrugged her shoulders. 'But you don't owe us anything at all.'

'Of course we do, you've spent many an hour helping out with the kids and sitting with Ma. Jimmy's helped us often enough. Now promise me if yer need any help you'll get in touch with me?'

She nodded almost with reluctance, and then bent down to scoop up Rosie in her arms.

There was a sudden knock at the front door. Kathryn and Dorrie exchanged glances but both knew who it would be. Kathryn's legs felt boneless as she walked towards the door.

As she drew it open she saw Jimmy's old familiar cocky smile and those eyes filled with light and hope as he stepped inside, and then she was in his arms and it felt so good. She couldn't believe he was leaving them all, particularly not the young 'uns.

'Oh Jimmy, do you really have to go?' she said as she wept on his shoulder.

'I do, yes. It's for the best and when I've earned my fortune I'll return, you'll see . . .' He drew away and, taking her hands in his, looked into her eyes. 'I'll never forget you, no fear!' he said. Then looking past her, he saw his sister and went over to her. 'I won't be away for long, Dorrie, don't cry me little sweetheart.' He embraced her. 'I've already said goodbye to Nick, now be a big girl for him, won't you?' She nodded with tears in her eyes. Then with one final wave, and hoisting his bag on his back, he left. Kathryn and Dorrie stood on the doorstep and watched until he was a little dot in the distance disappearing around the corner.

'He never even turned around to wave goodbye!' Dorrie complained.

'Aw, that'll be because it would have been too upsetting for him,' Kathryn explained. 'I bet if he'd have turned around, he might have lost heart and come back to us,' she said with a lump in her throat.

Dorrie sniffed and wiped away a tear with the back of her hand. It wasn't going to be easy for any of them.

'You go now, Kathryn, I'll take care of the kids.' It was obvious the girl was doing her best to act grown up, but how lost she must feel without her brother to care for her.

Kathryn furrowed her brow. 'Do you know where Jimmy will sail to?'

'North Africa. He said valuable goods were being taken there and cottons, fine silks, oils and things like that will be brought back with the ship.'

'How did he seem to you when he first told you he was off?'

'Quite excited to be honest with yer. I haven't seen such a gleam in his eyes for a long time. He was right looking forward to it I reckon.'

Downcast, Kathryn lowered her head. It was all her fault that Jimmy had been so down lately. As if Dorrie could read her neighbour's thoughts flitting through her mind, she touched Kathryn's hand. 'Hey, my brother's a big boy, he wouldn't do anything he didn't want to, yer can be sure of that! And he's told my aunt and uncle who live nearby to keep an eye out for me and Nick.'

Kathryn nodded through glazed-over eyes. Dorrie was right, it was her brother's decision to leave and he probably had his reasons, thinking he'd return in a year or two with plenty in his pocket to support his family. He'd never let them down, would he? Meanwhile, there were more pressing problems at hand.

'Listen, Dorrie, you take care and don't go letting anyone in or the kids out tonight, keep the door bolted.' She didn't want to alarm the girl but with a killer on the prowl they couldn't afford to take chances.

'Yes, I will, have no worries about that. I'll take good care of the kids.'

Aware she'd left Squire standing outside, she kissed Rosie, who was now snuggled into Dorrie's neck as she held her in her arms. 'Shaun, Damon!' She beckoned the boys over. 'Now you both be good for Dorrie until Mags and myself return, won't you?'

Shaun frowned. 'Where's our Ma gone?'

Kathryn ruffled his hair. 'She's gone on holiday until she gets better, you'll see if she don't return looking a picture of good 'ealth!'

'Will that mean she won't be in bed all the time when she gets back?' He looked at her with such longing in his eyes that she could have broken down there and then and held him to her. But she didn't want to upset them all, she had to appear strong even if she sometimes didn't feel that way.

'Yes, she's going to come back fit and well with rosy cheeks.' She smiled.

Shaun nodded, apparently happy with the explanation.

'I'll bring you all back a poke of fudge when I return!' she promised, and left them all in Dorrie's care.

When Kathryn had shut the front door behind her and was standing in the street beside Squire, she noticed he had a curious look on his face.

'Who was that young man who just called at your house?' he enquired as his eyes met hers.

Of course, he would have seen Jimmy knock at the door and be invited inside, she realised.

'He's just a neighbour, that's all. I've known him for years.' But she failed to add that Jimmy had once been a competitor for her affections and she wondered what Squire would make of that if he knew.

He smiled, looking reassured, and took her hand to hail a cab to take them to the West End. 'I need you to get fitted for a few more demure dresses,' he explained, as the cab rattled along the streets.

What did he have in mind?

'Why do I need more dresses like that?'

He drew a breath. 'So we can make ourselves more money of course, Kathryn.' He shot her a wolfish grin. 'Surely another auction isn't out of the question for the future, my dear?'

Kathryn nodded, but felt it was morally wrong to go ahead with duping men into parting with large sums of money to constantly claim her honour. Yet, what about those men?

The ones she'd encountered at the auction had been vile creatures and that was enough to change her mind about the issue. She supposed they were only going to get what they deserved. She had her family to think about and they obviously weren't thinking about theirs when they took their pleasures with women of easy virtue. At least she hadn't gone that far with any man as yet, and still maintained her honour.

'I'll drop you off at the outfitters and Mrs Harrington shall take care of you. She has your measurements noted down and I've told her the sort of dresses we wish to purchase.'

Kathryn blinked hard. 'You've told her already?'

'Yes, we have an agreement in place.' As if he had already said too much he tried to change the subject. 'Then tonight I'm taking you out to dine and we shall discuss our future plans.' He tapped her on the hand in reassurance, but she wasn't consoled at all.

'You mean to say you've done this kind of thing before?' Her eyes widened.

He shook his head. 'No, of course not,' he said quickly. 'I meant our current arrangement with the store.'

She narrowed her gaze with suspicion. Was he being truthful? She wasn't quite sure.

He asked the cab driver to wait while he escorted her inside the store, then left her in Mrs Harrington's capable hands. There was something about the woman that made Kathryn's skin crawl. She was clean and well dressed, but there was something she sensed that was so false about her, she felt it was as if the woman was keeping some sort of secret from her. It was a shame they had to be here at all really, but Brutus had ruined the last dress when he'd got carried away with his lustful urges and ripped it off her body.

'Right, *Miss Cartwright*, we don't have exactly the same material to make the white silk-style dress you last wore, but we have a muslin version which my assistant will bring in for you to try on. If it fits, I've been informed that I am to make three of them for you, is that understood?' She spoke to her as if she was a nuisance or a child at school.

Kathryn pulled herself up to her full height and met the woman's eyes with her own. 'If that's what Mr Curtis-Browne instructed then please get on with the job!'

The woman blinked several times and her upper lip twitched as her faced reddened with fury. But what could she do? Squire was bringing her good custom, very good custom indeed. Kathryn watched as the woman balled her hands into fists at her sides. Then as if realising she had to be nice to her, the redness disappeared, and she flexed her hands. Then her voice took on an almost sweet, sickly tone.

All I need to do is get through this then I'm out of here . . .

She slipped on the dress but for some reason it seemed slightly smaller than the last and she wondered why that was.

'You should have worn that corset we provided you with!' Mrs Harrington said, then more formally, 'Not to worry, we have a spare you can try on here.'

She was about to protest that Squire would no more want her to wear corsetry with that dress than with the other silk one, but how could she tell the woman it was to be her 'virginity gown'? And if three were being made, then he was obviously expecting her to 'lose her maidenhood' at least three times. That meant he intended her to have relations with three different men, other than himself. A voice inside her screamed that she should get out of this right now, but the thought of Ma needing help and the promise she'd made kept her rooted to the spot.

Kathryn nodded at the woman; she needed to keep her on side so she could get out of the store as quickly as possible. After being laced up in the corset, she found the dress fitted beautifully. Mrs Harrington smiled and then summoned her assistant. 'We'll make another, but with slightly different dimensions this time, this one only just fits.'

The assistant nodded. 'Very well, ma'am.'

Weren't people supposed to lose weight when they were in love, not the other way around? Maybe the dress she'd tried on was a fraction smaller than the other? Or perhaps Mrs Harrington and her assistant had used the wrong measurements by mistake?

She was about to ask Mrs Harrington about this, when someone else entered the communal section of the changing room, a dark-eyed young woman with a beauty spot on her left cheek.

'Ah, Miss Evangeline,' the assistant enthused, as if really pleased to see her. 'Mrs Harrington will be with you shortly when she's finished seeing to Miss Bella. Is anyone accompanying you today?'

'I'm supposed to be meeting someone 'ere,' the young woman explained, her eyes searching the room as if surprised whoever she was meeting had not yet arrived. She looked Kathryn up and down with curiosity. 'Hello,' she said. 'Nice to meet yer. I have a dress just like that one.'

Kathryn smiled, she felt almost as though she were looking at a mirror image of herself, except Evangeline's hair was almost black. She wondered what the chances of someone wanting that same white dress were. There was something so familiar about the woman though, she felt like she'd seen her somewhere before but couldn't think where or when. Maybe it would come back to her eventually.

'Nice to meet you too, Evangeline. I'm Bella Cartwright.'

Evangeline coughed. 'Me real name is Jess,' she whispered. 'Evangeline's me professional name, if yer get my drift?'

Kathryn nodded.

Jess? There was something familiar about that name.

'I'll just leave you two ladies alone for a moment while my assistant makes a pot of coffee for you both and Miss Bella waits for her lift home,' Mrs Harrington said. The woman's demeanour had now totally changed as if she was happy for them both to become acquainted.

Once Kathryn and changed out of the white muslin dress, she returned to her normal day clothes and sat one side of a low wooden table and chatted amicably with Jess who sat at the other, telling her she was also from the Whitechapel area.

They knew a lot of the same people and places; it was uncanny. What a coincidence! Two working-class girls being in a place like this? As the assistant entered the room with the tray of coffee, Kathryn caught sight of Jess's left hand. No, it couldn't be, could it? The engagement ring she wore looked very similar to the one Squire had given her not so long ago. Her stomach lurched.

Once the assistant had placed the coffee pot on the table and filled the awaiting cups and departed, with thudding heart Kathryn said, 'I . . . I couldn't help admiring your ring. You're engaged?' The girl nodded. 'So, your fiancé is he from the East End, too?'

'No, 'e lives around these parts actually . . .' She was about to elaborate as Mrs Harrington swept into the dressing room with a huge smirk on her face.

'Ladies, there appears to be some sort of mistake. Miss Evangeline, you are booked in for tomorrow, not for today.'

Jess shook her head with a vacant look on her face. 'But I don't understand. I'm sure you told me today, Mrs Harrington.'

Mrs Harrington sniffed loudly. 'No, it's you who has made the mistake.'

At that point, Squire hovered at the doorway. He blinked hard several times, looking at Kathryn then Jess and back again. 'H . . . hello,' he said, his eyes widening. He seemed thrown off guard.

Now it was Jess's turn to look surprised.

Mrs Harrington smirked again. 'It appears your *nieces* have just been introduced to one another, Mr Curtis-Browne.'

'I . . . I'm so terribly sorry, Kathryn, let me explain things to you . . .' It was then Kathryn remembered where she had seen the woman before. It was at The Horse and Harness pub, she'd been the drunken woman in the company of those two men, and it seemed to Kathryn that Squire knew her quite well. Now she understood why.

Not wishing to make a fool of herself in front of Mrs Harrington and adding to her merriment, Kathryn stood and walked over to the coat stand in the corner to snatch her cape. She put it on and, turning towards Squire, said, 'Is the cab still outside?'

He nodded.

'Then I shall leave you to it.' She swallowed hard, not wanting to cry in front of anyone. 'Nice to meet you, Jess. I am sure you are in the dark as much as I am. Would you like to get out of here?'

Jess stood, pursed her lips in annoyance, and then stared at Squire for the longest time, her eyes flashing dangerously. Then she turned to Kathryn. 'Yes, please.'

'Ladies, let me explain things to you, it's not how it appears . . .' Squire pleaded, but neither listened to him as they strode out of the store and into the waiting cab. The problem was, Kathryn wasn't quite sure where they should go. She didn't particularly want to return to the apartment and they couldn't discuss things at her family home, so she chose to go to a tea room that Squire had recently taken her to.

Things felt a little awkward between the women as they waited for their pot of tea to arrive; neither felt like eating.

'So,' Kathryn said finally, 'Squire, as he calls himself, was your fiancé, too?' She looked at Jess with avid interest.

Jess nodded, staring at the white linen table cloth for the longest time until she brought her gaze up to meet Kathryn's. 'I had fallen on hard times and went for a couple of gins at The Horse and Harness. You've heard of it?'

'Yes, I know of it.' She didn't want to tell the girl she had picked Squire up there one night and that's what had led to all of this. 'Go on . . .'

'He could see I was upset as I really needed to make some money. I was on strike with the matchgirls from Bryant and May at the time.'

'So, he approached you in the first instance?'

'Yes. He told me he could get a nice pretty young girl like me some easy work, all I'd 'ave to do would be to escort gentlemen if they wanted to go to the theatre or they needed someone to talk to. When yer down on yer luck yer think your ship 'as come in when someone tells yer that.'

Kathryn nodded. She could well imagine as it had happened to her too, though not in quite the same manner as it was she who had approached Squire and not the other way around. 'So what happened then?'

'Well, I soon found out . . .' – she glanced nervously around the tea room to ensure she wasn't being overheard, then in a hushed tone carried on so Kathryn had to strain to hear – 'that it wasn't as simple as just going to the theatre with a gentleman, they were going to expect something else in return. Then he suggested auctioning my virginity.'

'He didn't take you to a large country house to do so, did he?'

Jess nodded. 'It was awful. I was paraded around in front of a bunch of letches and the man what bid for me was old enough to be me father. My first time was terrible.' She closed her eyes as if the memory had come flooding back and she was trying to block it out. 'The man treated me roughly, I was left covered in cuts and bruises, but Squire said I had done well and he handed me five pounds for my time. At first I thought I was rich, but by the time I'd paid the rent for our home back in the East End and other things it began to run out over time, so Squire put me out to work again. Only this time I earned far less and got regular beatings from that first punter. It got so bad that I ran off back home and began to work the streets near me house. But Squire came after me telling me he loved me and then he gave me this ring.' She fingered it as if now it meant nothing to her. 'He got me away by reminding me that there was a madman on the loose who had already killed two working women and he reckoned I might be The Whitechapel Murderer's next victim. Like a fool I went with him and he set me up in an apartment, but then just a couple of weeks or so ago he turned me out and packed all me bags ready for me to go, reckoned he couldn't pay the rent no more and I'd have to go back home. So I ended up just walking the streets for money.'

'Oh Jess, I knew I recognised you when you walked into Gilmour's. I remember seeing you in the pub one night.'

She nodded her head. 'Yes, I'm often in there or The Ten Bells. That's what I've now resorted to. Me lavish lifestyle all but disappeared overnight when Squire said I had to get out of that lovely apartment . . .'

Kathryn felt a sickening weight in the pit of her stomach. 'Because he wanted to move me into the place, that's why . . .' She looked at Jess. 'He claimed he had rented the rooms. Is it over a flower shop on the High Street by any chance?'

Jess slowly nodded her head. 'Yes.' She bit her lip as her eyes filled with tears. 'It was such a lovely place, I'd never lived anywhere like that before . . .'

'What a cad!' Kathryn couldn't believe her ears that someone who treated her so tenderly could do that to someone as vulnerable as Jess. Did she really know the man at all? It seemed obvious to her that he'd abandoned Jess and had been seeking a new girl to take her place the night she'd encountered him at the pub.

When the bill was paid, Kathryn ordered another cab to take them both back to the East End. There was no way now she could carry on her association with Squire. The man was a bounder with little regard for women. She pitied his poor wife and all she had to put up with, maybe even unknowingly, the prostitution and the gambling, too.

The cab drew up at a very rundown-looking house a few streets over from where Kathryn lived.

I have to get out of this place and fast, it's the only way! Ma needs a decent roof over her head when she returns from the convalescent home. One where there's no peeling wallpaper due to damp running down the walls, no mould to infect and inflame her delicate lungs.

She now had some decent money in her pocket and she didn't intend wasting a farthing of it. Initially, she'd felt guilty for accepting what should have been Squire's share of the spoils, but no longer, now she felt he deserved it. He had been prepared to whore her out and take his fun into the bargain while at the same time running another girl and maybe even more. Horror of horrors, she didn't know what she might discover about the man next.

Jess thanked her as she went to dismount from the cab.

'If you need anything, you know you can call on me,' she reminded the girl.

'I'll manage, but thanks anyhow, Kathryn. I'd rather walk the streets with no man to protect me than have someone like Squire mess me around. I was a virgin when I first met him.'

Kathryn squeezed her hand in reassurance. 'Have you any money to be getting on with though?' She was concerned as the girl had been turfed out of that fancy apartment just so Squire could install her there. She thought it odd he'd found the apartment for her so quickly.

Jess shrugged. 'Enough, I suppose, and what I don't 'ave, I can always earn overnight . . .'

Kathryn watched the girl make her way across the bustling street and around the corner, and she wondered if she'd ever see her again.

Chapter Nine

Alone in the cab, Kathryn smarted with indignation at what Squire had done to both her and Jess. He'd played them like a violin! She was disgusted that he could dupe the pair of them for his own ends, then discard one of them like he would drop a hot potato from his hands. She was so angry she felt like screaming at the top of her voice, but feared the cab driver might hear her and think she was being murdered in his cab.

When she alighted from the cab, she spotted a young lad selling newspapers on the corner of the street.

'A double murder overnight!' he shouted. 'Police search for The Whitechapel Murderer carries on!'

A cold shiver ran down her spine. If The Whitechapel Murderer, as the press referred to him, wasn't caught soon, who knew how many more women would be butchered?

Cold tentacles of fear gripped her heart. *All the more reason to move, then*, a little voice reminded her. She feared for young women like Jess when there was a killer on the loose; they were easy meat for the likes of him.

She approached her house with trepidation. What if something had happened during her absence? Scrambling for her house key from her jacket pocket, she glanced around nervously. What if someone was watching her now?

As soon as she entered, she heard the kids' voices and she let out a deep sigh of relief. All seemed normal. After she'd spent time catching up with them, she went in search of Dorrie, who was in the yard outside. If Dorrie was surprised she'd returned sooner than expected, then she wasn't saying so, as she finished pegging up the washing and stood back to admire the bedsheets and pillow cases flapping on the line.

'Be careful Dorrie, there were another couple of murders in the area last night. Don't go out after dark if yer can help it . . .'

'I 'eard about it all from yer next door neighbour, Stan, a few minutes ago when he spoke to me over the wall. He warned me to take care. Yer think they'd 'ave caught the murderer by now. Some people fink he's a city gent. I saw in one newspaper a drawing of him wearing a hat and long frock coat. It gives me the bleedin' creeps!'

Kathryn nodded and let out a long breath. 'You and me both. Thanks for helping yesterday and overnight, Dorrie.' She reached into her pocket and gave the girl a silver florin.

Dorrie held it between her thumb and forefinger as if she'd never seen one before in all her life.

'Cor, thanks, Kathryn. I can buy me and Nick a good slap-up meal later. Maybe I'll get him some cod and chips and some mushy peas. Jimmy used to treat us now and again when he 'ad the money to . . .' She broke off wistfully.

'Well, Jimmy looked after me and my brothers and sisters often enough, it's only fair to return the favour. Any time you need anything, just say so. After all . . .'

Dorrie's eyes clouded over with concern. 'Please don't keep blaming yerself, Kathryn. It was Jimmy's own 'eart that led him astray and out to the ocean, it's not yer fault. Yer didn't make him go, gal!'

'But I can't help thinking if I had done as he asked, he'd still be here today. He asked me to marry him lots of times and I always refused him . . .' She hung her head in shame.

'That's because yer independent. Don't really need no man I suppose, 'cept what about that Mr Squire? Are you sweet on him, Kathryn? Is that why you didn't want to marry our Jimmy?'

She met Dorrie's intense gaze and shook her head vehemently as she blinked back the tears. 'I've just been doing a bit of business with him up West that's all, working as a seamstress in one of his factories.' It was partly the truth, she had been doing business with him.

'Don't be so 'ard on yerself, gal,' Dorrie said sympathetically. 'Jimmy spoke of going to sea when he was younger. It'll be a great adventure for him.'

Kathryn nodded. 'Maybe you're right. Perhaps he'd have gone anyhow.'

Dorrie smiled. 'I'll just be off to pick up Nick from me auntie's house then, if yer don't mind?'

'Not at all. I'll be in the rest of the day waiting for Mags to return from Kent to see how Ma is.'

Dorrie cocked her a cheeky grin which reminded her so much of Jimmy. 'Well, if yer need me, yer know where I am.'

As Dorrie paused with her hand on the latch of the back gate, Kathryn said, 'You take care now, Dorrie. I don't like the thought of you and your brother being alone in that house with that madman on the loose. Make sure you bolt the door!'

Dorrie smiled. 'Our auntie and uncle only live a couple of streets away, they're always popping in. We could move in with them but they have a houseful as it is.'

Kathryn nodded as she lifted the wicker laundry basket, resting it on her hip. 'Anyhow, you know if you ever need anything . . .'

'I know.' The girl smiled, opened the latch, and closed the gate behind her.

Kathryn bit her lip, she was going to have to sort out something soon, for all their sakes.

Following a nice cup of tea while the kids played out in the backyard, she scoured the newspaper adverts. Most of the jobs weren't suitable, but one that stood out looked interesting. She circled it with a pencil. It read:

Young woman urgently required to live in premises over shop. Duties include sale of general goods to public, packaging items for home delivery, overseeing deliveries to shop, management of junior sales staff. Please enquire within.

Strangely though, underneath that advert was another advert for the same shop:

Junior assistant required urgently. Duties include serving customers, dealing with home deliveries and shop deliveries.

What could have happened to cause two situations to become vacant at the same time? Maybe there could be a job for both herself and Mags there, and a roof over their heads to boot?

Where was Mags, anyhow? She should have returned by now. She was hanging on so they could all eat their evening meal together. Reluctantly, she decided to feed the kids and put them to bed.

It was almost midnight by the time she heard the horse and carriage draw up outside the house. She had been snoozing in the armchair near the fire. She jumped up and rushed to the door to find her sister in a most distressed state.

'What's wrong, Mags?' she asked.

'I just feel a bit frightened being out after dark, you know, with everything that's been going on lately. I only had to walk a few footsteps to the house but I felt creeped out . . .'

Kathryn nodded, understanding completely how her sister felt out on the street at this time of a night. She didn't like walking the dark streets alone either and Squire had warned her not to, but what if she had to return to those streets to ply her trade now that he was out of the picture? A shiver ran the length of her spine. Pulling herself together she asked, 'So, how was Ma when yer dropped her off? Did she settle all right?'

'Yes, she seemed to like it there, it's a lovely place, you should see it. Ma's even got a lovely room of her own that overlooks the sea and the staff are wonderful, they can't do enough for her. She said she's never had such attention in all her born days and feels like a member of the royal family!'

Kathryn smiled, pleased that the place seemed nice. 'You look perished, Mags, let's get you a nice cup of tea and I expect you're hungry, too. I have plans to get us out of this place.' She encouraged her sister to sit by the fireside while she brought her some bread and a hunk of cheese and a hot cup of tea.

As the heat from the fire warmed Mags to the core, she sipped the sweet brew and looked questioningly at her elder sister. 'You said earlier you planned on getting us all out of 'ere, but how?'

'I've got a bit of money saved up from my job up West, but I looked at the newspaper earlier and noticed an advert for two jobs which might suit me and you down to the ground, if they haven't gone already. And there's living quarters thrown in. They're looking for a shop manageress and a junior assistant. The ad was placed in the evening edition of the newspaper, so what do yer say? We can dress up and go over there very early tomorrow morning?'

Mags nodded. 'But where is it exactly?'

'It's a street or two away, but a much nicer area than here, bit posher than this place, I hope.'

'But what about my friends and Dorrie?'

'Let's cross that bridge when we get to it. We ain't got the jobs yet.'

The following day the sisters rose at the crack of dawn to go to the shop, as Kathryn reckoned it would be open early for deliveries. She left Shaun in charge: as the eldest boy, he was almost thirteen, and could hold the fort for an hour or two.

The shop was located at the end of a terraced row of houses a few streets over from their home. It wasn't an area they usually frequented. Outside on the pavement were some wooden pallets containing all kinds of fruits and vegetables and several sacks of potatoes. The sign above the door read *E. J. Bailey, purveyor of fruit and vegetables and household goods.*

From the outside looking in through the misted windows, Kathryn could see a middle-aged woman scurrying hither and thither in a most flustered state. She took a deep breath and pushed the door open. The bell jangled.

'Sorry, we're not open yet!' the woman yelled out.

'But we ain't here to buy anything,' Kathryn said calmly, 'we just wondered if yer want any 'elp as I read your advert in last night's newspaper.' Almost immediately the woman's face relaxed, causing her wrinkles to smooth out. She tucked a strand of salt-and-pepper hair that had worked loose from her bun, behind her ear.

She sighed deeply. 'Forgive me, please. I am in such a pickle here. This is my father's shop and he's taken ill. I need someone to run it for me. Yesterday morning his only assistant walked out when I asked if she could work extra hours to cover.'

So that explained why there were two jobs going.

'Look,' Kathryn said, gently touching her arm. 'I'm 'ere now and I can help yer if yer like, I have to send me sister back home shortly to help with the kids, but if we can move into the quarters above the shop we'll all be on the premises. I know this is a cheek as I've caught yer bright and early, but the early bird catches the worm and all that.'

The woman smiled. 'Maybe you and your sister can help me sort these deliveries on a trial basis? If you do well, then you're both hired. I'm Georgina Smethurst by the way.'

Kathryn winked at Mags, who had already started to roll up her sleeves. Within the hour all the home deliveries were sorted by Mags, and Kathryn and Georgina had unpacked all the sacks and boxes at the far end of the shop. They were about to take a break for a welcome cup of tea when the first customer arrived.

An elderly lady dressed in a long black coat, with an umbrella tucked in the crook of her arm, came bustling in shaking her head. 'Dear, dear, when your father was running this place, Georgina, he'd have had it all sorted by now. Is Edward still poorly then?'

Georgina visibly stiffened, obviously intimidated by the woman. 'I'm afraid so, M . . . Mrs Jefferson. How can I help you this morning?' She forced a smile.

The lady sniffed and glanced at Kathryn and Mags. 'And who might these young ladies be? Taken on new staff, have you? And what happened to Betsy, may I ask?'

Before Georgina had a chance to answer, Mags had ushered her to a nearby chair. ''Ere ducks, take the weight orf yer plates of meat. I'm Mags Flynn and that's me older sister, Kathryn. We're 'oping Miss Georgina will take us on as staff 'ere. Now, can I 'elp yer with anything?'

The woman, whose face up until now had remained as stiff as a papier mâché mask, broke into a grin. 'This one's a keeper, Georgina,' she guffawed.

Georgina smiled and nodded.

'Thanks, I think.' Mags glanced at Kathryn, who winked at her.

'Well, if that's the case I'd like a quarter of tea, some of those King Edward potatoes out the front, just a few for me husband's dinner — make sure there's no eyes in them neither – four ounces of that cheese there,' she pointed to a large round of cheese beneath a glass dome on the counter, 'and when you've got time, miss, I wouldn't mind looking at the gloves you have for sale.' There was a section at the back of the shop where items such as gloves, socks, umbrellas and toiletries were sold.

Kathryn glanced at her sister as she went off to get the required items while old Mrs Jefferson settled herself on the customer chair, hand crossed over hand, as she began gassing away about all and sundry. She covered every topic from her husband's bad drinking habits to the next-door neighbour's brawls out in the middle of the street.

When Mags had finally finished serving the lady, having found her a pair of pristine white gloves that not only fitted but were at a favourable price, then watched her leave the store with a big smile on her face, Georgina said, 'You did well there, Mags. Mrs Jefferson can be an awkward old cuss, a bit of a battle axe at times. She really seemed to take a shine to you.' Mags beamed and looked very proud of herself as Georgina extolled her virtues. 'Shall we have that nice cup of tea now?'

Both girls were in need of a rest and were more than happy to put their feet up in the back room, which was packed to the rafters with boxes of goods, tinned cans on the shelves and several hessian sacks of who knew what. Kathryn and Georgina took the two available seats while Mags plonked herself down on an old tea chest.

'Now then,' said Georgina when she had rested her weary

legs in front of the small fireplace, 'I'll just go and fetch us this brew.'

When she had departed, Kathryn looked at Mags. 'Well, what do yer think?'

'I think it's great 'ere to be honest. 'Ard work though, but that never killed anyone, did it?'

Kathryn nodded, she'd been thinking the same thing herself. It would be back-breaking work lifting heavy sacks and on their feet all day, and of course, Mags would be needed to make deliveries, but they were young and fit and they could cope with it all, she was sure of that.

'I think we're going to like it here, it will be a fresh start for all of us,' she smiled.

Mags looked puzzled for a moment. 'Speaking of fresh starts . . . How come I don't ever see that Squire sort hanging around you any more, Kathryn?'

Kathryn felt her cheeks burn. 'Oh, that's because I don't work for him any more.'

'But yer suddenly packed in a good job to come 'ere, I just don't get it.'

Oh dear, Kathryn realised her sister had a bee in her bonnet and if she didn't placate her fast, Georgina was going to enter the room and hear what was being said and she didn't want that at all. 'Look, if you must know, me and Squire, well there was something between us.'

Mags blinked several times. 'I knew it! I bleedin' well did!' she exclaimed in excitement.

'Sssh,' Kathryn warned, holding an index finger to her lips. 'I don't want everyone to know that he had romantic designs on me. But in any case, it's over now.'

Mags's face fell. 'Well, he was very 'andsome and all. Wealthy too. I can see what the attraction must have been, he seemed like a man of the world compared to Saucy Sailor Jimmy!' She chuckled, causing Kathryn to smile.

Their heads both turned as the door opened and Georgina entered carrying a tray. 'Now then,' she said, as she handed them their tea in proper china cups – she's a real lady this one, Kathryn thought. 'We have living quarters upstairs but I need to know how many of you there are in the family.'

Kathryn smiled. 'There are five of us at the moment as our mother is staying at a convalescent home in Kent.'

Georgina raised a brow as if she wondered why they'd need jobs like this if they had the money to afford such care for their mother in the first place.

'I came into some money recently,' Kathryn explained. 'But it won't be enough to keep us all. The kids are too young to work in my opinion, and I wouldn't want them to neither.'

'What are their ages?' Georgina asked thoughtfully.

'The youngest Rosie is just three years old, then there's Damon who's five, Shaun is almost thirteen, Mags is almost fourteen. The money I have won't be enough to keep us all. Ma is going to need very special care for some time to come.

Please, I promise we'll work hard for you and your father and keep the rooms clean and tidy, too.'

Georgina set down her tea cup on its saucer. 'That's quite all right, please don't concern yourself. I wasn't about to go back on my word. There's just something I haven't told you yet. It's my father, he's ill and elderly and he also lives on the premises. I'll have to square things up with him first as he might not like children running around the place. But then again, he is lonely and the rooms above this shop are quite spacious. There's also the back yard the children can play in, and a park nearby. But there is one other thing . . .' Georgina paused as she bit her bottom lip as if deliberating about something. 'He needs care. Not a lot really, just the odd thing like helping him out of bed in the morning and putting him to bed at night and for his naps. He needs taking to the privy, meals made for him. Other than that he's quite independent. It's his old bones, you see, bad arthritis, some days are better than others. I'm afraid I don't really have the time to keep popping back and forth here several times a day to see to him and leaving my husband and home neglected.'

Kathryn wondered why she didn't take her father to live at her house but thought it rude to ask. 'I'm sure we can sort something out.' She sounded more confident than she felt; what if the old man was a cantankerous sort?

'Very well then, once you've finished your tea, I'll take you to show you around, then Mags can return home to see to the children.'

The rooms were far bigger and grander than Kathryn was expecting them to be. There was no odour of musty damp here, or paper peeling off the walls.

Georgina showed the girls the two unoccupied bedrooms. One had a double bed and even a dressing table and wardrobe, the other just one single bed and a tallboy-style cupboard. Kathryn reckoned she and Mags could sleep in the biggest and put a straw pallet down nearby for Rosie. The boys could top-and-tail in the other room. There was a nice-sized comfortable living room, with shelves full of books either side of the fireplace.

'What's in that room, there?' Mags asked, pointing at a firmly shut white door.

'It's Father's room. He won't bother you. Since he's been ill he hardly comes out. He's happy either sleeping in bed or sitting in the chair reading one of his books or newspapers. He's an avid reader.'

'What 'appened to make him want to stay in that room all the time?' Mags blurted out, causing Kathryn to give her a hard stare so that she added, 'Sorry, it's none of my bleedin' business.' She bit her bottom lip as if she'd already said too much.

'It's all right,' Georgina said gently. 'Father seems to have disappeared into himself since I've taken over the shop. It was his life. He worked here as man and boy. He started off as a simple errand boy and worked here for ten years until the owner, Mr Price, who was by then elderly and childless, offered him the chance to take it over. Father didn't have enough money to buy it of course, but Mr Price made provision in his will to leave it to my father as he was like a son to him.'

'Your father did well for himself then!' Kathryn thought there must be a lot to the old gent if he went from being simply an errand boy to running a store like this. 'When would you like us to move in?' she asked.

'Well, as soon as possible if that's permissible. Just give me time to explain to Father. It would make life far easier for me to have someone on the premises, as I explained. I have a brother who hardly ever calls to see him, so he's not much help.'

'What's 'is name?' Mags looked at Georgina.

'Walter. I'm afraid he's as wet as an old discarded dishcloth and as much use as one, too!'

Kathryn watched as Mags fought to hold back a fit of giggles, so she said, 'Mags, you better get off to see to the kids. I'll be back later.' She didn't want Georgina to think she might be poking fun at her brother.

Mags smiled and nodded, then turned on her heel and left.

Kathryn smiled. 'Thank you for showing us around, Georgina. I'll carry on helping you today, but if I could please leave a little earlier than planned, then I can get home to pack our belongings and hopefully we can move in here tomorrow.'

Georgina beamed, with tears in her eyes. 'That's fine, dear.' They were interrupted as the bell over the shop door jangled as customers drifted in and Kathryn wondered what the next few days had in store for them all.

Kathryn sighed. How she longed to put her feet up, but there was no time now she was back home. As soon as the kids had been washed and put to bed after she'd explained that tomorrow they'd be moving out, she and Mags had begun packing all their clothing into carpet bags and some old sacks Georgina had loaned them. For the time being, Kathryn was determined that they'd only move the essentials such as clothing, and anything of sentimental value or necessity. Rosie was quite happy to go as long as she could take her one and only beloved dolly – a rag doll named Jemmy that their mother had stayed up making one Christmas Eve from old scraps of material Kathryn had brought home from the slop shop.

The boys, however, were not keen on the move at all, until Mags explained that if they stayed put and were unable to pay the rent, they could all end up in the workhouse, and once inside, they would hardly see one another again. Then they soon came around to her way of thinking.

When they'd finished packing their essentials, Kathryn knocked at Stan's house next door. He owned a horse and cart which would be very useful with the intended move, if he'd agree to help them all.

Stanley stood on the doorstep gazing at her in a quizzical fashion. 'Hello, Kathryn.'

She smiled. 'Hello, Mr Morgan. I was wondering if yer could do us a little favour?'

His kindly eyes twinkled. 'What's that, lass?'

'Early tomorrow morning we need a lift over to a shop where me and our Mags 'ave found jobs. There's rooms for our family above it. We need to get out of 'ere as O'Shay is going to put up the rent.'

'I see . . .' He scratched his head. 'I expect you want me to help move you all and some of your belongings with me hoss and cart, then?'

For a moment, she thought he wouldn't do it. She nodded. 'Yes, please.'

Then his face broke out into a big grin. 'Aye, course I will, lass. I'll be sad to see you go, mind, but I've heard all about that rent collector afore and he isn't a nice man at all.'

Kathryn went to hand him a half crown for his time, but he waved it away. 'No, I won't hear of it! Yer Ma was good to me and my Nellie when she was dying of the cancer. She was in 'ere all day and every day. Didn't know what I'd have done without her help. And afterwards when she passed over, your Ma'd cook me a nice stew when I didn't feel like eating. She's an angel that lady. Now, put yer money away lass, it's no good here!'

Kathryn touched his shoulder, 'Thank you, Stanley.'

Breathing out a sigh of relief, she was thankful that at last things were going her way.

*

The following day, they were all up bright and early. Kathryn insisted they leave the house on empty stomachs as they'd be getting something to eat when they arrived at the shop. That way there'd be no shilly-shallying and no dishes to wash up afterwards either. Stanley said he'd keep an eye on the place for them until they could move their furniture out, as the rent was paid up for another week. She warned him O'Shay might return, and he said he knew the sort so he'd keep a special eye out for the likes of him. She'd written a letter to Dorrie explaining where they'd gone, giving the address of the shop. Stan pulled the horse up outside Dorrie's house on the way so Kathryn could drop it through the letter box. As she paused on the doorstep, her thoughts turned to Jimmy and what he was doing right now.

The clipper was sailing through choppy waters. Waves crashed against the bow of the boat, the sea spray hitting Jimmy full in the face. He could taste the briny water, but he didn't care somehow as the ocean washed his cares away.

He'd been at sea now for a couple of weeks and the ship was headed towards Morocco. Captain Tobias Blake was a fine upstanding man, who seemed to respect every member of his crew, no matter how lowly they were.

Some of the sailors had already been taken ill with dysentery and the ship's doctor had informed the captain there would probably be at least a couple of burials at sea to contend with.

Jimmy, who had never been much further than the London Victoria Embankment, delighted in the thought he was so far away from home. So far, but he could never forget – Kathryn. Didn't want to really, even though she'd taken up with that Squire sort who looked old enough to be her father. What did she see in him, for heaven's sake? What did that man have that he didn't? Maybe it was money. When money came along, common sense seemed to fly out of the window for some. He hadn't taken Kathryn for the materialistic sort though, he'd thought better of her than that. It was his plan to work a year or two at sea and return with a bit more money in his pocket for Dorrie and Nick; he was doing it for them. They'd be all right until then as his aunt and uncle had reassured him they'd watch out for them, and he'd left money for their keep so they wouldn't go without.

Suddenly, he felt himself slide across the deck, slipping as his hands reached out to grab for something, but there was nothing to hold on to except for thin air. He was thrown off his feet and hit his head with a crack and then he began dreaming.

Chapter Ten

The kids were thrilled when the cart pulled up outside the shop. The temperature had dipped lately and Kathryn felt a chill wind whipping up; she could hardly wait to get inside to the warmth of the shop. In their excitement, it didn't seem to bother her siblings.

'Are we really going to live here?' Damon asked, wide-eyed with wonder.

'Yes.' Kathryn patted his head. 'We're really going to live here.' She blew on her hands which felt numb to the bone.

'I bet there's plenty of sweets in there,' Shaun exclaimed.

'There might be,' said Mags, 'but you ain't getting yer mitts on any. We 'ave to pay for them just like anyone else. Just cos we'll be living over the shop it don't mean we can 'ave what we want when we want it!'

'Aw, maybe we can save up and buy some then,' he suggested, with a hopeful look on his face.

'And maybe you can get a job as a newspaper lad to pay for them,' warned Kathryn, taking the wind out of his sails. She had five mouths to feed and Shaun had to learn that there was no pay-off for doing nothing in this world. Their father had instilled that into her years ago.

She roused Rosie who had fallen asleep on the ride over. 'Come on darlin' we're 'ere now. Once we're inside Georgina says she'll make us all breakfast.'

After they'd taken the kids inside to meet Georgina, who explained to them how her father was living there too, Kathryn and Mags helped Stanley unload the cart. 'You sure you'll be all right 'ere, lass?' he asked, as he tipped back the peak of his flat cap so he could look her square in the eyes.

'Yes, thanks, Stan,' she reassured him, 'we'll be much better off 'ere. I'll be around in a couple of days to sort out the furniture and would appreciate it if you can help us once more?'

'Course I can, now get inside and 'ave your breakfast, looks like you'll be busy soon enough.' He smiled and turned to climb back on the cart. She stood to watch him take the reins and ride off, then turned her attention back to their new living quarters. Georgina, bless her, had prepared a lovely breakfast for them all of porridge and toast, and there were even boiled eggs to go around.

'Aw, you've gone to a lot of trouble,' Kathryn said. 'How can I ever repay you?'

'Look, it's you who is doing me a favour.' Georgina touched her shoulder as she placed yet another plate of toasted bread on the table. 'You don't know what a weight this is off my mind, knowing that both my father and the shop will be taken care of. I've taken his breakfast in already, so if one of you can help him wash and dress when you've finished then we'll open the shop.'

Kathryn nodded. She supposed she should be the one to do it, but she was surprised when Shaun stepped up to offer. She guessed he was hankering after some sweets from downstairs but she didn't mind at all and admired his initiative. She decided though, on this first occasion, to go along with Shaun and introduce herself and explain that her brother would be helping him, to see how he felt about it. Then if all went well she and Mags could go down to serve in the shop, while the kids set off for school. It would be a longer walk from where they were now living, but they were young and fit and could cope with it. It was a small price to pay for a roof over their heads.

Georgina knocked on her father's door. 'Father, I've brought Kathryn and her brother to meet you, are you decent?'

'Yes of course I am!' he growled, which immediately set Kathryn on guard; she hadn't been expecting that sort of a reaction.

'Don't worry,' Georgina reassured them. 'His bark is always worse than his bite!' She gently pushed at the door.

Shaun looked at Kathryn with apprehension, but he remained rooted to the spot. The door slowly opened and there was Georgina's father, Edward Bailey, sitting up in bed wearing an expensive-looking brocade dressing gown with a monocle in one eye as he read the newspaper. 'I see they reckon they're getting close to catching that Jack the Ripper!' he exclaimed, which caused Shaun to rush over to the bedside and peer at the newspaper over his shoulder. 'And who might you be, boy?' Mr Bailey asked with some amusement.

'I'm Shaun Flynn, sir. I've come to live 'ere with me brother and sisters.'

'And tell me, how old are you, Shaun?'

'Almost thirteen, sir.'

'Too big to go up the chimney I'll be bound, and too small to do a man's job. What are you doing in my room, anyhow?'

'I'm going to 'elp you, sir. It was my own idea so me sisters can work in the shop downstairs. I figured if I was the one who 'elps you get dressed and to go to the privy, Kathryn standing by there might buy me some sweets from your shop!'

'By Jove, this lad is very enterprising, isn't he?' he said to Kathryn.

'He is, Mr Bailey. Is that all right by you?' Kathryn watched the old man's face for any sign of a reaction.

'I suppose it will have to be. Well, leave us alone as I need him to help me wash and dress and then he can take me to the privy.' With a brush of his hand he shooed the women out of the room.

Georgina laughed. 'I think he likes your brother,' she said, when they'd got outside the bedroom. 'Father really misses

Walter, I really can't understand why he never wishes to visit. I think it hurts him so much.'

Maybe it will be good for him to have Shaun around, then, Kathryn thought.

The rest of the day flew by in a whirl of sorting out deliveries and packing them on to a handcart for Mags to take out, and she and Georgina serving customers in the shop. By the end of the day when Kathryn sat down feeling totally whacked out in the back room with Georgina, she said, 'You know what would make things easier for us? Instead of sending out Mags several times a day with that handcart, we should use a 'orse and cart.'

Georgina quirked a brow. 'That sounds a novel idea but I don't know anyone in these parts who owns one we might borrow.'

'Leave that to me.' Kathryn took a sip of her well-earned cup of tea and warmed herself near the fire. 'Stanley Morgan, my neighbour, who brought me 'ere, might enjoy helping us out as long as we pay him something for his time. He's lonely since his wife died last year, it would give him something else to think about.'

Georgina frowned. 'I don't know if I could afford another wage though, unless he'd be happy to be paid with leftovers, you know, the sort that are more difficult to sell like bruised fruit and things that are about to go off.'

'I can always ask him, no 'arm in that I suppose. I 'ave to go there this evening to bring some of the furniture and belongings over 'ere, though we haven't got much to speak of, just an old table and chairs, pots and pans, those sorts of things . . . O'Shay the landlord owns the rest.'

'You can always store it all in the old stable at the back of the shop. Thinking about it, that would be good for Stanley's horse. You see, in the old days, the man who owned this store who took on my father as an errand boy, he owned a couple of horses. Father's kept the stables as they're handy when we get deliveries, the men can rest their horses as they deliver and they often stop for refreshments for themselves.'

Kathryn nodded. 'I've had another idea too, Georgina.'

'Oh?' She swept a strand of hair that had worked loose from her bun behind her ear.

'Someone came into the shop earlier and asked if we had any meat and potato pies to sell . . .'

Georgina's eyes widened. 'No, I'm afraid we don't sell those, only the ingredients to make them.'

'This man wanted to purchase a hot pie to eat there and then. It got me thinking, what if we made pies and sold them hot as well?'

Georgina shook her head. 'Oh, I don't know. That would be a lot of work for us, Kathryn, and I don't know what my father would think about that. It's never been done here before.'

'Ma made the best pies going with only a few ingredients. We could make them in the evening and warm them next day. We could try it out for a few weeks to see what happens. It might be a bit of extra work but if we all pitch in . . .'

Georgina sighed. 'Very well, I'll mention it to Father later. Can you make the pies though as I have never made a pie in my entire life!'

'Then maybe it's time you learned how!' Kathryn chuckled.

The whole family loved the pie idea, especially Shaun and Damon whose stomachs always seemed to growl with hunger even when they'd been fed.

'Just like Ma used to make,' Mags said, with a wistful look in her eyes. 'I'd love to eat one as it will make me think of her when she's not here.'

Kathryn nodded and smiled. Everyone was on board. The only one now who needed convincing was Mr Bailey himself.

Later that evening, Mags and Kathryn, both wearing their thick shawls and gloves to combat the cold, headed back to their old house to load their meagre furniture on to Stan's cart. The only items left were the old scratched table and four chairs her parents had bought not long after they wed from a flea market in Petticoat Lane, a small bedroom chest of drawers, a wooden stool, Rosie's straw pallet and some pots and pans. The beds and wardrobes belonged to Mr O'Shay so would remain behind.

Before leaving, Kathryn scribbled a note for him saying they'd left to live elsewhere and she'd put the key on the mantelpiece inside. She also stated in the note that there was now no money owing to him whatsoever. Of course, she didn't mention where they'd moved to; she hoped she'd never set eyes on the man ever again, the thuggish brute. The only person in the street who knew where they'd gone was Stanley, and he wasn't about to tell anyone of their whereabouts.

'C'mon then, ladies,' he said, when they'd loaded the final piece of furniture aboard the cart. As the horse plodded along the cobbled streets, Kathryn took it as an opportunity to ask him about working as a delivery man for the shop.

Stanley let out a low whistle of surprise. 'Eee, I dunno, lass. My last job was working at the docks and I've only been doing odd jobs ever since my wife died, tha' knows. Won't this Georgina woman think I'm too old for it?'

'No, not at all. The only thing is for the time being she'll only be able to pay you in kind with leftover fruit and vegetables, stale bread, and maybe a bit of meat now and again and the odd hot meal. And I forgot to mention, I'm going to start baking pies to sell, like Ma used to make. So maybe we'd need you to deliver those an' all if it takes off, and you can have some of those too for your services.'

'By heck, lass, you've got it all worked out, haven't you!' He chuckled. 'Aye, I think that might work out very well indeed. I'm sick to death of staring at the four walls all day. It's beginning to feel like a prison indoors. I'll take a gamble then!'

The mention of the word gamble turned her thoughts to Squire and his gambling habits. She wondered where he was and whether she'd ever run into him again. And how would she react if she did? There was still a well of anger simmering under the surface and she feared it might bubble over, given the right provocation. He'd duped her good and proper and she didn't know if or when she'd ever forgive him.

The following evening Mags and Kathryn began to prepare the pies in the kitchen while Georgina watched the entire process. 'Yer need nice cool hands to prepare the pastry,' Kathryn explained as she rolled it out, and then Mags cut out circular shapes from it using an upturned tea cup. So far Edward Bailey had not left his room to eat any meals or converse with the family. Georgina had sent his meals in on a tray, but when the pies began to cook in the oven and the aroma drifted towards him, she heard the bang of his cane on the floorboards. Shaun jumped up to check on him, a worried frown on his face, then returned grinning from ear to ear. 'Mr Bailey has asked if he might try one of those meat and potato pies later as he didn't enjoy Georgina's burnt offering earlier.'

Kathryn's mouth popped open. She'd thought Shaun would have used a little tact and not mentioned that. She expected Georgina to be upset but she just laughed. 'Father has never cared much for my culinary skills. In fact, in all the time I've cooked for him, only once has he complimented me, but it was for an apple tart a customer had baked for him. I didn't tell him it wasn't my own. I allowed him to believe I had baked it myself!' They all laughed. It sounded as if Edward Bailey was a hard man to please.

The following morning, Kathryn affixed a large sign to the shop window: 'GET YOUR PIES HERE, SMALL FOR THRUPPENCE, LARGE FOR SIXPENCE. HOT OR COLD! THE BEST PIES IN THE WHOLE OF WHITECHAPEL!'

Kathryn had thought this a wild claim when Georgina had written it, but she explained that if her father had gone overboard about them, then they had to be ruddy good. Kathryn had been surprised to hear her use such choice language.

The pies were slow to sell at first, but by lunchtime word had got around and a queue had started forming at the counter. Mags was in charge of cooking and warming them in the oven. Kathryn watched through the window as some of the young workers from one of the nearby factories ate them outside on the street.

'No manners these days, young men!' Georgina exclaimed.

Kathryn was about to reply when Dorrie walked in through the door with her brother Nick beside her. 'You found us then!' Kathryn beamed.

'Aye, it took some doing, mind, I had to keep asking about!' She gazed around in awe. 'Cor, this is a right lovely shop, do you run it?'

'She will do in time,' Georgina told her. 'I'm the owner's daughter. And you are Dorrie? I've heard so much about you. And so you must be young Nick?'

The little boy smiled. 'Yes, miss.'

'Now then Nick, how'd you like a ha'penny twist?'

He nodded as Georgina led him away to the counter to choose one from a glass jar packed full of boiled sweets.

'Any news from your brother?' Kathryn asked Dorrie, hopefully.

Dorrie shook her head. 'No, nothing as yet.'

Noticing the girl was looking a bit pale and thin she said, 'Look, we've started baking pies. I'm going to give you and Nick a couple to take home with you.'

'Thank you, we are a bit hungry.'

Kathryn shook her head. She still couldn't believe Jimmy would set sail around the world leaving his siblings behind like that. They were supposedly being cared for by their aunt and uncle, but the kids didn't look as well nourished as the last time she'd set eyes on them. 'You look worried, Dorrie. What's wrong?'

Suddenly, Kathryn noticed tears in the girl's eyes. 'It's Mr O'Shay. He came to get the rent from us earlier and Nick let him inside. I told him not to, but O'Shay, h . . . he . . .'

'What's the matter, Dorrie?' She placed a comforting arm around her shoulder.

'He told me if I don't cough up the money soon, then he'll take what he's owed in kind. I think I know what he meant an' all. It was the way he was looking at me, leering like.' She began to sob as Kathryn held her close.

'Now you listen to me, Dorrie. That man has no right to say that to you. He's taking advantage as he probably realises your Jimmy is no longer around and you have no mother or father alive. I can't allow you to go back there.' Biting her lip, she looked at Georgina who seemed to be besotted with Nick as he sat on a wooden stool, licking his way through his ha'penny twist. She would ask her if both children could stay over the shop for now. Dorrie was a good worker. She could help if the pie business took off. They could squeeze another girl into her bedroom and Nick could sleep with the boys; they'd get another couple of straw pallets from somewhere. That's if Georgina were to agree of course. It would be better than leaving them to their own devices with that aunt and uncle only occasionally checking up on them.

'What do you think this is, a flaming doss house?' Kathryn heard Mr Bailey shouting at his daughter through the bedroom door. 'You've only just allowed the Flynn family to move in here and now you want to add another two down-and-outs! That pair should be in the workhouse if their parents are no longer alive and they've been abandoned by their elder brother as he sails half way around the world. I won't allow it! I tell you I won't. I can't go taking in all the waifs and strays of Whitechapel!'

Kathryn chewed on her bottom lip. Now the elderly man was angry with his daughter because of her. She stood with her hand on the doorknob prepared to barge in and fight their corner when Shaun appeared beside her. 'Leave it to me,' he said quietly.

Kathryn nodded as he knocked on the door.

'Enter!' boomed Mr Bailey. Georgina was standing by the side of his bed, trembling.

'I've come to speak to you, Mr Bailey!' Shaun said with an air of authority. 'Miss Georgina, can you leave please? I want to say what I have to say man to man.'

Kathryn was so proud of him, she could have hugged him there and then. She ushered Georgina away to make her a cup of tea. All she could hear on the other side of the door were muffled voices. At least the shouting had now ceased.

Ten minutes later, Edward Bailey summoned his daughter to the room saying he might have been a little hasty and to please forgive his outburst. Of course the children were free to stay, as long as they helped out in some way or another to pay for their keep.

'What did you say to him to make him change his mind?' Kathryn asked her brother.

'I just said to him, do you remember when you were a young man, Mr Bailey, and someone helped you out? That was all. He'd told me the story of how this shop owner had taken him on as a young man. He was from a poor family and he ended up taking over this place. It made him remember that he, too, came from a poor background and went on to make a success of his life because someone had given him 'alf a chance.'

Kathryn hugged him. 'Shaun, I'm so bleedin' proud of you!'

'Aw thank you. Now please can I have those sweets you promised me a couple of days ago?'

She smiled at his candour. 'Of course you can, and you can have the biggest pie of the lot for yer trouble, yer deserve it an' all!'

Word had got out about the pies being served at the shop. They were a great success as people came from far and wide to try a mouth-watering steak and kidney or a chicken and mushroom pie.

'I don't know how to thank you, Kathryn,' Georgina said, taking both of Kathryn's hands in her own. 'This shop was starting to go under. Father had let it run down in recent months as he was becoming ill, and by the time he took to his bed only his regulars were coming back, as they cared about him. I was too busy with my own husband and home to see what was going on under my nose.'

Business had become very brisk indeed, and so, on Kathryn's insistence, Dorrie had been taken on to help with the pie-making process as Mags and Stanley attended to the home deliveries with the help of his trusty horse and cart.

So far, though, Kathryn hadn't persuaded Dorrie and Nick to move in with them at the living quarters above the shop. It would have been a little cramped but at least she'd have known they were safe and cared for. Sometimes she found herself feeling angry at Jimmy for abandoning his siblings when they needed him so much. But on the other hand, she thanked her lucky stars to be shot of Squire, even though, she had to admit, she missed him at times. But did she need someone like him in her life who was only after his own ends? In some respects both men were like two sides of the same coin: both were doing things for what they felt were entirely the right reasons, but only one had a strong moral streak running through his body.

Chapter Eleven

One day a couple of weeks later, Dorrie failed to show up for work. She always brought Nick to work with her in the evenings and he played with the other kids while Dorrie helped prepare and cook the pies for the following day. But now, as it was half past five and still no sign of her, Kathryn was starting to get worried. 'I must go and search for her,' she told Mags with a worried frown. 'She's not the unreliable sort, something must be wrong. It's so unlike her to let us down.'

She pulled her shawl from the nail on the back of the staff room door and wrapped it around herself as she explained to Georgina. 'Can you manage without me for a while?'

Georgina nodded, realising by the look on Kathryn's face how concerned she was. 'If you find her, mind you make her come back here. Don't take no for an answer!' she called after her, as Kathryn closed the shop door behind herself with a jangle of the bell. Oh why hadn't she insisted the girl and her brother move in sooner? She was sure she'd have persuaded her eventually, though Dorrie had insisted that they were waiting for Jimmy to return with his fortune. *He'll be home soon!* she'd said. *Yer'll see if he isn't!* Dorrie's eyes had widened as she told Kathryn all about buried treasure, gold coins and precious jewels all the colours of the rainbow. It was then that Kathryn guessed Jimmy had been embellishing stories with his vivid imagination before he'd set sail for distant shores, the way he had done for her own siblings. Maybe the girl had received a letter from him by now? But surely if she had then Dorrie would have dashed over to the shop to show her, she would have been that excited. She guessed the reason Dorrie was holding off from moving into the shop was in case Jimmy came home and couldn't find them.

As Kathryn trudged along the grimy streets, pulling her shawl tighter around her shoulders to ward off the biting northerly wind, she shivered and her teeth chattered. It was now mid-October and the police weren't any nearer to catching Jack the Ripper, as the press now referred to him. Women were afraid to go out alone at night, and even during the day many went around in pairs. It was certainly no weather for two youngsters to be out and about in.

When she finally arrived on Dorrie's doorstep, she rapped the door knocker three times but there was no answer. So she tried the knocker again, but still no response from inside. She bent down and peered through the letter box but couldn't see any movement. Next she approached a grimy window, cupping her hands to peer inside, but there was no sign of life. So she returned to the letter box and called out, 'Dorrie! Nick! It's me, Kathryn!'

A feeling of dread seeped into every pore of her body. Something was wrong. Rushing over to Stan's house, she found him outside, feeding his horse some old vegetable peelings in a bucket, having already finished the shop deliveries for that day.

'Hey up, lass!' he exclaimed, when he saw how frantic she looked. 'What's troubling you?'

Breathless with anxiety, she blurted out, 'It's Dorrie and Nick. She didn't turn up for work this afternoon. I've been over to the house and there's no one in.'

He rubbed his chin in contemplation. 'Maybe they're gone round to a neighbour's or a relative's?'

She calmed momentarily. 'I'm probably being daft, Stan, and panicking for nothing. I've just remembered they've got an aunt and uncle who live in the next street over, Maisie and Thomas Wright. I'll call over there and check! They're supposed to be looking out for them, maybe they're over there.'

'Right you are, lass. I expect they're feeding them up and Dorrie's forgotten the time, it will be summat like that, I expect. You may be worrying for nowt . . .'

Darkness was falling by the time she found the house. She knocked on the door and heard a muffled noise inside, then it slowly opened with a creak. A middle-aged woman stood there in a soiled pinafore with her hands in both pockets. 'Whatcha want?' she asked.

'I'm looking for Dorrie and Nick,' she explained. 'I understand that you've been keeping an eye on them for their brother, Jimmy.'

She nodded and then folded her arms across her chest. 'What's it to you, anyhow?'

'It's just that they've not been seen for a while.'

The woman shook her head. 'Look, I 'ave me own brood to take care of, I can't keep an eye on them all of the day and all of the night, can I?'

Kathryn felt a sudden pang of disappointment. This woman just didn't seem to care a jot for the children's welfare even though they were related. 'Well, if they do show up, please let me know, I'm working at Bailey's Stores.'

'Don't hold your breath,' she muttered, then she closed the door in Kathryn's face.

It surprised her that the woman didn't seem to be all that concerned, so maybe Dorrie and Nick had gone missing before.

Blinking back tears of frustration, Kathryn walked away. Where to now? She remembered that sometimes Dorrie had done little odd jobs for the landlady at The Horse and Harness. She'd try there, and hope no one recognised her from the night she'd encountered Squire while all tarted up. What if she bumped into him? She didn't know how she'd react. Whenever an image of him came to mind recently she'd forced it into a box called 'The Past' and kept the lid firmly shut.

As she entered the pub, she noticed it was quieter than it had been that first night, probably because it was still early. A couple of dockers she vaguely recognised sat at a table playing dominoes, while a man was laughing uproariously as he pressed his face deep into the bosom of a woman in a gaudy dress. She was obviously a working girl who had been at the game for many years as her face had hard features and she was doing her best to look youthful.

Blossom, the landlady, spotted her. 'What's a nice gal like you doing in 'ere, missy?' she asked good-naturedly. Her hair was as white as driven snow and pinned up in a neat bun, and the sleeves of her flowered blouse were rolled up to the elbow. She looked like a woman who wasn't afraid of a little hard work.

Kathryn swallowed. 'I'm looking for Dorrie Dawkins. I understand she used to do odd jobs for you?'

The woman's gaze narrowed. 'And who's asking?'

'I'm Kathryn Flynn, a friend. I was concerned as her brother is working on a ship and he left her and their younger brother to fend for themselves while he's away.'

The woman's features softened. 'Are you Kathryn from that shop what makes the pies?'

'I am indeed.'

'Dorrie told me all about you, no fear. She said she's got a job with you. She was supposed to call here this morning to tidy up for me as I know she works evenings for you, but she didn't show up. I just assumed she was busy as it's not a firm arrangement.'

Kathryn was about to thank the woman and depart when Fergus O'Shay came lumbering into the pub. Spotting him, she turned her head away.

'Give us a pint of your finest ale, Blossom!' he bellowed, as he stood tapping at the bar with some sort of coin in his hand.

'Sorry I couldn't 'elp yer, ducks,' she said quietly to Kathryn. 'If she does show up, I'll tell 'er you was looking for 'er.' Then she went behind the wooden bar to serve O'Shay.

His eyes widened with surprise as they suddenly met Kathryn's. 'Thought you'd slip away without paying me what I was owed when you moved, Miss Flynn?' he yelled.

The hairs on the back of Kathryn's neck bristled with fear as her head shrunk down into her shoulders.

Got to get a grip on the situation, she thought, and immediately drew herself up straight to her full height. She needed to face the man head on and show no fear.

She turned. 'Mr O'Shay, I do not owe you any money at all. I left you the rent money on the mantelpiece along with a note of explanation before we left.'

'But the rent had increased by then. I make it you still owe me another couple of bob!'

'Then you shall just have to whistle for it!' she replied quite boldly, and Blossom winked at her from behind the bar.

'You're lucky, Miss High 'n' Mighty, you got away so easily. Not like that pair of orphans from Dock Street!'

Kathryn felt the heavy thud of her own heartbeat. 'Which

orphans do you refer to, Mr O'Shay?' Yet she knew in her heart who they were, she just wanted confirmation.

'The Dawkins kids!' he snarled, then he turned his back on her to take a sip of his foaming pint.

'What's happened to them?' she demanded.

He turned back to face her, wiping the beery foam from his moustached lips with the back of his hand, before letting out a loud belch.

'They couldn't afford to pay the new rent, so I hauled both their backsides over to the Spike . . .'

'The workhouse?' She could hardly believe her ears.

He nodded. 'That's right. I know one of the guardians on the board there. He'll make the lazy little blighters work for their keep!'

'But it weren't their fault, Mr O'Shay. Their brother abandoned them and went off to sea!'

'Aye, well, he should have thought about leaving them some extra money behind. Those houses I own are costing me money. You owe me that last week's extra rent and more as I can't get any new tenants for it so soon. You didn't give me adequate notice to quit!'

'Well, what can you do about it? I paid up fair and square as far as I'm concerned, Mr O'Shay. It wasn't no moonlight flit like many 'ave done. If yer not happy perhaps we should make it a police matter as I have a witness I left that money, one of the neighbours saw me leave it there.'

He scowled. She knew she did well to call his bluff, as he

was a wrong 'un who had his finger in many pies and wouldn't wish to see the police poke their noses into his affairs.

Blossom, as if sensing things might get out of hand, stepped in between them.

'You heard what the lady said, she did pay you, Mr O'Shay. And if yer want to carry on supping 'ere in future, let it drop once and for all! What you did to Dorrie and her little brother was wrong, throwing them to that pack of wolves at the workhouse!'

He glared at both women, then downed his pint in one go. 'What you're both missing is how I did them kids a big favour. They've got a roof over their heads and food in their bellies, no rent to pay now. Their brother didn't do that for them, did he? I'm a right charitable gent, I am!' He slammed down his tankard and belched once more. 'I'm off to The Ten Bells. Shan't get any hassle there. Need to see Mary Kelly about some business.'

When he'd departed and Kathryn had stopped trembling, she asked, 'Who's Mary Kelly?'

The landlady took a deep breath in and let it out again. 'She's one of the unfortunates, dearie. For a while she was living up West and dressing in fancy garb. There's even rumours she once ended up in Paris of all places, taken by a well-heeled gentleman an' all . . . That's why they say she changed her name from Mary Jane to Marie Jeanette to sound more French at the time. But now she's gorn to seed. Been knocking around with a young woman who's hit on 'ard times.'

Kathryn looked at her pleadingly. 'I really fear for those kids at the workhouse, we might never see them again!'

Blossom bit on her bottom lip. 'Well the workhouse might be a better option than—'

'Than what?'

'O'Shay has been running young girls as well as renting out 'ouses, ducks. I 'ope he hasn't just put Nick in the workhouse but kept Dorrie to work the streets!'

Kathryn was appalled. 'But she's only sixteen years old! What kind of age is that?'

Blossom looked at her with compassion in her turquoise eyes. 'It 'appens, love, some men 'ave a taste for such things. I ain't saying it's right, cos it ain't, but she won't be the first and won't be the last gal to hit 'ard times and end up working for the likes of him. I think the best thing you can do is get over to the workhouse and check to see if they're both there.'

'You're right, thank you.'

'Let me know if they're both orite!' Blossom shouted after her. 'I do care about 'em, poor mites!' But Kathryn didn't hear the last part as she was already out the door.

It was completely dark save for the dimly lit gas lamps on the street corners. As she walked along, her footsteps echoing back at her, she found herself turning at every sudden noise for fear someone was following her. What if O'Shay was in hiding in the shadows waiting for her? What if Jack the Ripper himself was around? *Don't be so silly, yer letting yer imagination run riot*, she chided herself as she walked on, realising it was vital to find out where those kids were before it was too late.

The walls of the Whitechapel and Spitalfields Union Workhouse were imposing. Kathryn had read in an East End newspaper that there were now around 108,000 paupers in the area, so many would need to use the workhouse at some point. She'd heard that the body of The Ripper's first victim, Mary Ann Nichols, had been taken to the infirmary part of the very same workhouse and she shivered at the thought of it.

Hesitantly, with her shawl now pulled over her head, as a light drizzle had begun to fall chilling her to the bone, she pressed the bell. Presently a man in a navy serge jacket and trousers and peaked cap appeared. She assumed he must be some sort of porter.

'I'm sorry we're not taking no more inmates tonight!' he announced brusquely.

'Excuse me, sir. I'm not looking for a bed for the night. I'm looking for two children who I've heard have been brought here.'

He sniffed beneath his whiskers. 'And what business would that be of yours?'

'I . . . I'm a relative of theirs, Maisie Wright,' she lied.

He stared at her for a moment. 'I'll just get the supervisor . . .'

'Can't you tell me whether they're here or not?' she pleaded.

'Ain't my job, miss. I don't keep the records here, we 'ave so many in and out, has to be recorded some place.'

He turned his back and walked away. The wait seemed

never-ending as she stood in the bitter cold. A chill wind whipped around the corner and she blew on her gloveless hands.

Finally a woman dressed in a long black gown with a high collar appeared, jangling a set of keys at her waist. 'Now then, I understand that you have relatives here?' She glared at Kathryn.

She nodded. 'Yes, ma'am.'

'What day would they have arrived?'

Kathryn fought to think when she'd seen Dorrie last, she hadn't baked at the weekend and today was a Monday, so she said, 'It would have been sometime over the weekend I reckon. Their names are Dorothy Dawkins, Dorrie for short, and Nick, Nicholas Dawkins. The girl is sixteen and Nicholas is eight. Both are small for their ages.'

The woman left to check her ledger and returned a short while later. 'Sorry, there's no sign of anyone by those names here. You could try one of the other workhouses in the area as sometimes they take the overspill.'

Weary and defeated for the time being, Kathryn thanked the woman and walked away.

Mags was looking out for her in the upstairs window of the shop, holding a candle. Kathryn waited as she left the bedroom and the flickering light came towards her as she unbolted the front door of the shop below.

'Where have you been, Kathryn? It's perishing outside . . .'

Kathryn could hardly speak. She felt like a block of ice.

Realising this, Mags ushered her inside to the warmth upstairs and helped her remove her damp shawl. 'Take off your clothes,' she commanded. So Kathryn stripped down to her underwear and Mags returned with a thick nightdress, dressing gown and carpet slippers. Then she sat her sister in the high-backed armchair nearest the fire. 'I'll be right back, I'm going to make us a cup of cocoa,' she said.

All the time Mags was away Kathryn stared into the dancing flames of the fire, wondering how she could trace Dorrie and Nick. She was running out of ideas.

Mags returned with the steaming cups of cocoa and a slice of fruit cake each. 'Now get that down you,' she ordered. Mags was fast becoming a proper grown-up lady. Kathryn studied her archly. 'When did you stop being a kid, Mags?'

Mags smiled. 'When Ma became ill I suppose, and I had to pitch in. It was only then I realised the responsibilities of running a home and looking after kids.' She turned and picked up a thick blanket that was lying on the settee to place over Kathryn's legs, carefully tucking her in.

Kathryn took a sip of the chocolatey drink, which was beginning to warm her up. 'Thank you,' she said, setting down the small cup on the table beside her.

'So what happened then?' Mags finally asked.

Kathryn sighed and told her all about her fruitless search, right up to the point where O'Shay came across her in The Horse and Harness and claimed she still owed him rent money.

'That we don't!' Mags said fiercely.

'I know we don't. He was just trying it on. Then he went on to say he'd recently taken a pair of orphans to the workhouse as they couldn't afford the new rent.'

'He's all heart, isn't he?' Then the penny dropped as Mags realised who her sister meant. 'Dorrie and Nick, you mean?'

Kathryn nodded slowly. 'So I went to check at the Whitechapel workhouse, spoke to the supervisor, but they hadn't any new inmates by either of those names. She suggested I try other workhouses in the area in case they were sent to one of those instead.'

'It's all very odd if you ask me.' Mags frowned.

'How'd you mean?'

'Well, we only have O'Shay's word for it that they're in the workhouse, don't we?'

Kathryn nodded, contemplating if she ought to tell her sister what Blossom had said. Finally she spoke. 'The landlady said that O'Shay is into all sorts, running prostitutes and things like that. She said it wouldn't surprise her if he tried to get Dorrie involved.'

Mags grimaced. 'Surely not, she's barely two years older than me. I can't believe that!'

Unfortunately, Kathryn could. 'If we can't find them at any of the other workhouses in the area, then I'm going to the police.'

'I don't know if they'd do much about it, Kathryn. Remember when that girl from the opposite street went missing a year ago, no one ever found her and the police didn't seem all that bothered. 'Er mother was heartbroken.'

Her sister spoke the truth. 'Then maybe if that's the case we need to follow O'Shay to find out what he's getting up to!' Kathryn said firmly. She had warmed up now and was thinking straight once again.

After checking out all the workhouses in the area and discovering that Dorrie and Nick weren't at any of them, Kathryn decided that Mags might have had a point and O'Shay was up to something really bad.

Blossom informed her where O'Shay and his wife were living, so one evening Kathryn and Mags approached the house from the back entry. They peered in through the back window and could see Dorrie at the old stone sink washing dishes. Kathryn tapped the window lightly, startling the girl and causing her to almost topple off the old wooden crate she was standing on. 'Dorrie, it's us, Kathryn and Mags!' Kathryn whispered through the door.

The door drew open slowly and Dorrie glanced behind her in case she was being watched. 'Oh Kathryn, Mags, what are yer both doing 'ere?' She looked genuinely pleased to see them but fearful at the same time.

'I couldn't find you the other day and O'Shay told me he'd evicted you and Nick from your home, he reckoned you were both interned at the workhouse!'

'The last part ain't true, but he did force us to go with him, though we didn't want to. I caught him with a kick to the shins which made him really angry . . . Nick has done nothing but cry since we've been here.'

'How's he treatin' you both?' Mags chipped in.

'Worse than slaves. I have to keep house, cook and clean for him and that fat lazy wife of his. They're both fast asleep snoring in the living room, they've been on the gin again.'

'Come with us, then,' Kathryn urged.

'I can't, Nick is in bed upstairs, they'll beat me if they find me even talking to you like this!' Her eyes widened with panic.

'Then we won't get you into trouble but before it's light in the morning, we'll get Stan with his cart at the end of the lane and you can slip out with Nick at the back gate, all right?'

Dorrie took a deep breath and nodded. There was a loud bellow from inside the house. 'Girl! Get me more gin!'

'I better go,' she whispered, and she closed the door behind her.

'Poor Dorrie, being treated like that. I'd like to march in there and grab her and Nick at this very moment!' Mags said, with sudden anger.

'Well, we can't,' said Kathryn wisely. 'If we do that we'll have to fight off O'Shay and his wife. It's best to catch them out when they least expect it.'

And so the following morning, Kathryn waited with Stan on his cart at the end of the lane. For a while she thought something must have happened to prevent the children leaving, but eventually the back gate eased open and both Dorrie and Nick emerged, furtively. In her hand Dorrie held an old sack with what Kathryn assumed were their belongings.

Kathryn jumped down from the cart and Nick came running towards her and into her waiting arms. The poor mite looked thin and he had a black eye too, courtesy, she guessed, of O'Shay.

'Quickly, you two!' she urged. 'Get on the cart!'

They clambered aboard and she covered them with an old tarpaulin Stan used to protect the goods.

'Keep down and stay quiet there until I say it's safe to come out,' Stan commanded.

They did as told, and it was just as well as the back gate opened suddenly and a large lady emerged with her hands on her hips. 'Fergus!' she shouted towards the house. 'Them kids have done a runner!' By the time her husband appeared on the scene the cart had disappeared around the corner.

'I'm so glad we've got you back with us!' Kathryn said later, when she'd bathed and changed them both. They were sitting down to a breakfast of porridge with tinned cream and Demerara sugar as a special treat, followed by hot buttered crumpets and warming cups of cocoa.

From the way they ate she could see they hadn't had a proper meal for days. She'd also noticed the bruising and welts on their bodies as she'd bathed them. 'You are to live with us from now on,' she said gently. 'You shall never have to go back there again. What did that man and his wife do to you both?'

'He was horrible to us,' Dorrie explained. Her eyes had lost their sparkle. 'I had to be up at the crack of dawn skivvying all day with hardly a break, and at the end of the day I had to sleep on the hard stone floor with the dogs in the scullery. I felt like an animal meself!'

Kathryn hugged her close to her chest as the girl wept. 'Then poor Nick had to go with O'Shay and he sent him up a chimney to see if he was the right size for a chimney sweep. He's small for his age, and he said he'd keep him small too so he could get plenty of work out of him!'

'It were 'orrible,' Nick grimaced. 'I nearly burnt meself and felt like I couldn't breathe. I was covered in soot when I got out too, coughing and splutterin' I was!'

Kathryn ruffled his hair. 'Nick, I promise you shall never, ever, have to go through that again.'

Following breakfast, she sent them both downstairs where Georgina had a selection of sweets and chocolate for them both as a treat after the ordeal they'd been through.

'Later, I'm taking you both to Vicky Park! And I bought you a little boat to sail on the lake!' she said, looking at Nick, whose eyes lit up.

'What about Jimmy, though?' Dorrie asked, with concern in her eyes.

'Oh, don't worry about him for now,' Kathryn soothed.

'But he might write us a letter and now we won't get it as we no longer live in the same house?'

Somehow Kathryn thought he might forget about the kids altogether, but she wasn't prepared to say so. After all, if he was in a distant land then maybe his thoughts would be distant too when focused on his exotic adventures. What was it Ma used to say: 'Out of sight out of mind'? But then again there was another old saying which seemed to contradict the first: 'Absence makes the heart grow fonder'. She hoped the latter would be true in Jimmy's case.

'Well, it can't be helped for now. I'm sure when he returns he will work 'ard to find you both.' Dorrie cheered up after that and looked forward to going to the park with Georgina.

It was later that afternoon when the doorbell jangled in the shop. Kathryn was on her own and she called from the back room, 'I'll be with you in a moment!'

'That's quite all right. I'm prepared to wait!' a male voice answered, and a tingle ran down her spine as she realised she recognised that voice. Oh, why did Mags have to be out on a delivery? The kids were at Victoria Park with Georgina, and the only other person was Mr Bailey upstairs and he could hardly take over. She wanted to flee on the spot. Instead, she carried on tidying up the store room, hoping the customer would leave, but he didn't. After a couple of minutes, the voice shouted, 'You can come out now, Kathryn, I know it's you!'

Gingerly, she brushed down her apron and patted her hair. Then, opening the door fully, she stood facing Squire, who had a very amused look on his face. 'I've come to take you out for dinner!' he announced.

Chapter Twelve

'How did you find me?' She trembled from top to toe, her legs seeming quite boneless, as she held on to the counter to support herself.

'It wasn't that difficult.' He twirled his moustache, his eyes twinkling with merriment.

'Please tell me how you knew where I was.' She was worried now in case word had got back to O'Shay they were all living over the shop.

'It was Jess who told me. She'd been talking to the landlady at The Horse and Harness, and Blossom said you knew her and that you'd left a message for her. Don't worry, she's only told me. I just had to track you down as you so misunderstood what went on, Kathryn. Let me take you out tonight and I'll explain, it's not what you think at all!'

She stuck out her chin in defiance. 'I really don't know what you can say that will make things any better between us. All I see is a cad and a bounder stood in front of me!'

Even if he is astonishingly handsome.

No way did she want him to melt her heart once again, there was a barrier in place now and it was pure iceberg.

'Look, if you just dine with me for one hour and you don't like what you hear, you are free to leave at any time. If you decide not to come, you know I won't leave you alone as I will always come to look for you.'

She might as well go, she thought, then she'd never have to see him again . . .

As she waited, gazing out of the shop window in her best emerald-green bombazine dress and matching wrap, a hansom cab drew up outside.

'He's here,' she said breathlessly, looking at Mags. The kids were all already bathed and put to bed, worn out by their earlier visit to the park. Mags said she would sit with Mr Bailey to keep him company. Secretly, she liked the cantankerous old man. His bark was much worse than his bite.

'I never understood why yer stopped bothering with Squire?' She studied Kathryn's face for an answer. 'I mean, it can't have just been because you stopped working for him. He must have liked you well enough as you said he had romantic designs on yer.'

'Never you mind, my girl, I had my reasons.'

'Then why are you going to see him tonight?' Mags stood with hands on hips.

That indeed was a very good question that deserved an

honest answer. Yet, she could think of none that made any sense. Because I'm curious? Because I need to see him? Because I miss him so? The last made more sense than she realised; she did indeed miss the man, but not his motives. She could do without those!

When she left the shop and Mags had secured the door behind her, she gazed at Squire as he stood on the pavement, his black cloak billowing out in the early evening breeze, his top hat cocked at a jaunty angle on his head. The presence of his gold-topped cane added to the ambience. He was such a dandy. Ordinarily, she would feel inferior in her old clothes, but this was one designer outfit she'd brought with her, though she hadn't had a chance to wear it before tonight.

His eyes widened as he studied her form beneath the street light. 'My dear, you look enchanting this evening,' he said, as he took her black velvet-gloved hand and laid a kiss upon it. She shivered with anticipation.

Why did her body have to betray her?

The restaurant he'd chosen was a French one called *La Mer* up West. It specialised in all sorts of sea foods and boasted that all the fish was freshly caught.

A waiter in a white jacket and black bow tie led them to a little alcove which was decorated with coloured lanterns, fishing nets and ornamental shells.

When they were both seated and the waiter had insisted on taking her wrap and Squire's top hat and cane, she began to feel slightly vulnerable and exposed as her shoulders and décolletage were on display.

The wine waiter appeared. Squire impressed her as he seemed to converse with the man in faultless French.

'What did you just order?' she asked him.

'A bottle of 1880 Château des Temps, it was a very good year!' He grinned and she caught the glint in his eyes over the flickering candle between them. He took her hand across the table. 'I am sorry that I upset you . . .'

She looked away as her eyes misted with tears. She hadn't expected to feel like this and was saved from saying anything as the waiter reappeared at the table with a bottle of white wine and two crystal glasses.

He poured some into a glass and handed it to Squire, who took a sip, then swirled it around in his mouth. He swallowed and smiled and nodded at the waiter, who topped up their glasses, then departed.

Squire was about to say something when yet another waiter appeared with the menu. Kathryn studied it but it was all in French, too difficult for her to decipher; besides, the only fish she'd ever eaten was from the marketplace or the fish and chip shop and likely to have been something like herring or haddock.

So she asked Squire to choose for her. He selected Salmon en Croûte with seasonal vegetables and Gratin Dauphinois, a potato dish with cream and garlic.

She had no idea what the salmon dish was but was surprised to find it was salmon encased in a puff pastry, very much like the pastry she made for the pies at the shop. It gave her an idea to maybe try selling some fish pies in the future.

When they'd eaten, having made idle chit-chat along the way, over a glass of brandy, Squire eventually began to tell her what had happened.

'. . . More than a year ago, I had accumulated severe gambling debts, so bad that a group of men who worked at the club were after me for payment, making all sorts of threats. One night after I'd been tossed out on to the pavement outside the club – this was in the East End – a middle-aged prostitute offered me her services. I declined, then she came after me, tugging on my jacket sleeve, offering me her daughter's virginity for a shilling. Absolutely appalled, I declined that offer too. Then I realised just how many women and girls were living like this in the area, selling themselves cheaply. I'd heard of a man who'd bid for a virgin's honour and paid her a fortune in return. So I thought, what if I help young women who need money to get the best possible price for themselves? After all, they were going to do it anyway!'

Kathryn felt anger and indignation. 'You're all heart!' she spat in disgust.

He shook his head. 'Please hear me out. Over the next couple of months I was approached by three young women, two before yourself . . .'

Her heart hammered wildly as the memory flooded back of what she'd been prepared to do for money.

'So I did it for those two. One was Jess of course. The other I'll not name to protect her identity . . . But when I met you, I hadn't banked on falling in love with you, Kathryn. The other two meant nothing to me, they got what they wanted, which was far better than dropping their bloomers for sixpence in Whitechapel!'

'Well, that's exactly what Jess is doing now after you led her on. She thought she was engaged to you, Squire! She's gone back to walking the streets around Spitalfields and mixing with all sorts!'

'I know.' His face reddened as he played with his napkin, folding and unfolding it. 'I shouldn't have bought her that ring and allowed her to feel she was betrothed to me. But when I met you I realised the feelings I had for Jess weren't real. But you for me, Kathryn, are the real deal and that ring I gave you was a token of my love for you . . . I feel bad about allowing Jess to think that I cared more than I did for her, but I had no control in her getting involved with Kelly and the others.'

'Kelly? Mary Jane Kelly?'

He nodded. 'Yes, that's the one. She was living with Joseph Barnett at Miller's Court. Do you know her?'

'No, but Blossom mentioned her.'

'Barnett and his brothers work at Billingsgate Fish Market. He told me he was fed up to the back teeth with Mary bringing back whores to their place and allowing them to spend the night, it's only a small place in Miller's Court. He's packed his bags and left, gone to digs. He said he had done everything he could to try to stop her walking the streets.'

'So, you know her well then?' She narrowed her eyes in suspicion. She remembered Blossom mentioning the French connection. Was it Squire who had taken the woman to France? Who was this man sat in front of her? Did she really know him at all?

Squire gazed at her with pleading eyes over the table, the candlelight reflected in them. 'Please, Kathryn. I beg you to give me another chance . . . I love you so much.' He reached out for her hand, but she quickly withdrew it.

'I don't really see any hope for us, Squire,' she snapped. 'You are married after all.'

'But I have a dreadful life with Constance. It's partly her fault I got myself into debt in the first place as she wants so much from me that I simply cannot give. Nothing's ever enough for her. If I get the house redecorated then a few months later, she'll say she wants it all changed again . . . If I buy her new furniture eventually she says it's old-fashioned and we need new to keep up with her friends. But they are far wealthier than us. That's why I started gambling, in the hope I could keep up with the lifestyle she has brought on us as a couple. And gambling is not without its consequence when you owe people money . . .'

Is he just trying it on so I feel pity for him?

It was hard to tell, as now she felt she was a poor judge of men. She'd thought Jimmy was the most loyal man she'd ever met until he abandoned Dorrie and Nick, and he hadn't even written to them all the time he'd been away.

She shook her head and bit her lip, forcing tears back before they fell because she did love him so, even though she didn't care to admit it to him. 'I made a mistake coming here this evening,' she sniffed.

He looked deeply into her eyes. 'No, you didn't, Kathryn. You came because you wanted to. No one held a gun to your head.'

She swallowed down her sadness. 'Tell me one thing,' she said.

He nodded. 'Anything you wish.'

'Mrs Harrington . . . was she somehow involved in your so-called nieces being togged up at the store?'

Hardly able to look her in the face, he lowered his eyelids. 'Yes, I am quite ashamed to say so. She knew all along, that's why I used to slip her the odd envelope of money for her assistance.'

'But no one else at the store knew?'

He shook his head. 'She could hardly tell them she was being bribed to get the dresses ready quickly for a couple of . . .'

'Harlots, you were about to say?'

He looked at her now and nodded.

'And that is the real problem, as now I could end up shop-soiled. No man would ever want me if I went with you.'

'That's simply not true. I want you for yourself.'

'But only on your terms. I can only ever be your mistress, don't you see? You ain't never going to be free to love me. Now I have that job at the shop with living quarters, I can't spoil that. I can't afford for no scandal to reach my employer's ears.' She gritted her teeth. How she'd love to slap his face right now after the way he'd lied to her and for how he'd allowed Jess to suffer for his misdemeanours. Trembling, she fought to bring her emotions under control.

He nodded. 'I quite understand, Kathryn. I shall wait for as long as it takes until you're ready to be mine.' Then changing the subject, he asked, 'How is your mother?'

Kathryn clenched her fists at her sides. How dare he bring up the subject of her mother at that rest home just so he could rub in how he helped to get her there!

'Damn you, Squire!' she said, standing. '*This is emotional blackmail!*'

'But you've got it all wrong . . . Please sit back down, Kathryn. It was a genuine question and one with no strings attached whatsoever.'

But she had already tossed her napkin on the table and, reaching into her reticule, she withdrew a few shillings and placed them down in front of him. 'This should cover the cost of my meal!' She held her head in the air. No man was ever going to buy her again. Heads had begun to turn towards their table.

'The show's well and truly over, folks!' she said. 'And as

for yer, Squire or whatever yer name happens to be today, please do not contact me again!' Then she turned and stopped a passing waiter to ask for her cloak.

She waited near the entrance of the restaurant as the doorman, on the waiter's orders, hailed a passing cab and helped her inside. She turned to look out of the cab window, but there was no sign of Squire following her and for that she was extremely grateful.

The next day, a letter arrived at the shop from Ma. The kids gathered around as Mags read it out. The handwriting didn't look like Ma's at all and Kathryn guessed someone had helped her write it.

> *Dear all,*
>
> *Hope you are all well? I am feeling so much better. The air here is doing me a power of good but I miss you all so much. Matron says I can now receive visitors. If you can arrange a suitable day, Matron says she can book a meal for you, but she will need numbers.*
>
> *I've met a lovely lady, who is an author. She's interesting to speak to. There's also a man who paints scenery. They all seem so upper class here to me, I really can't understand how you afforded for me to stay here, but I am feeling more my old self. I don't cough half so much and I've put on a little weight too.*

Anyhow, I must close now as we are due to have our supper soon, then we're expected to be in bed for lights out at eight o'clock.

All my love,
Ma

Mags and the kids beamed when she'd read the letter out, but Kathryn wasn't so certain that things were going all that well. She guessed maybe the lady author had helped her compose that letter as it didn't really sound like Ma's tone of voice.

'I'm going to write back and go and visit her on Sunday,' she whispered to Mags. She needed to check things out for herself.

'Can I come, too?' Mags asked.

'Better stay and look after the kids as Georgina won't be around.'

'You look worried, Kathryn. Did something happen last night?'

She shook her head. 'We had a nice meal, that was all, but I ain't going to be seeing Squire again.'

On Sunday morning, Kathryn took the train to the Kent coast. She'd packed a little carpet bag in case she missed the last train home and needed to stay overnight. For once, it was a sunny and bright autumnal day. The views out of the train window were spectacular, as rows of East End houses and large factories and warehouses gave way to green fields and trees with leaves of russet and burnished gold and farmhouses and finally the sea.

She'd worried a lot about Ma lately as she hadn't seen her for a few weeks, but it was better than hearing that hacking cough in that damp back bedroom, and at least she trusted she was in good hands.

When the train reached her destination there were several hansom cabs, carriages and people with carts waiting outside. She noticed an elderly man sat atop one of the carts who reminded her of her father, and as it was such a nice day, she asked if he could take her to the rest home.

'Hop aboard, young lady!' he shouted, then shot her a wizened smile. He clambered down and placed her carpet bag on the back of the cart and helped her into her seat, then handed her a woollen rug to place over her legs. Even though the sun shone brightly, the trees rustled with the breeze and she was grateful for the warmth the rug provided.

'Gee up!' he shouted to the large black and white Shire horse as it pulled away. The horse let out a loud whinny and a large puff of steam as they set off leaving the small country railway station behind.

They chatted amicably as the cart plodded along winding country lanes. Beside them, stone-walled boundaries separated farmers' fields filled with patchwork colours of green and gold. 'Corn,' her driver announced. He'd told her his name was Ned. 'The gold fields. Bet you ain't ever seen those before?'

Kathryn drew in an astonished breath and shook her head. 'No, I ain't. It really is a lovely sight. 'Ave you lived here long, Ned?'

'All me life. Wouldn't want to go and live in the city with all that foul air clogging up me lungs!' He thumped his chest with his left hand while the other kept hold of the reins.

Kathryn nodded. She knew what he meant, the streets near the match factory at Bow stank of sulphur, and other areas were thick with industrial smells from various factories and warehouses. And worst of all were the pea-souper fogs from people's chimneys, tanneries, breweries and other industrial sites in the area. Sometimes they were so thick you could barely see a hand in front of you. Criminals took advantage of those times to dip into pockets and whip whatever they could. It was so bad for Ma's chest, living in the East End.

'So you say your mother's been at the rest home for a few weeks now?' Ned asked.

'Yes. She was right poorly, but in her last letter she said she feels so much better and has even put on a bit of weight.'

'Well that's good then.' He glanced at her. 'You look troubled, lass.'

Kathryn chewed her bottom lip. 'I am. I will 'ave to bring her back to London soon as I can't keep her there forever, it costs too much money. And of course, she'll want to return to be with the kids. She misses them so much!'

'That's understandable, but I think you've done a great kindness for your mother and maybe she will feel better in time to cope with it all.'

Kathryn hoped so.

Jimmy opened his eyes. All he could see were wooden planks all around him which were swaying back and forth. Where was he? It looked like a small dark cellar and stank to high heaven of human waste.

'Stay still, lad,' someone beside him advised. 'You've been out cold for weeks. I thought we'd lost you.'

He groaned. 'Where am I?'

'Don't you remember?' A man's face drew up close to him and he thought he detected a faint whiff of rum in amongst the stale smell of human bodies that appeared to be lying close by.

'No.' He brought his hand to his head. He had vague recollections of being semi-awake and people feeding him something sloppy on a spoon during that time, but he had no idea how long it had been as he'd found it hard to stay awake long enough to be fully conscious until now.

'You fell on deck and hit your head. We thought you were a goner for a time, but you must be a strong lad as you've survived all that on the high seas while some of the men are falling like flies with dysentery . . .'

Then it came back to him full force — he was on board a ship! It all started to make sense. He'd left his brother and sister behind. 'Nick! Dorrie!' he shouted, as he began to pull himself up in a blind panic.

'Lie still, lad,' the man advised, settling him back down on the narrow bunk bed. 'I'll get the ship's doctor and tell him you're awake.

There's no use you crying out for Nick and Dorrie, whoever they are, as they ain't on this ship.'

'Where are we?'

'We're off the coast of Morocco . . .'

Jimmy felt his eyes brimming with tears. What had made him leave his home and come all this way? How could he have abandoned the kids like that? Then he remembered he'd asked his aunt and uncle to watch out for them. He'd figured he'd make his fortune and return home sooner or later and they'd all have a better life. But who and what had he been running away from? He just couldn't remember a thing.

Chapter Thirteen

The cart eventually took a turning that led up to a path banked on either side by low stone walls which housed lush green fields. There were sheep dotted here and there, put out to pasture. The steep incline was very rickety as the cart bumped over the stones and the horse worked hard to get to the top as he puffed out clouds of steam.

Kathryn glanced at Ned, who appeared to be unconcerned. 'Are you sure this is the right way, Ned?'

He nodded, then taking a puff on his pipe, said, 'This is the shortest route. Haven't been asked to take anyone up here for years, mind you.'

Now he tells me! Suddenly, she wondered as the place was so remote how she could get a lift back to the station as she didn't know how long she'd be staying for.

'Ned, are you likely to come this way again?'

He took another puff on his pipe, savouring the taste of tobacco, and said, 'Maybe I will and maybe I won't . . .'

What kind of an answer was that? 'It's just that I'll need to get back to the railway station either tonight or tomorrow.'

He smiled. 'You're not used to the ways of us country folk, are you, lass?'

Not if they were as laid back as Ned, she wasn't, but she didn't want to show her irritation. He didn't have a job where he had to get up at the crack of dawn to open up a shop, see to kids, and at night bake several dozen pies for people. All he had to do was pick passengers up from the railway station by the look of it, and it didn't seem to matter that much to him whether he returned for them or not.

But she was mistaken about his intentions as next he said, 'Look, what I'll do is get you settled at the rest home. Maybe I'll stay for a cup of tea and then you can decide whether you want me to stop on with you for a couple of hours and then take you back if your Ma is fine, or if not, I can be about my way and return for you at an agreed time tomorrow.'

She could have wept with relief. She had chosen the best driver for the job as she couldn't imagine those who drove a hansom cab or carriage would put themselves out so much for her.

Eventually, they arrived at the brow of the hill. Just a few more feet and then Kathryn's eyes took in the sweep of the landscape, for as high as they were she could see the green rolling hills in front of her and the sparkling blue sea beyond. It had been years since she'd seen the sea; it fair near took her breath away. Ma was certainly in the right place.

'What wonderful scenery!' she exclaimed, as the breeze blew her hair into her face. She moved it out of the way with a sweep of her hand. Oh to live out here, wouldn't that be wonderful? It would be like looking at one of those old landscape paintings that hung in the museum, every day. 'I've never seen anything so beautiful in all me life!'

'Aye, it is that an' all, but beauty comes with a price . . .' He puffed on his pipe. 'It can be dangerous too, there are steep cliffs at the edge there and many a farmer has lost livestock over the other side, so you be careful, my girl.'

'I will,' she said, catching her breath.

Ned turned the cart left and through a small wooded area which Kathryn imagined, when no one was around, was inhabited by pixies, elves and fairies! How enchanting. They emerged out of the forest to be faced with Clifftop Towers, the rest home. Oh it was grand and all. Covered in ivy, with four towers attached one to each corner of the house and in the middle of the roof there was a clock tower which displayed the time as half past two.

As the cart rumbled along, Kathryn felt her excitement mounting up.

She was going to see Ma at last.

The cart entered the large black wrought-iron gates, which were already open. It passed underneath a small stonework arch with a lion's head on the top and drew up outside the side entrance of the house.

As if already watching out for visitors, a liveried footman appeared to ask what their business was.

'Hello,' Kathryn said, unsure whether to shake his hand or not. 'My name is Kathryn Flynn and I am expected. I am due to visit my mother 'ere this afternoon.'

'Very well, miss, and what is your mother's name?'

'Enid. Enid Flynn.'

'Just one moment, please.' He returned inside the house, then reappeared at Kathryn's side a few minutes later.

'I'm afraid your mother isn't here at the moment, Miss Flynn. I'm sorry if it has been a wasted journey for you.'

Kathryn shook her head vehemently. 'But that ain't right, there must be a mistake! I wrote to her to arrange today's visit. Can you check again, please?'

He gazed at her as if she was something of pity before him, sighed and walked back in the direction of the house, only to return with a large middle-aged woman at his side. The woman wore a long black dress with a high collar. Her hair was styled as two coiled-up plaits secured either side of her head, a style Kathryn was unfamiliar with. 'This is Mrs Plumley, she's the matron here, Miss Flynn,' he explained, then turned on his heel to leave the woman to deal with Kathryn.

Mrs Plumley smiled. 'But I thought you'd have known, your uncle turned up early this morning to take your mother home with him, Miss Flynn.'

'B . . . but I don't have an uncle . . .' she stammered.

Matron's eyes clouded over. 'I . . . I . . . don't know what to say. He was a nice gentleman and your mother seemed pleased to see him. She said she felt so much better and she couldn't wait to go home.'

For a moment, Kathryn wondered if it was Doctor Beck who had called and maybe Ma had insisted on returning home with him, but then another thought occurred to her. 'What did the man look like, Mrs Plumley?'

'He was a rather handsome gentleman . . .' Kathryn could tell by the look in Matron's eyes that whoever it was had won her over. 'Dark hair, blue eyes, a twirled moustache. A man of fine breeding, to be perfectly honest with you.'

'Can't you remember his name?' It had to be Squire going by Matron's description but she just needed to know for her own benefit.

'Something Arthur, I believe.'

'Ronald Arthur?'

'Yes, that's the name. I don't think your mother will come to any harm, dear.'

'How can you be sure of that, Mrs Plumley? I haven't seen my mother for weeks and have had to save up for the journey here today to discover she's been taken away by a gentleman without my consent. What grounds did you have to allow her to leave anyhow?'

'Our resident doctor said she was in better health and there was money owing, dear. Mr Arthur paid the rest of the bill and took her with him. She was more than happy to leave here.'

Kathryn felt furious and gritted her teeth. If she wasn't such a lady she'd have booted the matron on the shin.

And the question was, where had Squire taken her mother to, anyhow?

Kathryn trembled all over, her heart racing so fast she could hardly think straight. *Calm down, think carefully . . . What can you do now?* She paced the gravelled drive, biting her lip as she watched Matron head off back to the house. It was no longer her problem, she'd obviously washed her hands of the whole affair.

'What's up, lass?' Ned asked, when he could see the state she was in.

'Someone has been here and taken my mother away . . .' She raised her hands in the air in desperation.

'But surely that's not possible? They wouldn't allow her to be taken by a stranger.'

'This is the problem though, Ned. It wasn't a stranger, the person concerned is known to me.'

'Do you think your mother might come to any harm with this person?' Old Ned's brow furrowed as if deeply concerned.

She let out a long breath. 'To be truthful, no. I think he will take care of her, but he just had no right to do that. The matron said Ma was better anyhow and he settled the bill.'

'Well there you are then, lass. What are you going to do now?'

'I can't stick around here. I better get back home.'

'If I were you, I'd take some time to cool down before leaving. I've got a bottle of ginger beer in my basket and a pork pie my sister made. We can have a little picnic before leaving. You must be famished.'

She shook her head. 'No, thank you. I don't think I could eat a thing to be honest with you.'

'Come on now, lass. You'll be neither use nor ornament to your ma if you make yourself ill. I'll take us back to the cliffs and set the blanket on the grass and we'll have a bite to eat. I could do with some nourishment anyhow. Then I'll take you back to the railway station and you can catch the next train back home.'

Kathryn could hardly believe Ned's kindness. 'Thank you, Ned.' She sniffed as her eyes filled up with tears.

'Here, don't be letting on so, miss.' He handed her a white cotton handkerchief. 'You'll see, your ma will be all right. I expect she couldn't wait to get home and see you all.'

Kathryn nodded through her tears as she followed Ned back to the cart and they made their way to the cliffs.

They chatted amicably as the cart wove through the copse and approached the breathtaking scenery of the cliffs overlooking the sea. But it wasn't the sea nor the scenery that made Kathryn gasp, it was the sight of a couple in the distance strolling arm in arm.

Squire and Ma!

'There they are!' she shrieked.

Ned took the cart as near as he could then Kathryn leapt out, not caring for her own safety, shouting 'How dare you, Squire!'

He and her mother turned, both looking surprised. Kathryn was far too angry to even hug her mother or notice how much healthier she now looked.

'Ah, Kathryn,' he said. And as she approached, his smile became uncertain at the sight of her obvious anger. She whipped her hand up in the air ready to bring it down on his cheek. He caught hold of it, drawing her close to him.

'No, not here, dearest. Not in front of your mother and that gentleman, please,' he whispered.

He released her hand. And she embraced her mother. 'Ma, are you all right? Did you want to leave the rest home?'

Her mother smiled. 'Oh, Kathryn, it has done me such a lot of good, but it's time to go 'ome now. You two have something to discuss, so I shall wait with this gentleman, if that is all right?' she asked diplomatically.

Kathryn nodded and Ned smiled.

He clambered off the cart and laid out the blanket. 'Come and sit here, Mrs Flynn. Your daughter has told me all about you. Please join me for a little refreshment.'

Kathryn accompanied her mother as far as the blanket and left her in Ned's capable hands while she returned to Squire's side and glared at him.

'I'm sorry, Kathryn. I had no idea you would be visiting here today. My intentions were to escort your mother home as a surprise for you.'

'But I didn't want to have any more to do with you. I can manage for myself!'

'All of that is very noble but I'm afraid there is no way you would have managed the fees at that rest home, there has been a price increase. In any case, your mother is over the worst of her illness, you can see by the look on her face. Her cheeks are plump and rosy, she looks so much better for it.' Kathryn had to admit this was true.

As they strolled along the cliff top, he reached out for her hand with his. She took it, and all of a sudden she was in his arms as he kissed her with such a passion she was giddy with love for him, and gratitude that he had wanted to bring Ma home for her. All thoughts of his previous misdemeanours disappeared from her mind.

'Kathryn,' he said, breaking away. 'Now that I've found you I never want to lose you again. I want us to be together forever.'

But then realisation dawned as she thought back to all he'd done in the past, his promises and his lies. 'But how can I possibly ever trust you again?' She blinked several times.

He took her hands in his. 'I think it will be a question of time for you to build up trust in me again, Kathryn. I'm so sorry for all I've put you through, but I am a changed man.

You've softened my heart and taught me what true love really is.' He lifted her hand and placed a kiss upon it.

She nodded, but at the back of her mind was Constance. If they were to see one another she could only ever be his mistress. But she loved him, so much so that she was just going to have to paint his wife out of the picture altogether. Besides, maybe he did deserve a second chance, after all he'd done for her mother. For that she would always be grateful.

There was no need now for Kathryn to return home by train as Squire accompanied her and Ma back to the shop in his carriage. When Kathryn had returned to her mother's side she couldn't help noticing how well she and Ned had been getting along as they shared his vittles together. It had been good to see the twinkle back in her eyes once again.

And now they both stood outside the shop as Squire made to leave. He stared at Kathryn for the longest time.

'I do love you, you know. I did this for you.'

She swallowed down a lump in her throat as she realised she had misjudged the man and his motives.

'Thank you,' she whispered. Then before she knew it, Ma had pushed open the shop door with a jangle of the bell and Mags greeted them, calling the kids down from upstairs to share the surprise. Never had Kathryn seen such a warm homecoming in her life. There were tears and laughter and such delight that for a moment it was impossible to get a word in edgeways.

And when Squire took Kathryn to the apartment later, she gladly let him sweep her up in his arms close to his chest. Breathlessly, he whispered, 'Kathryn, I want you so much, my darling.'

She melted in his embrace, finding herself succumbing to his fervent kisses. Could this really be happening at last? It seemed strange that when they first met she had been prepared to offer her honour at a price and he was the one to hold back. Then she had been the one to become coy. But now there were no misgivings on either side, and when he began to unbutton the bodice of her dress, she did not resist. This man, although he had his faults, had done a lot for her and her family.

'My Kathryn,' he said as he carried her in his arms into the bedroom, and gently laid her on the bed as if she were a precious piece of porcelain. She was about to become a woman at last.

This was so different to the night she'd been almost ravished by Brutus. He would have treated her cruelly, she was sure of it. If it had not been for the fact he'd been unable to perform, she would never have known what it felt like to be treated so gently.

If she had one misgiving though, it was that Squire was

married, but for the time being she forced the picture she had of him and his wife together out of her mind. This was her night and her night only. A chance finally to act on the dammed up feelings she had inside of her, remembering all the times she'd trembled at a mere touch from his hand or felt pleasurable sensations coursing through her body when he'd whispered suggestively in her ear. He was all man and he knew it. But she was all woman too and he wanted her as much as she wanted him.

Ma settled in well at the shop. A spare pallet was brought into the girls' bedroom and Mags gave up her bed for her mother to sleep in. When Ma discovered that Kathryn had been using her pie recipes she was thrilled to bits, wanting to come on board to help out.

'Are you sure you're up to it?' Kathryn asked, as her mother sat in the armchair nearest the fire, darning an old sock.

'Aw be off with you, of course I am. I might include my corned beef pie and some mincemeat recipes as Christmas is fast approaching.'

'That sounds great, Ma, but don't go overdoing things,' Kathryn warned. 'I have to nip out later, can you keep an eye on Mr Bailey for me? He'll need his elevenses soon.'

'Sure thing. I know the man seems like a tyrant, but he's all right with me, he 'as to be or he'll be getting the sharp edge of me tongue!' Ma threw her head back and laughed, then set down her darning on a small wooden table at her side. It was then Kathryn realised it had been a long time since Ma had laughed quite like that. It had been ages since her mother had had the strength to even conjure up a feeble smile. There were no two ways about it, that rest home had done her a power of good.

Kathryn lifted her bonnet and shawl from a peg on the back of the door.

'Where're you off to?'

'Just need to see someone, it's a lady I need to check up on. Someone less fortunate than ourselves . . .'

Ma took hold of her daughter's hand. 'You're so good to everyone, Kathryn. You're a real selfless person, I've always admired that about you.'

Kathryn smiled as she squeezed her mother's hand in reassurance. 'But before I go, I have something to give you . . .' She dipped her hand into her skirt pocket and placed something small in her mother's palm.

'Well if it ain't me wedding ring!' Ma exclaimed.

'There was no way I was ever going to pawn that. Slip it back on your finger, Ma. You've put on some weight, it should fit now.'

Ma sat there for a moment, her eyes glistening with tears. Then she slipped the ring on her wedding finger. 'Aye, it does fit and all, just like it used to!' she said, staring at it as if seeing it for the first time.

Although it gladdened Kathryn's heart to see Ma reunited

with her precious ring, she swallowed a lump in her throat as she dreaded her mother finding out what she'd been prepared to do for money. And if she ever discovered it was all for her welfare, she would be thoroughly mortified.

Chapter Fourteen

Kathryn passed through Itchy Park, a railed area at the rear of Christ Church, Spitalfields. The shadow of the church fell across the garden in the early afternoon sun. She wrapped her shawl tightly around her shoulders to protect herself from the cold. An old man walked towards her, pushing a small handcart containing a big bundle of rags, tightly wrapped, as though they were all his worldly possessions. Kathryn realised that often the homeless ended up dossing down here, for it was not a park in the ordinary sense with a lake and boats and lots of pretty flowers like Victoria Park, but a site where the destitute came to beg, sleep or otherwise collapse from sheer exhaustion. Some were simply too proud to knock on the workhouse door while others, due to their inability to work, would have been refused entry anyhow.

The despair etched on the faces of the people on the benches, where they huddled together in their ragged attire, showed her the truth of the poverty in this part of the city. *There but for the grace of God go I.*

A raw, bitter wind whipped up and she turned to see the face of a mother and child seated on a wooden bench, the mother's eyes pleading and the child's face practically blue as she clung her tightly to her mother's breast. Reaching into her reticule, Kathryn withdrew a shilling. 'For the babe,' she said, as she pressed it into the mother's grubby palm. The woman nodded her thanks, but Kathryn's benevolence had attracted the eyes of onlookers, and some were now staring in their direction while one or two of the men started to walk towards them. 'Let's get you out of 'ere darlin', and to some place warm,' she said kindly. She placed an arm around the woman and led her away from the letches and lepers of Itchy Park, who, she now realised with regret, would knock the woman and baby flat to the ground to get hold of that shilling.

After settling the young woman and baby in a nearby chop house and ordering her a cup of tea and a meal, she left knowing they would be warm for a little while yet with food in the mother's belly so her child could suckle a while longer. She would even still have that shilling in her pocket for later . . . though Kathryn guessed in an hour or two the woman might return, begging again, to that same park bench.

Standing on the corner of Commercial Street and Fournier Street was The Ten Bells pub, which faced the side of the church. Kathryn heard raucous laughter drift on to the pavement outside as a couple of men stood on the street supping from pewter tankards. She bypassed them to push open the pub door and was met with the strong odour of tobacco and ale. A group of men were being entertained by a woman in a low-cut red dress who raised her skirts and sang, 'I'm a good girl when I'm able!' The men loved it as they tossed ha'pennies and other coins at her feet as she sang and danced on the table. Some tried to leer up her dress as she waved her skirts, showing off her frilled petticoat and black button-up ankle-length boots.

Kathryn's eyes searched for Jess, but she couldn't see her anywhere.

She nudged a man who was enthralled watching the woman's performance. 'Have you seen Jess or Mary Kelly, please?'

The man, who looked more than a little irritated at being disturbed, averted his gaze from the performer towards Kathryn, then pointed to a corner of the room. Kathryn's eyes were drawn to two women huddled together clinking their glasses and laughing, already appearing inebriated at this early hour. So it was correct what Squire had told her about the pair knocking around with one another after all.

There was no mistaking Jess in a bright-blue, low-cut dress, which looked as if it might have been one that Squire had formerly purchased for her, but which had now seen better days.

Mary Jane Kelly, who had dark shoulder-length tresses and a slightly chubby face, wore a grey linsey frock and white apron, and her shoulders were covered with a red shawl.

As Kathryn approached their table, Jess's eyes showed a flicker of recognition as she squinted and blinked, and then she was on her feet, beaming. 'Well if it ain't me old mucker Kathryn, or should I say *Miss Bella*!' She threw back her head and laughed uproariously, sending a shiver down Kathryn's spine. She didn't want to be reminded of her past.

'Hello, Jess. I just wandered in to see how you were keeping,' she said.

'I'm keepin' fine, ducks. Wanna join us for a drop of porter? Mary don't mind, do you, Mary?'

Mary closed one eye, raised her glass, belched and said, 'Cheers, love. The more the merrier, I say.'

Feeling totally out of her depth but realising she stood out like a sore thumb, Kathryn took a seat in between the women.

'I'll gerrus a drink now!' Jess bellowed. 'Oi Frank!' A large man wearing a leather waistcoat and striped shirt stood at the bar with his back to them.

'He's the cellarman,' Mary whispered. 'A good sort. Will get us a free drink for a fumble, don't 'e, Jess?'

Jess nodded and laughed.

Kathryn could see this wasn't going to be easy. 'Sorry ladies, I haven't come here for anything like that. I'll get the drinks instead.' She pushed past Mary and made her way to the wooden bar, nudging past groups of men as she went until she got there, thankfully without being accosted.

She tried to call the landlord but he was busy serving a man at the other end of the bar. Then the barmaid spotted her. 'What's a nice-looking young lady like yerself doing in a place like this?' she enquired.

'I've just called to see Jess, that's all.'

'Oh 'er. She's gorn to seed since she's been knocking around with that Kelly one. You be mindful of that, gel.'

Kathryn nodded. 'I will. Thank you.'

The barmaid smiled. 'Now what can I get you?'

'Whatever they've been drinking and I'll have a small gin and lemon, please.'

'You go and sit yourself down dear, I'll bring them over. A lady such as yourself shouldn't be standing by no bar. Now Jess and Mary, well it's in their blood see, but you're more refined, like.'

If only the woman knew the truth of the situation. Yes, she had changed her ways but she had been prepared to prostitute herself for her cause and was now in a relationship with a married man. It hadn't been of her choosing, but she couldn't help who she fell in love with, could she?

The barmaid arrived at the table within a couple of minutes with their drinks on a wooden tray. 'Now you behave yourself, Mary,' she warned. 'You too, Jess. Don't want to be slinging you out like what we had to last time . . .'

'Cross me heart and hope to die!' Mary threw back her head and laughed.

The barmaid leaned over to pass Kathryn her drink and whispered, 'She's not the same since Joe left her, poor dear. He loved her to pieces, but couldn't take any more of the goings-on at Miller's Court. He never wanted to see her on the game in the first place.' Mary and Jess were too busy chatting to one another to notice anything the woman was saying to Kathryn, it was as if they were in a world of their own; one Kathryn could never be a part of, she realised, as she saw the leering looks of the men who seemed to be eyeing them up like pieces of meat for the taking. And now some were watching her too, assuming no doubt that she was cut from the same cloth. It gave her the creeps.

When Kathryn finally managed to get a word in edgewise she said to Jess, 'How about I help you out, Jess? I can try to get you somewhere better to live than around these parts.'

Jess blinked profusely. 'I don't need yer help. I've got a room in a lodging house over there at Dorset Street.'

Weren't Dorset Street and Miller's Court in the same area?

'You mean you're staying with Mary at Miller's Court?'

'No, just around the corner. A gentleman is paying for it as long as he gets his privileges, if you know what I mean!' She gave a dirty laugh and tapped the side of her nose, causing Mary to join in.

'You're a card, an' all, Jess! You know you can stay at my place any time if the landlady slings you out!' Mary shouted.

'Please, the two of yer . . . I want to help you out.' Kathryn tried to explain.

Jess frowned. 'Hark at her, *Miss High and Mighty*! Who do you think you are?'

'I'm sorry, Jess. I don't mean no offence, but you know how dangerous it is around here. Come back with me tonight.

I can give you somewhere safe to stay and a hot meal, I'm living over Bailey's Stores with the rest of the family . . .'

'Sorry, ducks. I'm on a promise. Gerroff home yerself before it gets dark,' Jess said, as she hiccupped quite suddenly and seemed to sober up. 'It's too late for the likes of me, but yer have a better life than this to go home to. Yer working at Bailey's then?'

Kathryn nodded. 'Any time you need me, call there,' she said.

Jess smiled and then turned her back to talk to Mary.

Sighing deeply, Kathryn stood as the barmaid appeared at her side. 'She's right, love. Ain't nothing you can do to protect the likes of those pair, they've made their choices in life. That Joe Barnett couldn't keep Mary off the game even when he was working, and how that man tried. They'd rather ply their trade than face up to life . . .'

Kathryn guessed there was truth in the woman's words. She nodded and left the pub without the pair even noticing she'd gone. Another hour or so and they'd have drunk so much they'd hardly remember she was there in the first place.

As she searched for a cab, the church bell chimed five times. Darkness would soon descend and she wanted to get back home. There was no more she could do for the time being.

The following morning Kathryn was up bright and early helping Mags to set up the shop for the day. The kids, including Dorrie and Nick, were getting themselves ready for school while Ma had a big pot of porridge on the go for everyone.

'Where were you yesterday?' Mags asked, as she hefted a heavy sack of spuds out to the front of the shop. She was a strong girl but sometimes Kathryn wished she'd slow down a little and accept help from others.

Kathryn felt her face flush red hot. 'I had to take a trip over to Whitechapel to visit a friend, that was all.'

'Who?' Mags slumped down on the sack she'd been carrying. It was obvious she wasn't going anywhere until she'd received a satisfactory answer; as far as she was concerned there'd been too many secrets of late.

Kathryn drew in a long breath and let it out again. 'If you must know, it was to see a young woman called Jess. She's hit hard times lately. I went to The Ten Bells to find her.'

'You went inside a pub?' Mags blinked several times. 'Pubs are for bad women, Ma's always warning us of that, Kathryn!'

'I just wanted to see if I could help her, that's all. I had hoped to bring her back here until she got back on her feet.'

Mags tittered. 'I expect she's more off her feet than on them!'

Kathryn gritted her teeth. It was hard to hear her sister speak that way about prostitutes when she herself had almost gone down that path, but of course Mags wouldn't know that. 'Please don't make light of it. Anyhow, she didn't want my 'elp so there's no more I can do for her.'

'I bet you Squire could help . . .'

If only Mags realised it was Squire who had got her on the game in the first place. But if truth be told, she knew that Jess would have gone that way anyhow; he'd just given her a push off the precipice.

Kathryn furrowed her brow. 'What makes you think he could help her?'

'Well ain't he the benevolent sort? He helped us to get Ma into that rest home.'

'That's perfectly true, but we can't expect him to help all the waifs and strays around here. Come on, we best get a move on, we should have been open five minutes ago. Don't want Georgina or Mr Bailey getting cross with us, do we?'

'Aw, Mr Bailey's a pussycat, Kathryn.'

She chuckled. 'Well my girl, he might be like that with you and even with our Shaun, but he's pretty snappy with the rest of us!'

'That's 'cos you don't know how to handle him like me and Shaun do. We don't take no nonsense, see. We stand up to the old codger!'

The doorbell jangled and Mrs Jefferson sauntered into the shop with her wicker basket tucked over her arm. She was often the earliest customer and always made a beeline for Mags. She was a tough cookie like Mr Bailey that Mags had won over.

'How can I 'elp yer today, Mrs Jefferson?' Mags asked, as she shot her a glowing smile.

'Good morning, young Mags, I think I'll have a quarter of tea and a half pound of flour, please. Oh, and a bloomer loaf, Mr Jefferson will be rising for his breakfast soon. Where's Georgina this morning?'

'She no longer does full days here, Mrs Jefferson,' Kathryn explained. 'She has her husband and house to see to, she'll be in for a couple of hours later on.'

Mrs Jefferson snorted. 'Husband? Pah! That husband of hers never got on with old Mr Bailey and that brother, Walter, is like a wet weekend. Poor gal needs a break in life.'

Although Kathryn agreed with Mrs Jefferson, she didn't like the idea of discussing the woman who had given her and Mags both employment and a roof over the family's heads, it didn't feel right somehow, so she changed the subject.

The remainder of the morning flew by. Trade was brisk at lunchtime as people formed an orderly queue for the pies. Word had got around how good they were, and now, thankfully, Ma was here to help on that score; after all, they'd been her special recipes Kathryn had been using in the first place.

They now had several types of pie on the go, meat and potato, corned beef, chicken and mushroom and now Ma was experimenting with some new recipes for sweet ones like apple and blackberry.

When the lunchtime trade had died down, the girls were

just enjoying a welcome cuppa in the back room when the doorbell jangled and Squire stepped into the shop, his face set in stone. Oh dear. What was wrong here? Kathryn immediately rushed to his side.

'Have you heard the news?' His eyes searched hers.

What news? 'No. What's going on?'

'I thought that one of your customers might have got word by now, but Mary Jane Kelly was found dead this morning . . .' He shook his head as if he couldn't quite believe his own words.

Kathryn's heart hammered. 'W . . . Where?'

'At her home at Miller's Court. Word is it was a very savage, frenzied attack . . .'

Kathryn had forgotten that Mags was stood close by. 'Oh my gawd, it's the work of The Ripper!' The whites of her eyes were on show. 'It has to be!' She let out a loud blood-curdling scream.

'Sssh for heaven's sake,' Kathryn chided. 'You don't want to go waking up old man Bailey upstairs, he's taking a nap and you don't want to go worrying people neither.'

'Word will get around soon enough,' Squire said, glancing at Mags, who had turned as white as a pail of milk.

Ma stepped on to the shop floor, the sleeves of her dress rolled up, her hands covered in flour. 'What's going on here?' she asked. 'Anyone would think someone has died, the looks on all yer ruddy faces!'

'They have an' all!' Mags cried. 'Ma, The Ripper's been at it again!'

Ma opened her mouth and closed it again. 'Aw, never to goodness! That man is a madman. Who is it this time? Anyone we know?'

'Mary Kelly, Ma,' Kathryn explained. 'She drinks . . . I mean used to drink at The Ten Bells.'

Mags narrowed her eyes at her sister. 'Hey, isn't that where you went yesterday afternoon?'

Kathryn nodded slowly. 'I did, and I was in her company together with Jess . . .'

She looked at Squire, who draped his hand around her shoulder and whispered in her ear, 'Can you get away from here for a while? My carriage is outside.'

She nodded, then leaving Ma in charge of the shop, she took her shawl and bonnet from the back room and they drove off to find somewhere to talk. All the while during the journey, Kathryn felt her mind drifting off as if she couldn't believe the horror of what she had just heard. Mary Kelly had been so full of life yesterday and now she was no more, as dead as a doornail.

She studied Squire's face, his strong jawline, his charming demeanour. What was he thinking about it all? she wondered.

'Come on,' he said, when the carriage had drawn up outside a small coffee shop. 'We'll go in here and have a bite of something.'

'I couldn't possibly eat a thing.' Her appetite had disappeared and there was now a sickening feeling in her gut, and then all of a sudden, she saw Jess's face dance before her eyes.

Jess, where are you?

Chapter Fifteen

The coffee shop was warm and welcoming; a fire blazed in the hearth and several smart waitresses breezed around taking care of their customers' needs. As Kathryn stirred Demerara sugar into her coffee, Squire gazed into her eyes. 'Come on now, Kathryn, what's the matter with you? I can tell something is up.'

Was it that obvious? She stopped stirring and set down her spoon in its saucer. 'It's all this stuff about The Ripper and where he'll strike next . . .'

He lifted her chin with his thumb and forefinger and, looking into her eyes, said, 'There's no need to worry. You're quite safe. You don't frequent those sorts of places, Kathryn.'

'No, but Jess does!' She couldn't help herself as the words came tumbling out, and she noticed a shadow of guilt pass over Squire's face.

'I know and I do feel partly responsible, although I daresay she'd have gone that way anyhow. I just tried to keep her from the streets.'

'Yes, but yer failed as once she found out about me it was the end for her, she believed she was your fiancée like I did. That ain't right in my book!'

He shook his head. 'And I'm sorry about all of that.'

'But you led her on, the other girl too by the sound of it . . .'

'Don't you think I realise that? I do want to make amends but am at a loss what to do about it.'

'Well for now I reckon we should try to find Jess to see 'ow she is. Maybe get her to a place of safety, just in case.'

He nodded. 'I suppose The Ten Bells would be a good start, though we'd best leave the carriage here or else those Spitalfields nippers will be begging us for pennies once they clap eyes on it.'

'Very well then, and if she's not there we could try to find her lodging house; she told me it's on Dorset Street.'

When they arrived at The Ten Bells, it was heaving. Many of the people who had been following the Lord Mayor's Procession at Fleet Street had flooded the area from sheer curiosity about another slaying, and were getting in the path of the police and regulars in the area. Two such men were being escorted from the premises by the scruff of their necks by the landlord. 'Blood sport spectators! You can get orf 'ome the lot of you!'

When the man had dumped them unceremoniously on the pavement and they bade a hasty retreat for fear of being followed by an angry mob, he stared at Kathryn and Squire. 'Weren't you in here yesterday afternoon, miss?'

'I was, yes.'

'And you were with Mary Kelly in the corner?'

'For a short while, yes.'

He narrowed his eyes as he glared at them both. 'And you, sir, haven't I seen you in my pub before, too?'

'You have indeed. We are looking for Jess who was with Mary yesterday to check on her whereabouts.'

Almost as if he were relieved about that he let out a breath. 'You 'ave to forgive me for being so cagey, like. I've had all sorts in here today: police, hacks from Fleet Street, nosy parkers, the lot. Me patience is wearing thin. They're all asking questions about Mary – a lot I can't even answer. They need to speak to Joe Barnett, he could tell them a tale or two!'

'Did you see much of Mary and Jess after I left?' Kathryn blinked.

'What time was that?'

'It was five o'clock as I 'eard the church bell chime the hour,' Kathryn said.

'I don't remember seeing them long after that to be truthful' – he paused a moment as he stroked his bewhiskered chin in contemplation – 'though someone says they saw Mary back in here with a friend called Maria. That was later in the evening. It was very busy.'

'No sign of Joe Barnett last night, either?' Squire asked.

'No, he left Mary a couple of weeks ago – he'd 'ad enough of her antics – but he has been back here a time or two. You could go to Jess's lodgings in Dorset Street and ask there.

Don't know the number but she's staying with a Mrs O'Connor.'

That seemed a sensible thing to do. They thanked the man and, battling their way through the crowds, made their way there.

Kathryn shivered as they entered the slum area, which was full of lodging houses. There were also a couple of pubs, one of which was called The Blue Boy. The area was densely populated anyhow, it not being unusual to see people of all descriptions out on the street. It was now teeming with onlookers and a horse-drawn Black Maria was parked at the end of the street.

'I can't help thinking about that poor young woman,' Kathryn said, shaking her head.

'Was she drunk when you encountered her yesterday?' Squire asked.

'No, just merry I'd say. Enjoying 'erself. The poor thing never even realised her life was all but over . . .'

A young lad who had been watching the police stared at them. 'Penny for a peep show, sir? I'll show yer where the grisly murder took place, plenty of blood and guts an' all!'

'What an enterprising young fellow you are!' Squire chuckled. 'You'll go far, lad.' He was obviously capitalising on the crowds who had descended on the place, but not doing any real harm other than trying to make some money for himself by showing them where Mary had met her untimely end.

Squire dipped into his pocket and gave the lad a shiny

silver sixpence. 'Put that in your pocket, boy, before anyone sees. We are looking for a Mrs O'Connor who has a lodging house, do you know it?'

'Cor thanks, mister!' His eyes lit up. 'Yes, I know of it. Come this way . . .'

He led them through the raucous crowds until they came to a door with steps leading up to it. 'Mrs O'Connor lives here!'

'Do you know a dark-headed lady called Jess, by any chance? She's very pretty,' Kathryn asked hopefully. But the lad just shook his head and walked away, digging his hands deep into the pockets of his threadbare breeches. Off to try to make even more money, no doubt. If he knew Jess then he wasn't saying so. Maybe he thought he'd get her into trouble, or maybe he just wanted to keep out of whatever was going on. Even so, Kathryn thought he was very wise for someone so young. What chance did a young boy have in the East End other than to live off his own wits?

Kathryn looked at Squire with some trepidation, glad to have him at her side. 'This is a really rough area here, ain't it?'

He nodded. 'It's mainly made up of lodging houses and had the reputation of being a place that housed stolen goods from the docks in years gone by. But I think the landlords here realised they were on to rich pickings by housing prostitutes these days instead. Some of the houses employ a few strong men to guard their doors to ensure punters pay up as well.'

No wonder Jess had ended up here then, where there was so much squalor and degradation. Although Kathryn hadn't been born with a silver spoon in her mouth, at least the street she'd been brought up on was a tidy enough area where largely folk worked to feed their families.

Tentatively, she rapped on the peeling door but there was no answer, so she rapped again. Eventually the door swung open to reveal an elderly, hunched-over, wizened woman. She was dressed all in black save for her white blouse which was now greyed with age, and she pulled her knitted shawl tightly around her shoulders. 'What do yer want? I ain't telling any tales about no Mary Kelly if that's what yer after!' The woman didn't have a tooth in her head, judging by her puckered lips and the way her cheeks appeared to be sucked in as she spoke.

Kathryn smiled. 'I'm sorry, we haven't come for that. Are you Mrs O'Connor?'

'Well, who's asking?' she replied gruffly.

'I'm Miss Kathryn Flynn and this is Mr er, Squire.' She didn't want to give his name of Curtis-Browne for fear their mission should somehow reach the ears of his wife.

'Pleased to meet you I'm sure, but what do yer pair want with the likes o' me? And yes, I am Mrs O'Connor.'

'We're looking for a young lady called Jess,' Squire said, turning on the charm, so that it put a smile on the woman's face. 'She's very pretty with long dark curly hair. I'm informed she's lodging with you.'

'Yes, she does stay here most nights, though I haven't seen her for a day or two. Why do yer want her anyhow?'

Kathryn softened her stance to appeal to the woman's better nature, if she had one. 'I'm very concerned about her, Mrs O'Connor. I was in her company in The Ten Bells yesterday afternoon and she was with Mary Kelly at the time, but no one seems to have seen her since.'

The elderly lady chewed a moment; it was then Kathryn realised she was chewing on a piece of tobacco. 'Lemme think now . . . last night I heard a lot of coming and going here, doors slamming woke me up but can't say I heard her voice. I'll tell you what I'll do as I don't like to think of anything happening to that girl meself, I'll go and check her room if you can give me a moment.'

Squire put his foot in the door so the old woman couldn't close it behind her. 'Please Mrs O'Connor, can we come and take a look at her room ourselves, in case there's a clue there?' He dipped into his pocket and held out a florin.

A big grin broke out on her face and Kathryn realised she wasn't totally toothless, there was one tooth in her bottom gum, but how that one had survived when the others hadn't, she hadn't a clue.

'That'll do nicely,' she said, snatching the coin from Squire's hand and dropping it into a little drawstring purse she had tied around her neck, which she quickly hid back beneath the folds of her blouse. No doubt she had to do that for safe keeping, living in this area, Kathryn assumed.

They followed the woman into the dark passageway, which smelled strongly of damp with a faint odour of alcohol, tobacco and unwashed bodies, then up a flight of stairs and then another. The elderly lady puffed and panted as she went, but didn't pause to draw breath; it was obvious she wanted rid of them as quickly as possible by the pace she was walking.

When they arrived at the landing outside Jess's room, Mrs O'Connor didn't bother to knock, she just turned the door knob. 'Didn't expect that to open,' she said under her breath. As the door opened wide to allow them access, it was obvious there was no one in the small room that housed a single bed that was made up and looked unslept in. In the corner was a wooden chest of drawers with a cracked mirror on top. In the opposite corner was a long washstand with a jug and bowl in place upon it, and in front of the window was an old wicker chair. Considering the house looked pretty shabby, the room itself was better than Kathryn expected.

'Wouldn't she have locked her room if she'd gone out somewhere?' she asked.

Mrs O'Connor chewed on her tobacco as if giving it some thought. 'It depends . . . Course it's safer to lock her room if she's leaving any valuables behind, but to be honest with yer, she lives pretty much hand to mouth. And I don't allow her to bring any gentlemen callers back with her neither, if that's what yer thinking an' all. No, sir, I don't. She can conduct her business elsewhere.'

Kathryn shook her head sadly. To think Jess had gone

from working out of a nice warm room up West to probably having a quickie in some dark alley or even Itchy Park . . . it appalled her. But the mystery was, why hadn't that bed been slept in, and why was the door left unlocked?

Kathryn had already scribbled down the address of her residence at the shop on a piece of paper, and she handed it to the woman. 'If you see Jess, please hand her this note and ask her to come to see me.'

The woman took the note from Kathryn's hand and placed it in her pinafore pocket. Still chewing on the tobacco, she said, 'Well I hope I do see her soon as she's owing this week's rent money.'

'How much?' Squire asked.

'A shilling.'

Squire dipped into his pocket again and handed the woman the silver coin. 'Don't give her any more money,' Kathryn whispered.

He just smiled; it was evident he felt more than a little responsible for the young woman's welfare and maybe deep down he even blamed himself for her disappearance.

In the back room of the shop later that day, Mags was in a foul mood. 'You left me working here all by myself,' she moaned to Kathryn.

'Well Georgina came in for a couple of hours to help out,

didn't she?' Kathryn couldn't understand why Mags appeared so upset.

'Yes, but she turned up late and left early before you came back. I'm right tired.' She blew a breath sending a strand of her own hair upwards, her face flushed.

Taking pity on her, Kathryn smiled. 'Go and have an hour to yourself, but if the kids come in from school, give them some leftover apple pie and a cup of milk each.'

Mags beamed. Kathryn didn't mind giving her sister the time off as she was such a hard worker who was worth her weight in gold.

'Thank you. I'll check in on old man Bailey as well. I've started reading a chapter a day from *Little Dorrit* to him as he can't see much with his eyesight as the print is too small.'

'That's very kind of you, Mags.'

'Well, I don't mind as I like reading and it's a good book,' she enthused.

Kathryn marvelled at how well her sister coped with difficult people. Although Georgina was by no means difficult herself, Kathryn noticed she was spending less and less time at the shop and was hardly ever popping upstairs to see her father any more.

As Kathryn busied herself in the shop seeing to customers, weighing this and that, packaging items and trying to remain cheery, she found her thoughts absorbed by Jess and what had happened to Mary Kelly. The trouble was, initially women in the East End had been wary after the first couple of Ripper murders, but as time passed they had become complacent and instead of ganging together in groups or pairs like before, some had reverted to going around unaccompanied at night, particularly if they were street walkers.

Every time the doorbell jangled, Kathryn's head turned with the hope that Jess would show up, and each time it was a customer waiting to be served. If only she would come to the shop just so Kathryn knew she was safe and could offer her a bed for the night.

As darkness fell and Kathryn began to bring in the sacks of potatoes and other items that were on display outside the shop, a shiver ran the length of her spine. Someone was watching her, but who? 'Jess!' she called out as a strong wind whipped up and hit her full in the face. There was no answer to her cry. Convinced she must be imagining things, she watched as a wooden sign suspended from the shop next door started to swing back and forth and make a creaking sound. She finally lugged the last sack of potatoes in through to the shop floor and was about to put the door on the latch when it burst open with such a loud jangle her heart began to hammer. Fergus O'Shay was looming over her, his eyes bulging with anger, face red with fury. 'Found you at last, yer little trollop!' he shouted.

'W . . . what do you want, Mr O'Shay?' She was in no mood for such an encounter when she felt so weary and worried.

His eyebrows rose. 'What do I want? You have thieved from me, Miss Flynn. You still owe me rent money.'

She let out a sigh of exasperation. 'I explained all of that. I put the rent money what was owing on the mantelpiece before I left.'

'Not only that . . .' he continued. 'I believe that you are unrightfully harbouring the Dawkins kids, Nick and Dorrie. You kidnapped them while me and the missus were fast asleep.'

'Stuff and nonsense. I haven't seen those kids for weeks, you said they were in the workhouse anyway.'

He rubbed his mutton chop whiskers. 'Don't try to be clever with me, missy. I want those kids now this very minute or else you and your family are going to suffer, believe me. I have the authority to keep the little blighters!'

Kathryn glared at him. 'And on whose authority might I bleedin' well ask, Mr O'Shay?'

'The Guardians, of course. I told you I know one of them . . .'

She could tell by his shifty manner that he was lying to her. Anything to get his hands on those kids to make himself some money. Kathryn squared up to him, pulling herself up to her full height. 'I am telling you now the Dawkins kids are not here with me. But if you insist on asking for more rent because the price went up as you claimed last time we met, then I shall pay up if it keeps you off my back!'

He smiled a sneaky smile as she dipped her hand into the

till and handed him a few shillings. She'd repay it later when she got her reticule from upstairs. But for the time being she couldn't afford to leave him alone on the shop floor with so much money under his nose.

'That'll do nicely for now, my dear. Next time I want paying we might be able to come to some other arrangement.' He leered at her, causing her to draw her shawl tightly around her shoulders. 'A nice-looking filly like yourself could go far. I've a few girls working for me at the moment. You'd do well, course there'd be something else in it for me too, boss's privileges and all that.'

'You filthy beast!' Kathryn spat, stepping back from him. 'Now I've just paid you what I didn't owe you in the first place, I owe you no more. Get out of here!'

He turned and walked towards the door, then looking back at her said, 'Just think about it, otherwise I'll send that Dorrie out to work. Men would pay a high price for her and that sister of yours with her flame-red hair. Two little beauties they are! I'll be back. Cheerio!'

As he left the shop, Kathryn picked up a stale loaf of bread that was on the counter and tossed it at the door. Then she quickly bolted it behind him. The man was insufferable, it was obvious he was never going to leave her alone, and now she had another concern: he'd mentioned Mags. Her sister was a feisty sort who could hold her own if need be, and she was nobody's fool, but she also feared for Nick and Dorrie. She needed to get them to a place of safety. O'Shay wasn't going to rest until he had those kids back in his clutches, that much was evident.

Jimmy was on his way home; one trip away had been enough for him, what with being ill and all. He'd been sick for days, but thankfully, he had managed to make it to Morocco. He hoped Nick and Dorrie were all right. His aunt and uncle had promised they'd take care of them at their home and he'd paid them well for doing so. He couldn't wait to see their faces. He'd bought a beautiful colourful dress for Dorrie and a wooden ship for Nick, and for Kathryn he'd bought a pretty necklace made from seashells. When he'd recovered, the memory of her and what she'd meant to him hit him full force. Now, as he stood on deck and gazed out to sea, there was no sign of any land but he knew somewhere in the distance was home, somewhere where there were white cliffs and green fields and a dark and sometimes dangerous bustling capital city that beckoned him. He saw Kathryn's face dance before his eyes. What was she doing right now? he wondered. Before he'd gone to sea, they hadn't been close as they once were, but he forgave her all that. He just wanted to see her again, at least one more time.

Chapter Sixteen

Kathryn deliberated whether she should tell the family about what had just occurred. She didn't want to alarm any of the children, but decided to tell both Ma and Mags later when the kids were fast asleep, to put them on their guard.

She made them all cups of cocoa after the last of the kids were tucked safely in bed and Mr Bailey was settled in his room. As she seated herself in the armchair by the fire and the other two sat opposite on an old horsehair couch, she said, 'I've got some news for you both and it isn't good.'

'What is it, child?' Ma asked, setting down her cup of cocoa on the small wooden occasional table beside her while Mags looked alarmed.

'It's Mr O'Shay. When I was in the shop alone earlier, he burst in through the door and made threats.'

'What sort of threats?' Mags wanted to know.

'He was asking for more rent money, which I gave him even though I don't feel we owe him a sausage, but worst of all he's discovered that Nick and Dorrie are here and he wants them back.'

'He's just guessing, that's all, Kathryn,' her mother said.

'Maybe, but I reckon they need to go to a place of safety for the time being, just in case.'

'Like where, though?' Mags asked.

'I was thinking we could ask Georgina to hide them at her 'ouse, if she's willing,' Kathryn said hopefully, though in all truth she wasn't that certain the woman would comply. She was kind-hearted, but they had yet to meet her husband. Would he be so keen to take in a couple of orphans?

'That's a possibility, I suppose,' Ma said. 'Them poor kids being pulled from pillar to post. I can't believe Jimmy would abandon them like that, it ain't fair.'

'I can't believe it either, Ma.' Kathryn stared into the flames of the fire. 'He's got a lot to answer for. So what do yer think we oughta do?'

Ma stretched her weary arms above her head and yawned. She'd been busy baking most of the day and Kathryn now wondered if she was expecting too much from her. Tomorrow, she resolved to help her more. She'd been far too busy today charging around hither and thither.

'I reckon you ought to ask Georgina first 'cos otherwise if the kids go to their auntie and uncle's house, they'll be too near to O'Shay. He's more likely to find them in that neck of the woods.'

'You're right, Ma. And I didn't get the impression their aunt and uncle were that concerned about them anyhow.'

Mags jumped out of her chair. 'Well that's that sorted then, now I think we should try one of Ma's baked apple pies!'

'Yer always thinking of that stomach of yers, me gal!' Ma chuckled. 'Go and get it then, there's one I took out of the oven not long since. Slice us a small piece each and there's a tin of condensed milk in the cupboard to go with it.'

Kathryn hadn't felt like eating all day, what with the worry about Jess and now O'Shay's threats, but being with her mother and sister comforted her. It was good to see Ma with a bit of life back inside her.

Ma looked at her for the longest time when Mags was out of the room. 'And what about you and Squire, my gal? Any wedding bells in the offing?'

Kathryn's cheeks flamed red hot. How could she tell her mother she couldn't marry the man as he was already married?

'Er, no. I'm an independent girl. I don't need no man to marry me.'

'Well don't leave it too long. Don't want to be left on the shelf like poor Paulina Wilkes. Remember her? Still an old maid at the age of thirty!'

'In any case what about you, Ma? And Ned? You seemed to be getting along well. Didn't he promise to visit you soon?'

'Aw go on with you . . .' Now it was her mother's turn to look all shy and bashful. 'They were only words from him. I expect he's forgotten all about me by now.'

'Don't be so sure,' Kathryn smiled. 'I think he was right sweet on yer. He has our address, anyhow.'

They carried on chatting for a while and then Mags appeared with a tray carrying the plates of pie and a jug of condensed milk. 'I'm just going to take one in for Mr Bailey,' she said. 'I'll be right back.'

'Why don't you ask him to join us for a while,' Ma offered. 'He's always stuck in that room on his own unless you or Shaun sit with him.'

'I'll ask, Ma, but I doubt he will.'

Mags was right in her assumption, as within minutes she returned.

'Well?' Ma looked at her, blinking.

'No.' She shook her head. 'He said, thanks but no thanks, he'd prefer to eat alone. Though I have promised to go and read to him later before bed. I think he's upset because Georgina hasn't been up to see him again today. He would never say so, though. I wonder what's the matter with her?'

Ma took her hand. 'You're a bright, understanding gal, our Mags. So kind to everyone.'

Kathryn stared at the latest newspaper headline over breakfast: 'PARDON OFFERED TO RIPPER ACCOMPLICE'. The article went on to explain that if anyone was aiding and abetting Jack the Ripper, if they came forward with information leading to his arrest, they'd get a pardon. All sorts of rumours were flying around, making women and young girls more petrified than ever to go out alone after dark as the Mary Kelly murder was said to be worse than all the others put together. Meanwhile, Georgina had agreed to take Nick and Dorrie into her home until their safety could be guaranteed. Never mind Jack the Ripper, there was someone much closer to home they needed to fear, Fergus O'Shay!

A sudden wave of nausea took over Kathryn's body. She thought that maybe if she ate a little oatmeal in warm milk it might curb the feeling, but she had to leave the table in front of the others and only just made it to the privy in time. What was the matter with her, had she eaten something that might have disagreed with her? Kathryn retched again and when there was no more to come up, went off to wash her face and rinse her mouth in plain water. Strange, she felt all right now. A moment ago she thought she'd have to leave Mags to fend for herself in the shop, now she felt as fit as a fiddle.

The rest of the day passed without incident and she managed to eat well, so she put the nausea business out of her mind, dismissing it as a bit of undigested food from the previous evening.

Georgina had shown up for work again but she still avoided going upstairs to see how her father was, prompting Kathryn to ask why.

Georgina's face flushed and she made herself busy measuring out bags of flour. 'I just feel he's better left to his own devices,' she muttered as she sealed a bag, and then went to fill another with a small silver scoop in her hand.

'But he's a sick, elderly man, he might not be with us much longer. The only attention he gets is when Mags goes to his bedroom to read to him or if Shaun helps him walk to the privy downstairs. He refuses to leave his room and sit with the rest of us of an evening. I 'ave tried.'

Georgina met her eyes with a steady, unwavering gaze. 'If you must know, though I think it none of your business, the last time I called to see him he was most rude to me and threatened to write me out of his will in favour of Walter! After all I've done for him . . .' Her bottom lip quivered. 'Is it Walter who attends to his every need? Oh, no!'

Kathryn rushed to her side and gently touching her arm said, 'No one has been better to your father than you have, Georgina, and I can see that your brother has not paid a visit in all the time we've lived here. No one could have done more for him. Is it getting too much for you, having Nick and Dorrie at your home?'

Georgina's eyes lit up at the mention of the children though her tears were glistening like dewdrops. 'Goodness, no. Those little cherubs keep me going. In fact, I was going to speak to you about them anyhow. Josiah and I were thinking, well, as we have no children of our own and I am past child-bearing days, maybe we could adopt them?'

Kathryn hugged the woman tightly. 'That would be wonderful! You would have to apply to the courts and I'd imagine you might have to consult somehow with their elder brother, Jimmy. Though if truth be told, maybe not, as he has abandoned them.' Kathryn paused to think for a moment; what would it take for him to write to any of them? But on the other hand maybe something had happened to him at sea? The not knowing was the worst thing, and a little pang of longing pierced her heart.

'So, you think it's a good idea?' Georgina said, intruding into her thoughts.

'I do, yes. But only if all is right in your own life – you don't want any upset hanging over your head, do you?' She glanced up at the ceiling above so that Georgina might understand she was talking about her father.

Georgina dried her eyes on a handkerchief she extracted from her pocket, and sniffed. 'You are right of course, Kathryn. I shouldn't take any notice of an old man's ramblings . . .'

'No, you shouldn't. He's probably forgotten he's even mentioned it by now. Could he be becoming confused, do you think?'

'Maybe. But sometimes he's sharp as a tack, particularly in regards to matters pertaining to the shop.'

'Why was he rude to you the last time you visited, anyhow?'

'We had a little disagreement, that was all.' She refused to say any more on the matter and turned her back on Kathryn to carry on scooping the flour from a hessian sack into small brown paper bags.

*

Squire showed up when the shop had closed that evening and insisted on taking Kathryn back to the seafood restaurant she had marched out of without finishing her meal that last time. She'd asked him no more about his wife, deciding to accept the relationship with him for what it was: she was a mistress, nothing more and nothing less. But if people should ever discover the truth she'd have to hang her head in shame. Maybe Georgina wouldn't want to employ her any more and would toss the entire family out on to the street. She wouldn't want a common whore under her father's roof. So, to be careful, she decided from now on there was to be no more intimate contact between herself and Squire. Not that there had been for weeks, but she decided to spell it out for him.

He took both her hands in his across the table as the candlelight flickered, casting a warm glow over his face and putting a gleam in his eyes.

'My dearest Kathryn, I shall wait for you until you are ready for me once again, and you will be, of that I am certain . . .'

A mischievous smile danced upon his lips. The sheer arrogance of the man! But she had to admit it was hard to keep away from him.

They spent a pleasant evening together but it was as Squire was leaving her at the shop that they noticed someone curled up on the floor in the doorway. At first, Kathryn thought it was a bundle of old rags, until she heard a loud groan. Squire had been about to return to the carriage when she shouted: 'Quick, over here!'

And as a cloud drifted past in the sky, revealing the illuminating light from a full moon, she could see it was a woman lying there, badly beaten up, by the look of her. Her swollen face was covered in blood. It was then Kathryn's heart broke to see that it was Jess.

At that moment, Squire realised the same thing and knelt down beside her to cradle her in his arms. 'Oh, Jess, what have I done to you?' he sobbed.

'You didn't do this to her!' Kathryn said angrily. 'Maybe it was the work of The Ripper.'

'Weren't no Ripper,' Jess moaned, 'it was O'Shay's doing. I owed him money and I made the mistake of working for him to pay him back.' She let out a long groan.

Kathryn's stomach plummeted to her boots, to think the man capable of doing such an evil deed. 'Let's get her inside,' she said, taking command of the situation and fumbling inside her reticule for the shop keys. Once inside, she went over to the window and lit an oil lamp.

Squire helped Jess to her feet and they both got the woman to safety inside. 'We'll take her to the back room,' Kathryn said. 'There's an old sofa we can lay her down on. Don't want to scare the kids by going upstairs at this hour.'

Squire lifted the barely conscious woman in his arms as Kathryn carried the oil lamp, lighting his path.

He laid Jess down on the sofa and Kathryn set down the lamp on the table, then she propped Jess up with cushions. 'Have you eaten?' she asked.

'No, but I could murder a bleedin' gin, me 'ead hurts something rotten.'

Kathryn left the room and returned with a bottle of sherry and a small glass. 'Here, drink this. You'll have to make do, we 'aven't got any gin I'm afraid.'

'Much obliged to you, ducks.' Jess drank it down in one go and returned the glass. Kathryn figured she daren't offer another as she had no idea how much she'd already drunk that evening.

'So what happened, then?' she asked, drawing a chair up beside Jess to sit on while Squire remained standing, almost as though he was on guard, fearing O'Shay might return.

'I've been working for O'Shay now for a couple of weeks but I objected once I saw he was putting young girls on the street. It broke me heart when he offered up a little twelve-year-old to an older man. She was only a tiny little mite, small for 'er age an' all. She reminded me of me little sister, Sophia, so much . . .' She took a ragged breath. 'Anyhow, I called him every name under the sun, then I managed to get the girl away from him to a relative of hers. Course I paid for that tonight, I took a right hammering for me good deed.'

Kathryn could have wept for Jess. 'You did the girl a great kindness,' she said. 'I'm going to clean up your cuts and put some liniment on those bruises. The man is the scum of the earth. He came around 'ere and threatened me a couple of days ago!'

Squire narrowed his gaze. 'Why didn't you tell me of this, Kathryn?'

She shrugged. 'I didn't want to concern you.'

He gave her a look as if to say, 'We'll speak of this later.'

Jess gasped. 'Aw, never to goodness, Kathryn. Keep well away from him, he's going to murder someone . . .' And as the words left her lips, Kathryn realised that Jess hadn't heard about Mary's murder yet. How on earth could she break it to her?

That night Kathryn allowed Jess to sleep on the sofa but decided she needed to move her somewhere else before the kids saw her in that state. So Squire arranged to pick her up early next morning in his carriage and take her to a place of safety. She definitely wouldn't be safe at the shop as O'Shay had made it clear he would return anyhow.

'Where will you take her to?' Kathryn whispered to Squire as he stood in the shop, his eyes looking full of concern.

'I'll take her back to the apartment. The rent is paid up until the end of the month.'

Kathryn chewed on her bottom lip. If it hadn't been for her coming along and replacing Jess as Squire's latest protégée, the girl wouldn't be in this trouble now, and she felt guilty about that. 'She hasn't felt like eating much up until now so I've put a basketful of groceries together for her. At least she'll be comfortable at the apartment and well away from the clutches of O'Shay. How often do you think you can be there to keep an eye on her?'

'Now don't you go worrying about that, I can call in at least once a day and we'll nurse her back to good health. Meanwhile, I'll make enquiries to see if there are any places going for fallen women at the various refuges in the area.'

'There's the Hanbury Street shelter,' Kathryn offered. 'Women get a mug of hot tea and a slice of bread and dripping for a penny. There's a room where they can chat to others in the same position and a washroom too! Supper and bed and breakfast are three pennies, but the women have to be in bed by nine o'clock at night, up at six in the morning and out of the place by eight o'clock each day . . .'

'Sounds like you've given it a lot of thought,' he said.

'I have, I enquired for Jess the other day, but as it's in Hanbury Street it's a little too close to O'Shay. We might have to see if we can find somewhere else, and employment for her as well.'

His lips curved into a smile. It was the first smile she'd seen since they'd discovered Jess last night. 'Where is she? I've got the carriage ready outside and some warm blankets as it's perishing this morning.'

'That was thoughtful of you. She's just getting dressed. I've given her one of my old dresses for the time being.'

'I'll get her kitted out, don't you worry about that.' He rubbed his chin in a circular motion.

Kathryn glared at him. 'I'm sure you will!' she said sharply.

Squire took her by the shoulders and gazed into her eyes. 'Kathryn, you have got to believe me, I am no longer that man. I shall take her to a different outfitter, or better still, bring in a seamstress to see her as I'm sure she doesn't want to be seen with two black eyes and a puffed-up face.'

'Very well.' What could she do? She was just going to have to trust the man for now, she had little choice.

Jess suddenly emerged from the back room dressed in Kathryn's old linsey-woolsey dress, her shoulders covered in an old shawl. She made a beeline for Kathryn. 'Thanks ever so much for taking me in last night and offering me breakfast this morning . . .' she said.

'It was nothing,' Kathryn said brightly, trying to keep the girl's spirits up. 'You can keep the dress and shawl, and you hardly ate enough to keep a sparrow alive so I've packed some food into a basket for you.'

'You're throwing me out?' Jess's eyes widened in horror.

'No. Squire is going to move you back into the apartment for the time being. The rent is paid up until the end of the month. It's been a good few weeks since I left the place, you won't recognise it now, Jess. It's all nicely decorated and everything, really luxurious it is, these days. We don't want O'Shay to find yer, mind, so we thought it best for you to move back in there.'

Jess fell to her knees in front of Squire and kissed his hand. 'Thank you. You are a true gent and I promise I'll work my keep again . . .'

Kathryn watched as Squire's face reddened. 'Oh, no, my dear, you shall never have to do anything like that ever again. Your working days in that respect are over. I am going to see that you find proper employment. Now please get to your feet, there's no need to thank me.'

She stood. 'Aw bless you both.' It was then Kathryn realised she hadn't broached the news about Mary Kelly, but she didn't feel now was the right time to tell the woman. Maybe Squire could tell her in a day or two when Jess was more her old self. She was likely to feel devastated when she found out about her friend, it was such shocking news.

Who could have been so brutal? Newspapers were selling like hot cakes in the area as people clamoured to read all about the latest frenzied attack. Apparently, Mary was unrecognisable when she was discovered by Thomas Bowyer, a shop assistant, who worked for the landlord, John McCarthy. She'd been behind with the rent money. All kinds of names had been bandied around by the press blaming certain people, and the Whitechapel Vigilante Committee was up in arms about it all. A reward had been offered for The Ripper's capture by Member of Parliament Samuel Montagu.

At least for the time being, Jess would be safe and so would Nick and Dorrie with Georgina.

*

'You worry too much about things, Kathryn,' Mags said next morning as they were setting up the shop for the day ahead.

Kathryn was about to reassure her sister all was well when it happened again, a wave of nausea swept over her. She had to rush from the shop floor as the contents of her stomach began to heave. She failed to reach the privy this time, only making it as far as the cobbled back yard. She retched until she could heave up no more, then was about to go inside to clean her face, and get a pail of soapy water to wash the yard, when she looked up at the upstairs windows to see Ma staring down at her. She had seen it all, and she was no one's fool either.

She might as well face the music, she thought, so she washed her face in the downstairs stone sink and swilled her mouth under the tap, then wiped her face on the towel and made her way upstairs. She could lie to Ma and say she had an upset tummy, but realised she would only be lying to herself. She had to face the inevitable – she was pregnant with Squire's baby, and it would be a bastard at that. How was she going to tell him and how was she going to explain to Ma?

Her mother was at the top of the stairs, waiting for her. 'Kathryn, I'm glad you decided to come to see me,' she said, leading her into the small kitchen. In the main living room Kathryn could hear the sound of the children's voices as they ate their breakfasts, ready for school. 'What's going on? Are you ill or is it something else?'

'Something else, Ma . . .' To her horror she broke down in tears, her shoulders shuddering with grief.

'You're pregnant, aren't you?' Her mother said the words she didn't want to hear or believe.

She nodded slowly. 'Oh, Ma, what am I to do?'

'Well, I think you're going to have to tell the father. Whose baby is it?'

'Squire's of course! Whose did you think it might be, Ma?' She couldn't understand why her mother would be so uncertain.

'I had thought it might be Jimmy's baby to be honest . . . he did ask you to marry him once!'

'No, we've never been close in that sort of way.'

Ma's lips pursed and her chin jutted out. 'Well then, more to the point, what will The Squire do about this? He's going to have to marry you, gal! I ain't having me daughter's name dragged through the mud for the likes of no toff, so he can have his pleasure and leave his spawn behind!'

'But Ma,' Kathryn said, through her tears, 'he can't marry me, he's already married.'

'Oh, I feel all wobbly,' her mother said, steadying herself by holding on to the old pine table.

'Sit down Ma, you've had a shock.'

'You too, I've no doubt. We'll both sit down, shall we, and decide what we're going to do about this.'

They sat facing one another at the table, unable to speak for a moment. 'Well, the way I see it is this,' Ma said finally, 'the man 'as to be told even if he ain't in a position to marry yer – he can help with money for his own child. Thankfully, as we've recently moved to these parts so no one knows us really, we shall tell people you are widowed. Yer'll have to start wearing your widow's weeds, mind.'

Kathryn frowned. 'Mourning clothes, Ma?'

'Yes, my gal.'

'But people will know I'm not widowed as they've seen me in me usual garb at the shop.'

'What we shall say is that yer husband was killed in an accident at sea. Yes, that's what we'll pretend. We'll say it was Jimmy and he went to sea but drowned.'

'Aw no, Ma. I can't do that!' Kathryn threw her hands up, aghast.

'Look, my gal, you'll go through a terrible time if people discover you're pregnant out of wedlock and by a married man. Jimmy is no longer around, yer can pretend yer just wed before he left to go to sea. It makes sense to me. And we'll have to tell Georgina the truth of course. Let's hope she doesn't turf us all out of 'ere. But in the first instance, yer'll have to tell The Squire!'

Kathryn nodded, realising her mother spoke sense. She could hardly jeopardise their positions at the shop. Squire was due to call to see her that evening, so she could inform him then. 'All right, Ma. I'll do as you suggest. Jimmy's gone away and might never come back anyhow, so what harm can it do? And I'll have a word with Squire later. I better go back and help Mags, she'll be huffing and puffing without me.'

'No, you don't, my gal. You'll stop and have a cup of tea with me for a few minutes to settle your stomach. A bit of dry toast too, if yer can manage it.' Kathryn nodded. She'd explain to Mags later. The girl was no fool; she'd cotton on soon enough, so she'd just as well tell her. Feeling a little better after eating half the toast and sipping a cup of hot sweet tea, Kathryn returned downstairs, but not before her mother gave her a big hug.

'Thank you, Ma,' she said with tears in her eyes.

'Don't thank me, Kathryn. That's what I'm 'ere for, I'm yer ma and you've done enough for me. And we can all cope with the baby between us. One extra mouth to feed won't make that much difference. We're a damn sight better off than we were a few months back.'

A sudden thought occurred to Kathryn. What would Mr Bailey think about a new baby being born into the household?

'That's true, Ma.'

'If I were you, I'd go and find your sister and tell her the news as soon as possible. You know how she gets if she feels you've been keeping things from her.'

Kathryn smiled. She knew that well enough. There had been too many secrets between them lately, but from now on all that was going to change.

Chapter Seventeen

Kathryn paced around the bedroom as she got ready to meet with Squire. She really couldn't seem to make the smallest of decisions. Gazing down on the cobblestoned yard below, and at the old stables which were now used only to store old wooden crates and sacks, she wondered about the future. If things were different, Squire could stable his horse there; but as it was, she didn't want to attract too much attention for fear questions would be asked.

She'd noticed too of late that the shop was getting busier by the day and strangers were popping in, including people with plummy accents. The atmosphere was becoming very carnival-like as people bought hot pies to take with them and she realised that it was all down to The Ripper's fifth victim, Mary Jane Kelly.

Although she found it ghoulish the way people came to gawp around the area, and there were even some profiting from guided tours showing The Ten Bells pub and Mary's house in Miller's Court, she could well understand it was a form of entertainment for them. What else did they have to look forward to? It was a time when the wealthy brushed shoulders with the impoverished to view the streets where The Ripper had walked, and they wondered who his next victim might be.

She glanced back at the dress hanging on the wardrobe door. It was a high-necked black bombazine one, which she decided to wear with a string of pearls that Squire had given her. From now on it was black only as her mother advised for her widow weeds, even though she felt odd wearing the colour. She had not worn it since her father's funeral and at least for now it still fitted; she hadn't put on any noticeable weight as yet, and no wonder, as the way the sickness was developing, she had trouble keeping food down.

Finally, she added a black cape and bonnet and went to the upstairs living room to watch for Squire's arrival down below. As if by magic, at seven o'clock on the dot, his carriage slid around the corner and pulled up outside the shop.

'Why yer all in black, Kathryn?' Mags asked.

Realising she was going to have some explaining to do, she said, 'Look, I know I told you about the baby earlier, but something I didn't tell you is that Ma told me to pretend I'm widowed so people won't think badly of me.'

Mags blinked. 'Well I don't think badly of you, do I?'

'No, of course not, you're my sister and I love you for it. But there are those that will and if word got out to any of the customers – or Mr Bailey, come to that – we could get turfed out of here, understood? You don't want to end up in the workhouse, do you?'

Mags shook her head, her hazel eyes creasing at the corners as if she was about to cry.

Oh what have I done, getting myself pregnant and ruining everything? It isn't as if I really want a baby.

'Good.' Kathryn placed both hands on Mags's shoulders and, gazing into her eyes, said, 'There is one other thing . . . Ma thinks it best if people believe I married Jimmy before he left here, and that it's his baby I'm carrying before he passed away at sea.'

'But it's not, is it?' Mags's eyes widened. 'Not only that, but it's wishing him dead. I don't like it!'

'What choice do we have though, Mags? Think about it.' She shook her sister's shoulders in frustration.

Mags pursed her lips but Kathryn knew that given time and understanding Mags would take the situation on board; it was still a shock to her. She pulled away. 'I'll try, but I'm not saying I like it, mind.'

'You don't have to like it, just pretend it's the truth!'

'What will I say to Nick and Dorrie though? If they find that out from someone else they might think yer did marry their brother and he really is dead.'

Kathryn honestly hadn't even considered that. 'We'll talk about it later. Now I have to go. Have you seen my reticule?'

'But why can't you marry Squire, then?'

Mags asked the question that up until now Kathryn had dreaded. She turned to face her sister. 'I can't, that's why.'

'I don't get it, doesn't he care enough to marry you, then?'

'Look, it's complicated.'

Mags huffed out a breath. 'Seems pretty simple to me.'

'He's married, that's why.' Before Mags had the chance to say any more, she changed the subject. 'You didn't answer my question, have you seen my reticule?'

'It's on the windowsill.' Mags pointed.

Seeing how upset her sister looked, Kathryn hugged her and kissed her warm cheek. 'It will be all right, I promise you. We have to keep our jobs and a roof over our heads.'

Wordlessly, Mags stood there as tears streamed down her face. Kathryn told herself as she left the room that Mags would be all right. She just had to be.

Squire was already waiting at the entrance of the shop when she arrived and as she opened the door, he took a step back, frowning. 'Kathryn, why the black? Has somebody died? Or is it a mark of respect because of poor old Mary?'

'Not at all. I shall explain while we are at the restaurant,' she said sharply, giving the door a tug behind her as the bell jangled. She gazed up at the upstairs window to see Mags there next to the oil lamp, watching her, as Squire took her by the arm and led her to the waiting carriage.

*

At the restaurant, Kathryn was quiet throughout the meal. Thankfully her stomach had settled by early afternoon, so she managed to eat fairly well and the banter between them was amicable with neither speaking about feelings, only about the recent goings-on in the area and how Jess was doing.

Then suddenly, Squire reached across the table and took her hand, causing her to flinch and almost reject his touch. It wasn't that she didn't want it, but more that she feared what she would have to say to him.

'Kathryn, I'm prepared to wait for you, but am I wasting my time?' he asked. His eyes looked sad and guarded as if he might get hurt at any given moment.

'No, no, you're not.' She bit her lip and turned her head to one side.

'Then tell me what's wrong, and why you are dressed in black.'

She swallowed hard. 'Ma told me to do so. She said to save my reputation I am to dress as if I am a widow in mourning, widow's weeds she called it.'

'I am sorry, but I do not understand. You are neither married, as far as I am aware, nor widowed.'

'But I am pregnant . . .'

There. She had said the words.

'By me?' He blinked several times.

'Yes, of course you. And as yer not free to marry, this baby will be a' – she lowered her voice – 'bastard.' She played with her napkin on the table, unfolding and refolding it, hardly daring to look into his face. But when she finally plucked up courage to do so, she only saw positive delight there.

'My darling, this is wonderful news!' His eyes shone. 'But you shall not have to wear your widow's weeds as you put it as I intend to marry you!'

She blinked several times. 'But how can that happen? You're a married man.'

'I shall divorce Constance. I think I have good grounds to do so, then I shall be free to marry you.'

'But what grounds could they possibly be?' Kathryn was truly astonished; after all, he couldn't really divorce her because she spent too much of his money, could he?

'It's more to do with her withdrawing her love and affection from me . . .' he said sadly. 'And her refusal to bear a child.'

'Even so, you can't just toss her out like a discarded piece of rubbish.'

'I won't throw her out on the street, of course not, but she shall have to understand. She no longer performs her wifely duties. We live very much separate lives.' Although she realised she should be happy, she wasn't. 'What's the matter, Kathryn? Doesn't my offer to marry you please you?'

She looked at him through unshed tears. 'It should. I know it should, but it doesn't feel right somehow.'

'Look, I'll sort it out. I was thinking of leaving her anyhow. I can't go on like this in a loveless marriage. I only married her in the first place as our families seemed to think it was a good idea – to keep the wealth between them, as it were. Her father and mine are some sort of cousins.'

Kathryn had heard of that before, with wealthy families marrying cousins, but that didn't happen where she came from. To her, it seemed incestuous. 'So that means you married your own cousin?'

He coughed. 'Well sort of. She's a distant cousin, mind you – we share some great-great-grandfather further up the line. Maybe that's why we've never really got on as we have too much of the same sort of blood coursing through our veins. In any case, I shall tell her soon.'

'I don't want you to break her heart,' Kathryn said quickly.

He threw back his head and laughed. 'Constance, a heart! Oh what a joke! She's the hardest woman I've ever known in my life. The only thing she cares about is spending my money.'

'That may be so, but no woman likes to be rejected.'

'Please do not worry your pretty little head about such matters, all shall be well.'

He might be sure, but I'm not convinced.

That night Kathryn slept fitfully, tossing and turning, and when she did finally manage to fall asleep she dreamt of a woman dressed in black who was chasing her around the streets of Whitechapel. When the woman finally caught up with her and lifted her mourning veil, it was the grinning face of Mary Kelly herself she was met with, horrifying her so much she let out a loud ear-piercing scream in her dream and promptly awoke, perspiring profusely, heart pounding out of her chest. In the distance she heard the church bell strike the hour. It was five o'clock; another hour, and it would be time for her to wake up anyhow and set up the shop for the day. She slowly rose out of bed feeling the familiar stir of nausea in her gut. It wasn't just the morning sickness, it was the feeling of anxiety attached to the fact she knew Squire would be speaking to his wife.

Quietly, she pulled her flannel dressing gown from the peg on the back of the door and slipped into her carpet slippers. Then she went to make herself a cup of tea to still her stomach. It was while she was drinking her tea in the living room and gazing down at the street below that she saw a man standing there, staring up at the shop. At first she thought it was O'Shay, but even in the semi-light, she could tell this man was younger than O'Shay. He wore a battered top hat on his head and a long tailcoat that looked as though it had seen better days.

She shivered. What if this was The Ripper? Perhaps she should go to the police? But it was hardly a crime to stare at the shop.

The man gave one final glance in her direction, then, turning, left the street. Maybe he was an early-bird customer who had hoped the shop was already open, she surmised. Thinking no more of it, she finished her cup of tea and got washed and dressed for the day ahead.

She was about to rouse Ma and the kids for breakfast when

the door to Mr Bailey's bedroom suddenly opened, causing her to jump.

'Oh, Mr Bailey, you frightened me for a moment there!'

He gazed at her for the longest time and then said sharply, 'Can't a man do what he wants to in his own home?'

Her emotions were all over the place and his dour tone of voice upset her greatly. She didn't want to break down and cry in front of him, so instead she plastered on a smile, swallowed and said, 'Of course you can, Mr Bailey. Maybe you'd like to join us all for breakfast, I was about to put a pan of porridge on the hob. Or I can boil an egg for you, if you like?'

He stood shakily on his legs as he pressed down hard on his walking stick, his knuckles white. 'Do you know what . . . that brother Shaun of yours has pestered me often enough to join you all, I think I will for a change. I'm pig sick of seeing that flowered wallpaper in my bedroom. But first I need the privy . . .'

She smiled. 'I'm about to wake Shaun anyhow, so he'll take you there, Mr Bailey.'

For the first time ever, Kathryn saw a small smile dance on the old man's lips.

He drew a breath as his rheumy eyes twinkled. 'I'm sorry I've been so cranky, m'dear, it's the pain you see, and not being able to do the things I used to do. I miss seeing the customers, too.'

An idea began to form in Kathryn's mind. 'I'll tell you what, after you've eaten breakfast with us, how about we bring you downstairs to join us in the shop for an hour or two? You can supervise the running of things.'

He nodded. 'I'd like that very much. Thank you.'

If the others were surprised to see Mr Bailey sat at the breakfast table with them, they weren't showing it. Of course, he was already familiar with Shaun and Mags, but the other kids and Ma herself had hardly met him as yet. But he settled in well with everyone and was most amused when at one point, Rosie and Damon insisted on tugging his white beard to see if he was Father Christmas. He threw back his head and laughed uproariously. And following breakfast, he not only sat in the shop and greeted his customers old and new, but he decided to stay longer than an hour, only retiring to his room once it was time for Georgina to come into work.

'I still don't understand why Mr Bailey and Georgina don't seem to want to speak to one another,' Mags sighed, as she packaged up goods into an elderly lady's basket.

'Sssh,' Kathryn scolded under her breath. 'Whatever it is, do not discuss it in front of his customers. Walls have ears. If it got back to Georgina that you and I were discussing her private business she wouldn't like it at all.'

Mags nodded. 'Sorry, but I just want to see everyone happy.'

'That may be so,' Kathryn said, brushing a strand of hair from her sister's face and tucking it behind her ear, 'but in this world I've discovered you can't please everyone.'

When it had quietened down later, Kathryn had time to

think about Squire. Had he told Constance he was leaving her? She had hoped he'd call by the shop to see her; each time the door opened she'd looked up expectantly. The waiting was most definitely the worst part. But he didn't call that day, nor the next. Her mind was racing. What was going on? Had something happened to him? Or Jess, even?

But she didn't have to think much longer as the following evening Mr Bailey was taken ill. Shaun called her from upstairs in such a frantic voice that she shut the shop and bounded up the stairs, taking them two at a time. When she got to the top his face was ashen. 'It's Mr Bailey . . .' he explained, pointing towards the man's bedroom.

'What's happened?' She tried to keep her tone as level as possible so as not to frighten Shaun further.

'I was just taking him back from the privy when he collapsed on to the bed. His face is a terrible colour and he keeps saying he feels sick.'

Kathryn dashed into the room to see the man lying flat out in the bed. His skin looked a puce colour and his breathing was rapid.

'Are you all right, Mr Bailey?' she asked.

'I just feel so sick . . .' he groaned. Suddenly he heaved.

'Quick, Shaun,' she commanded. 'Fetch me a bucket from the storage closet.' He dashed out of the room as Kathryn attended to Mr Bailey. There was nothing for it, she would have to fetch Georgina.

*

As Kathryn hurried down the street to inform Georgina of her father's condition, a dense fog had descended. It was a real pea-souper combining all the chimney smoke and industrial fumes from the tanneries and factories in the area, mixed with freezing fog. She drew her shawl tightly around her. It was a while since she'd had to walk through one of these, let alone go through it alone.

It was no use her hurrying as she could hardly see her own hand in front of her face. Poor Georgina would be devastated to hear that her father had taken a turn for the worse. She didn't live too far away but Kathryn feared she'd get lost in this fog. There were so many alleyways and courts in the area, all looking pretty much the same. In the distance, she heard raucous laughter and muffled voices as she realised she was nearing a tavern. Shouldn't be much further now to Georgina's home: she'd have to cross the road, pass the park and cut through another alleyway.

A couple of men were standing outside the pub and she almost bumped into one of them, who steadied her with his hand. 'Go careful there, darlin',' he warned. She was getting really scared.

As she walked on from the pub and the voices faded away, she began to hear footsteps echoing behind her. She quickened her pace; so did the approaching footsteps. Fear seized her by the throat. There was no going back as she couldn't even see behind her; fingers of fog furled and obliterated her backward and forward views.

Someone grunted loudly as if in pain, then a hand clamped onto her shoulder and tingles of terror skittered down her spine. It was him, The Ripper, she just knew it. She was about to scream when a male voice said, 'Sorry, miss. Please stop, you dropped this!'

She paused and saw an elderly man standing there, huffing and puffing as if he'd been rushing after her. In his hand he held a small drawstring purse which she recognised as her own.

'Oh, thank you so much,' she gasped, hardly wanting to inform him that his pursuit had frightened the living daylights out of her. 'I can't believe that someone would be so honest and so kind.'

The bag contained the shop keys and a couple of shillings for emergencies. Thank goodness it was safe. She must have dropped it in all the commotion outside the pub when she was jostled about.

'No trouble at all, ma'am,' he said doffing his cap. 'I shall escort you on your way, if you like?'

Relief flooded through her as she nodded, and he took her by the elbow for the remainder of her journey. When she arrived at Georgina's home, she worried about waking up Dorrie and Nick, so she knocked quietly on the back door. But the place was in darkness, so she rapped on the front door, causing an upstairs light to go on.

A couple of minutes later, the front door flew open and a middle-aged man stood there in his dressing gown, scratching his head. 'Where's the fire, young lady?'

'Hello. I'm Kathryn Flynn, I work at the shop with your wife. I've come to inform Georgina that her father is poorly . . .'

There was the sound of footsteps and Kathryn noticed Georgina had appeared behind her husband. 'Father is ill?' she asked, blinking, as if not quite taking in the situation.

'Yes. He's been retching and is bathed in perspiration. I've had to change his sheets. We need to get hold of a doctor.'

'There's our family doctor, Doctor Robinson, who lives a couple of streets away. I'll fetch him, you two get on back to the shop,' Georgina's husband advised.

'What about Nick and Dorrie?' Kathryn asked.

'They won't be left alone for long, I'll only be a couple of minutes,' he replied, dragging his coat from the hallstand. 'They won't even realise I've gone.'

Kathryn nodded and waited while Georgina grabbed her cape from the hook. She was so concerned about her father, it appeared she didn't care she was still in her dressing gown. Who was going to see her in the fog anyhow? And Kathryn could always loan her a dress if need be.

When they arrived back at the shop, Mr Bailey was sitting up as Mags attended to him, holding a small tin bowl in front of his face with one hand. In the other she held a damp towel. 'Am I glad to see you both. He hasn't stopped being ill since yer left, Kathryn.'

'Thank you, Mags. Get off to bed, I'll take over for now and Georgina is on her way up the stairs. Her husband has just gone for the doctor.'

Mags nodded. 'If you need me, wake me up!' she warned.

It was another half an hour before the doctor arrived to see the old man. When he'd finally finished examining him, he took both women to one side. 'I suspect he has a stomach tumour,' he said gravely. 'It will only be a question of time. All I can do is give him something for his pain.'

When they were out of earshot of both the doctor and Georgina's father, Georgina began to weep profusely, her shoulders convulsing. When she'd finally calmed down, Kathryn placed a hand on her shoulder. 'It will be all right,' she soothed.

'How can it be, though? I had no idea he was so ill,' Georgina said, through misty eyes. 'I fear it's all my fault. I should have been here, maybe I'd have noticed he was getting sick. I've been keeping away from him lately as I was so mad at him!'

'Now, don't talk foolish. We've all been here and your father has been eating with us. If it is a tumour then it's happened awful quickly. I think we need to get a second opinion on this.'

'But Doctor Robinson is our family physician, I completely trust him, as does Father.'

Kathryn placed both hands on Georgina's shoulders and stared into her eyes. She had to get through to her somehow. 'Look Georgina, I really think it odd that the symptoms have come on so quickly. Tomorrow, I'll bring my family doctor here. He was responsible for getting Ma into that rest home that did her so much good.'

Georgina appeared to mull things over in her mind for a couple of moments. 'Very well. If you can bring your doctor here tomorrow, I should be much obliged to you,' she said firmly. She put her hand to her forehead.

'What's the matter?' Kathryn asked gently, drawing near.

'It's all that business with me avoiding Father. I've been so silly. It wasn't just over him saying he'd leave everything to my brother, he made out that Josiah wasn't good enough for me and that's just not true . . .' She sniffed. 'Josiah is a good man. Father never took to him as he viewed him as taking his only daughter away from him.'

'I know. You have to think of his age and rise above it, I suppose. Between you and me, I don't think he means 'alf what he says. Yer'd better stop here the rest of the night. You can't walk home now, it's not safe in that pea-souper and a madman on the prowl. I'll sleep on the settee in the living room and you can have my bed. That way you'll be near in the night should your father call out.'

But instead, Georgina chose to sleep in the armchair beside her father's bed, and when Kathryn entered early next morning, the woman was sound asleep, while her father was sitting up wide awake wondering what all the fuss was about. He even fancied some breakfast, but Kathryn was fearful of feeding him until Doctor Beck arrived to examine him. And when Georgina finally awoke, Kathryn was pleased to see that both father and daughter appeared to have settled their differences and were chatting amicably.

'Ah, Kathryn,' the doctor said, when he arrived. 'Did Shaun come to fetch me to examine your mother? He didn't seem to know.'

'No, it's not Ma, she is fine, thankfully. I didn't want to alarm him as I sent for you to examine Mr Bailey, the proprietor of this shop. He had stomach pains and a fever last night, he couldn't keep his food down, but this morning he appears back to normal. His usual doctor was sent for but he said he thinks it's a stomach tumour and it's only a question of time.'

Doctor Beck shook his head gravely. 'I see, so what makes you doubt that diagnosis?'

'He'd been fine up until last night, eating normally. He's even started to leave his room and join us at the table.'

Doctor Beck rubbed his chin. 'I see. Well I shall examine him. I don't like to undermine another's diagnosis but . . .'

'There is one other thing, Doctor . . .'

'Yes?'

'He gave us this bottle of medicine for him but didn't say what it was.' She handed the brown bottle over to the doctor, who took a sniff.

'Have you a glass I might have?' he enquired.

She nodded and left the room to return with one and watched as he poured some of the thick liquid into it, examining it closely. 'If I'm not mistaken I think it's . . .' He took a small sip as Kathryn gasped. 'Sugared water! As I suspected, the man is a poor quack! How much did you pay for this stuff?'

'Well I didn't, but Georgina coughed up a florin for it. He told her it would kill the pain.'

'And I bet when it had run out, he would have sold you more and more. That would not kill any pain but it would eventually rot any teeth if Mr Bailey has his own?'

'He does have his own teeth, yes.'

'Take me to the fellow and I shall examine him and I won't sell you any sugared water either. I shall be reporting that doctor.' Kathryn could see how angry he was about it all. 'It's people like him who give the rest of us a bad name,' he said, lifting his leather Gladstone bag.

When they arrived at the bedroom, Georgina was in the middle of propping her father up with pillows and he was now wearing fresh pyjamas. The examination took a few minutes as Doctor Beck inspected the old man thoroughly while the women waited outside. Eventually, he opened the bedroom door and turned to Georgina. 'I think what we have here is a bad case of constipation. Your father's stomach was very hard when I examined him and his tongue's a bit yellow as if he's dehydrated.'

Georgina nodded and she and Kathryn followed the doctor back into the bedroom. He turned to Mr Bailey. 'When did you last have a bowel movement?' he asked the old man.

Mr Bailey shook his head. 'Not for some days, Doctor.'

'Make sure he drinks plenty of fluids and eats lots of roughage, fruit and vegetables in particular. Give him some prunes and if they don't work, then you can purchase some opening medicine. Exercise he needs, fresh air. Get Shaun to take him out for a little daily walk as far as the park and you'll see a big difference.'

'So, you don't think he has a tumour then, Doctor?' Georgina asked.

'Oh good grief, no. The tumour the other doctor felt was the hardening of his bowel from waste matter, and he vomited due to a build-up of gas in his gut. I really don't think there is any cause for alarm, just a change of daily activity and his diet needs amending.' And with that he lifted his bag and left the room.

'What's the charge, Doctor?' Kathryn asked, following behind him.

'None whatsoever, m'dear,' Doctor Beck said, turning.

'Please, I insist as you have come out of your way.'

'I tell you what then, I'll try one of those tasty pies I've been hearing all about, if you don't mind . . . The delicious smell was wafting towards me as I entered the shop, no wonder people are clamouring for them.'

Kathryn nodded as her mother stepped into the room wearing her pinafore, her hands covered in flour dust. She was beaming to hear the doctor's kind words.

'I might have known you were responsible for those

pies, Mrs Flynn,' Doctor Beck said. 'And how are you these days?'

'Very well, Doctor. That rest home did me a power of good and thank you so much for getting me into that place.' Ma was beaming, and Kathryn wondered what had put her in such a good mood today; it couldn't just have been a throwaway compliment from Doctor Beck, surely?

Later that day, Kathryn was to discover it was because Stan had asked to take her mother out. Ma had got herself all dolled up in her best dress and had even borrowed a new shawl from Georgina for the occasion.

'You don't think badly of me going to meet with Stan, do you, Kathryn?' she asked.

'No, of course not, Ma. You seemed to get on well with one another.'

'Aye, well, he's been keeping me company sometimes since I got back here. He's lonely, and although I can't say I'm lonely with you lot around to keep me company, I do miss yer father.'

Kathryn placed a hand on her mother's shoulder. 'You deserve a bit of happiness, Ma. Stan is a true gentleman, he took good care of you that day he offered to sit with you before you went to the convalescent home.'

'I'm glad you like him.'

Kathryn hugged her mother to her. 'Of course I do. He was always a good neighbour to us and has helped us out a lot recently.'

Stan turned up later and he had a hansom cab waiting outside to take Ma out for dinner. It was good to see the sparkle back in her mother's eyes. She hadn't seen that in such a long time.

Chapter Eighteen

When all was quiet later, Kathryn had time to reflect about Squire. Why hadn't he been in touch? She could hardly go to his house to see him. Had he even told his wife about them? And the baby? She patted her stomach. Quite soon it would be impossible to hide this pregnancy from anyone. Inside she felt so disappointed in him, yet again he had promised things would be different and he was a changed man; had he forgotten that promise? If he was running true to form then she guessed he probably had. It made her heart sink to think of how foolish and naïve she had been.

If he didn't show up soon she would have to visit his home to find out where she stood. Blossom would know where he lived, she knew everything. As she patted her stomach she felt a little flutter for the first time, just like a little butterfly. It gave her a wonderful feeling of fulfilment. Although she hadn't initially desired to become a mother, she was now warming to the idea. Soon she'd have to tell the whole family of this pregnancy whether she liked it or not, and it would be better if she had Squire's backing to do so.

Blossom was surprised to see her later that day. Kathryn scanned the bar room to ensure O'Shay was nowhere to be seen. ''Ere, you look edgy, ducks!' she exclaimed.

'I'm worried in case Fergus O'Shay calls in again. I just know he won't let things rest.'

Blossom shook her head. 'Ain't seen him in this pub for a matter of weeks as it 'appens. Now what was it yer wanted?' She wiped the long wooden bar with a cloth, then lifted a glass, studied it carefully with one eye closed, breathed on it so it misted and wiped it with the same cloth.

'I need some information about Squire . . .' Kathryn let out a long breath.

Blossom dropped the cleaning cloth and placed the glass on the bar, then looked Kathryn in the eyes. 'The Squire? Why do you need information about him, luvvie?'

'Is there somewhere we could speak in private?'

Blossom nodded and led her to her private rooms and gestured for her to sit down on a floral armchair, while she sat on a matching one opposite. The living room was a sharp contrast to the bar; here everything was orderly and in place, and well kept. Blossom had good taste by the look of it. 'So what did you want to speak to me about, ducks?'

Kathryn swallowed hard. 'I'm having a baby . . .' she said.

Blossom's eyes rounded. 'And it's The Squire's I assume?'

'Yes, yer assume right. Trouble is, I need to find him.'

'I bet yer do. What a rotter leaving you in the family way!'

'No, he knows about the baby and told me he would inform his wife. He intends leaving her.'

Blossom chuckled. 'Aw gal, that's the oldest trick in the book. He won't leave her. It's her what's keeping him in a manner he's accustomed to.'

'But I don't understand. He claims she's the one spending his money.'

'No darlin', it's the other way around. His wife Constance is the daughter of Sir James Davenport. The Squire has severe gambling debts. She's even been in this pub looking for him a time or two. That's how he got the nickname, The Squire. You see he's from these parts himself. Puts on a posh accent and all that, but I knew him when he was a lad, simple little Ronald Arthur. Her father didn't like her marrying a commoner, oh no.'

A sense of fury overtook Kathryn. 'I . . . I find all this hard to believe.' Yet as she said the words she knew Blossom wasn't a liar. It was just hard to take in, though she had heard him use the name Ronald Arthur previously.

'Look, luvvie, I'd forget all about him. The Squire is a confidence trickster and a bloody fine actor to boot! See if yer can find someone else to marry you before it's too late. You can pretend the baby is premature, the father need never know.'

'But I'd know all about it,' she said sadly, shaking her head.

There was only one man she knew who would marry her in this state as he loved her so much, and that was Jimmy. Why hadn't she married him when he'd asked her?

'I can see yer've had a nasty surprise. I'll get Marie, my helper, to make us a nice cup of tea, she's a good girl.'

Kathryn nodded gratefully. 'That would be lovely.' Her head was swimming with thoughts and anxiety for the future. She pressed her cold hand to her forehead as she struggled to take it all in. *How could Squire have lied to me like that about marrying his cousin to keep the wealth in the family?* She felt as if the rug had been pulled from beneath her feet.

'I'll ask her to put some sugar in it for the shock . . .' Blossom carried on. 'I can let you know where Squire lives, but don't know what good it will do.'

'Please Blossom, I need to find out what's going on,' Kathryn pleaded. Blossom sighed and shook her head and then, going over to a small walnut bureau, she took a piece of paper and a pencil from the drawer and scribbled down a name: Gatesford Manor. 'It's not too far away. I'll explain how to get there now,' she said.

From outside the impressive manor house, Kathryn could see it was far grander than anything she'd ever expected, with its copious lawns, and there was even a set of stables and a pond. Anger seeped through every pore in her body. Squire had lied to her about being born to nobility, which made her wonder what else he'd lied about. And why hadn't he got in touch these past few days?

She watched from a distance as two footmen drew open the large black wrought-iron gates and then a coach came rattling through pulled by two black horses wearing black plums on their headdresses. She swallowed hard. It looked like a funeral carriage – but whose? Whose funeral could it possibly be? Her heart skipped a beat. Another coach carrying several people followed after it. She turned her head to one side so as not to be seen, and was just making to walk away when she spotted a young girl in a shawl, with mob cap askew, leaving the house. Maybe she worked there? Kathryn turned and began walking after her, falling into step with her as she reached her side. 'Excuse me, miss. Do you have any dealings at Gateford Manor?'

'I do indeed,' the girl replied sharply, 'but I don't see what business it is of yers. I'm a kitchen maid and I've been sent on an errand.'

The girl walked quicker which made Kathryn increase her pace too.

'For the funeral?'

She nodded. 'Yes, now if you'll excuse me I'll be on my way – I ain't got time for this!' The girl tried to walk away from her, but Kathryn grabbed her by the arm. 'Lemme go!' she shouted.

'Please, one more moment of your time,' Kathryn said gently, as she blocked her path. 'Who is it who has passed away?'

The girl's face flushed. 'I'm not at liberty to say, you might be from one of those rags what writes rubbish about the family. I've been warned about yer sort!'

Kathryn smiled. 'No. I'm not working for a newspaper. I just know the family and I'm concerned, that's all.' She dipped her hand into her reticule and held out a threepenny bit. 'Might this change yer mind?'

The girl's eyes widened and she made to snatch at the coin, but Kathryn pulled her hand away. 'Could you hang on a moment, please?' she asked. 'I need to know the name of the deceased and details of how they died. It is important to me.'

The girl huffed out a breath. 'It were the mistress, Constance. She was found dead in the pond a couple of nights ago. The master says he blames himself.'

Kathryn's hands flew to her face in horror. 'Oh lawd, no,' she mumbled under her breath as she fought to compose herself, and then, realising the girl was still waiting for her reward for imparting the information, she dropped the coin into her palm. 'One more thing, do you think your mistress took it upon herself to take her own life or was it an accident?'

'I don't know, miss. I heard Cook saying she was distressed just before it happened though.' The girl looked around fearfully as if she might have said too much.

A sense of dread swept over Kathryn. Was it her fault Constance had died? Had Squire told his wife of his plans to leave her for another woman, who was bearing his child? It would be enough to tip any woman over the edge. There was only one other person who might know the answer – Jess. Maybe he had called to keep an eye on her at the apartment and he'd said something to her then. After all, they'd been close to one another once upon a time.

Feeling shocked and distressed, Kathryn thanked the girl and hailed a cab to take her to the West End apartment.

She paid the cab driver and picked up a bunch of mixed blooms from the florist's shop on the corner of the street. Poor Jess didn't deserve to get beaten to a pulp by that pimp, O'Shay. He was evil personified.

She tapped on the apartment door, but there was no answer from inside. She was about to leave the blooms outside and depart when she heard muffled voices and laughter from inside. Oh no, it was evident that Jess was entertaining. Wasn't Squire supposed to be helping her leave that lifestyle behind? Not putting her back in jeopardy?

Biting her lip, she hammered forcefully on the door. 'Jess, I know you're in there, now open up. It's me, Kathryn!'

Slowly, the door opened a fraction.

Jess stood there, swaying slightly. 'Kathryn,' she slurred. 'Come and join the party . . .'

The woman smelled like the inside of a brewery. 'No, thank you. I've come to check on your welfare. Are yer all right?'

'Yes.' She held on to the door jamb for support. 'All me bruises are fading.'

Kathryn tried to peer into the room behind her. 'Who have you got in there with you?' There was a scuffling sound coming from inside and it dawned on her that maybe the girl was with a punter and it sickened her to the core.

'Come on, Jess, you're coming with me!' Kathryn said firmly. She needed sobering up and removing from this place if she was going to keep away from her lascivious lifestyle.

'Aw come on, Kathryn. I want to stay 'ere in this lovely apartment. It was yer fault I was pushed out in the first place.'

Feeling consumed with guilt when the girl's words hit home, Kathryn realised there was nothing she could do about the situation. She was in no mood to wrestle with her in her present condition and felt too weary to make a fuss.

Admitting defeat for the time being, she handed Jess the bunch of flowers and, turning, walked away.

The following day, Constance's obituary appeared in *The Times* and several local newspapers. It didn't give any details of her untimely death at the age of thirty, it just stated she had passed away. Kathryn noted the date of death was the day after she'd informed Squire of her pregnancy.

However, in one newspaper there was some speculation that something seemed amiss and an inquiry into her death was to be held.

A shiver ran the length of her spine. She could never believe that Squire would harm his wife in any way, but what did she really know about him anyhow? Maybe her feelings towards him had blinded her to the truth.

It was with a heavy heart she closed the newspaper, just as Georgina came rushing breathlessly into the shop, her cheeks crimson. 'Kathryn, you know that night you came to get me, and my husband left the kids to summon the doctor?'

'Yes?'

'Well, he's only just told me, when he returned to the house, he found a strange man loitering in the vicinity. He thinks he might have tried to break in.'

'Tell me, what did he look like?'

'Tall, he said. He wore a battered top hat and a scruffy long tailcoat. It was hard to see any more than that due to the pea-souper.'

Kathryn gasped. 'It sounds like the same man who was watching this shop a few days back. I think he might be working for O'Shay and he's probably after Nick and Dorrie.'

All the colour drained from Georgina's face. 'Heavens above, I can't let his happen. The sooner the adoption goes through, the better. How the heck did O'Shay find out they were living at my house in the first place?'

It was then Kathryn noticed Mags was stood behind them, her cheeks flaming red. 'I'm sorry, I think that may have been my fault. You see, a woman called here a week ago looking for them. She said she was a teacher from the board school and needed to speak to them both as their aunt had been in touch and it was to do with their brother, Jimmy.'

'How could you have been so foolish?' Kathryn snapped at her sister.

'Come on now,' Georgina said gently. 'We don't know she isn't a teacher. Did she look like one to you, Mags?'

'Well, yes. She was well dressed and spoke nicely.'

'That proves nothing!' Kathryn slammed down a can of pears on the counter with such force that a bag of wrapped toffees toppled off the edge, causing Mags and Georgina both to flinch. The truth was, it was Squire she was really upset with and poor Mags had just got herself in the firing line.

'I'm sorry, Mags,' she said, 'I shouldn't have snapped at you like that but we do need to take care. We don't want to come home one day to discover that Nick has been sent to work as a chimney sweep again or worse, and poor Dorrie – who knows what he might do to her? None of us are safe while O'Shay's around. He's got it in for this family good and proper.'

Mags began to sob, causing Georgina to glare at Kathryn. 'Don't go frightening the girl, Kathryn.' Then she turned to Mags and speaking softly said, 'Look, he can't touch us if we all stick together, can he?'

Kathryn shrugged. It was now that her family all needed one another more than ever.

The Horse and Harness looked different by day; there was no one stood outside as it hadn't yet opened for service. Kathryn would need to speak to Blossom before any customers arrived.

As she entered the wooden double doors, she inhaled a

powerful fragrance which seemed to be a mixture of lavender and beeswax. Cleaning had obviously been in progress.

'Well, I never!' Blossom said, with one arm propped up on the bar. 'What yer doing in these parts again, gal?'

Kathryn inhaled deeply then let it out again. 'I've come to tell you that Squire's wife has died . . .'

Blossom's eyes widened. 'Constance, dead? I ain't read the papers the last couple of days, it's a wonder that none of me customers told me. 'Aving said that, they knew him as "The Squire", not by his real name. There's few what remember him as a lad around these parts as his appearance 'as changed so much.'

'Trouble is, I feel like Constance might have taken her own life because he may have told her he was leaving her for me and our baby. She was found drowned in a pond on their estate.' She lowered her head.

Blossom placed a reassuring hand on Kathryn's forearm. 'I'm sorry to tell you this, ducks, but the only person Squire cares for is himself. I reckon he won't have told her about you at all. There's probably some other reason for it. He did once hint she was feeble of mind after the birth of a baby that died a couple of years back.'

Why hadn't he told her of this? It was a lie by omission in her book. Now she felt she didn't know the man at all. He had been prepared to put her on the game and it wasn't all for her benefit, was it? There would have been something originally in it for him even though he had eventually forfeited the purse of money for her virginity. Maybe he'd felt sorry for her. He'd even helped to get Ma to that rest home and it was the reason he hadn't taken his share of the spoils, so she would always be grateful for that. But most of all it was the feeling of betrayal that got to her. He was someone she had trusted implicitly and her mother had thought highly of him too. That's what hurt the most.

'Aw don't upset yourself, Kathryn,' Blossom said kindly. 'What are you going to do now about the baby?'

'Carry on without him, I suppose,' she sighed. 'We'll manage well enough. I'll do what Ma suggests about wearing black to pretend I'm a widow. No one knows my background where I'm living now.'

'That's a good idea. I've got an old brass ring I can give you. Had to do something similar meself at one time and didn't want people to know that me and his lordship upstairs weren't wed when we took over this pub. Some would have frowned at the fact we were living over the brush, so for a full two years I wore that brass ring until we had enough money to really get wed. We did it on the quiet with only a couple of friends as witnesses. He made an honest woman of me in the end, but don't go telling folk, will you?' She winked.

Kathryn smiled. 'No, of course not. And thank you, Blossom, I'd appreciate it.'

'Who knows, one day it might bring you luck and you'll really wed someone who is worthy of you and your new baby.'

Kathryn stared wistfully at the highly polished bar, then

watched as Blossom left to get the ring for her. When she returned, Kathryn felt there was something she needed to warn the woman about. 'Please, if you see O'Shay let me know. I think he's had a man watching the shop and I think the same man was loitering around Georgina's house and might have been trying to abduct Nick and Dorrie.'

'That's awful, ducks. Who's Georgina when she's at home?'

'She's Mr Bailey's daughter, he owns the shop. She and 'er husband are making an application to adopt the children.'

'Oh, I see. That's marvellous. But what about Jimmy, won't he mind? They're his brother and sister after all.'

'Hmmm, well, Jimmy should never have left those young kids to their own devices and gone to sea, should he?'

'I suppose not, but maybe he thought he'd earn enough money to come back and give them a better life. What about their auntie and uncle who live close by?'

'They didn't want to know, Blossom. It didn't matter to them if Dorrie and Nick ended up in the workhouse or out on their backsides living on the streets. I feel so angry with Jimmy, it's like he tossed his brother and sister to a pack of wolves when he left on his big adventure.'

'Oh Kathryn, you don't know if it was really like that?'

'No, maybe not, but O'Shay was prepared to send young Nick up chimneys and was working Dorrie to death. You know he pimps out young women?'

Blossom nodded. 'You don't think he'd have done that to Dorrie, do you?'

'Yes, I do. Maybe not straight away, but there are men who have a taste for young girls.' She turned her head away. 'It doesn't bear thinking about ... .' She bit back the tears for girls like Dorrie.

'Well at least the girl and her brother now have a good home. I hope the adoption goes ahead, but Jimmy must be told about this.'

'There's no way of telling him at the moment, but if he ever shows up here, go ahead and inform him of the situation. But please be mindful to tell him that O'Shay is a huge danger to those kids.'

And anyone else who crosses his path, Kathryn thought mournfully.

Chapter Nineteen

The following day, Kathryn dressed once more in black and wore Blossom's brass ring on her wedding finger. She had explained to Mags and Georgina why she was doing what she did, under the watchful eyes of Ma.

'But I thought Squire would have married you, Kathryn!' Mags explained, blinking.

'You are such a romantic, Mags,' Kathryn smiled. 'But you know Squire was already married. He had told me he planned to leave his wife for me, but since then she has passed away. I can hardly expect him to marry me now as it would look bad on him, wouldn't it?'

'But that means he's free to marry you now!' To Mags things were either black or white, she didn't understand that there needed to be a period of mourning and respectability.

'Look, when Pa died, how would you have felt if Ma had married someone else right away?'

'I'd have hated him whoever he was, no one can take the place of Pa!' she said crossly, her long red hair bouncing on her shoulders as she tossed her head in annoyance. Kathryn noticed Ma had a worried look on her face as Mags spoke and she wondered if she was thinking about her blossoming relationship with Stan.

'There you go then.' Kathryn turned to Georgina. 'How do you feel about this, Georgina? I don't want to bring down the good name of your shop.'

'And you won't either,' Georgina said softly. 'There's no need for anyone to know the truth, not even my father. We can stick to that story you just told me, that Jimmy is the father.'

'I already told you I don't like that at all.' Mags stamped her foot.

'Now look here, Mags Flynn,' Ma said, taking command of the situation. 'Jimmy might never return home at all, so where's the harm? People from the area we lived knew that he and Kathryn were close, so it makes sense. It also fits a purpose. He abandoned those kids, so he deserves everything he gets in my book!'

'Aw Ma, he doesn't,' Kathryn said, thinking about Blossom's words from yesterday. 'He's a good man, you know that. I'm still baffled by it all, to be honest.'

Ma nodded. 'Maybe that was a bit unkind of me. He was good in my eyes up until he left. I always thought you'd 'ave married him anyhow, so it was a shock when he left like he did.' Ma narrowed her eyes as if she was mulling things over. 'Come to think of it, didn't he leave just around the time you began knocking around with that Squire?'

Kathryn nodded slowly, realising the truth of Ma's words. 'Yes. I have wondered if that was the real reason he left.'

'He was heartbroken no doubt, poor lad,' Ma said, now changing her tune.

'Still, he shouldn't have abandoned his flesh and blood like that,' Georgina said. 'Those children are very dear to me and Josiah.'

'Aye, well it's all water under the bridge now,' Ma said philosophically. 'Before long you shall have adopted two of your own, Georgina. Those kids were orphans, so you're doing them a kindness. And Kathryn, while you are pregnant and it might not be what you planned for your future, there's new life inside you. And who knows what that young baby might grow up to be . . .' She sniffed loudly. 'We have a lot to be thankful for, especially towards you and your father, Georgina, who have both put a roof over our 'eads and given us jobs.'

Ma's words were like a soothing liniment on an inflamed wound. They all needed to look to the future now, and with Christmas around the corner there was a lot to look forward to.

The nearby streets were bustling as people prepared for the Christmas festivities. Outside Harper's the poulterer's hung all manner of birds for the season: plump turkeys, geese, chickens and ducks too. Soon to be plucked, roasted and dished up on dining tables on Christmas Day. Shops were nicely decorated with sprigs of holly and colourful candles and in Mr Henderson's toy shop down the road, the display had been changed to a wooden fort with colourful marching soldiers for the boys and pretty china dolls with bright-as-a-button eyes and long luxurious locks for the girls. A sense of expectation and merriment filled the air everywhere Kathryn turned, so much so that she felt herself swept up in the excitement of it all.

The Flynn children in particular were excited about the festive season. The shop and the living quarters above were decorated with garlands of holly and ivy, and even Mr Bailey seemed to be getting into the spirit of the season as he helped Rosie and Damon assemble colourful paper chains and cut out paper snowflakes to suspend from the walls and ceilings. Kathryn often wondered what Squire was doing now and if he was happy. She had called by the apartment a couple of times to see if she could find Jess, but there was never any answer. It seemed as though anything connected to Squire and the life he'd left behind had now disappeared forever.

Business at the shop was brisk as Ma now invested a lot of her time in baking the most succulent mince pies and chocolate Yule logs as well as her usual meat pies, especially for the season. The baby in Kathryn's belly was now well and truly kicking, and a little bump had started to show, so much so that Ma had needed to take out the seams of her dresses. The customers in the shop had begun to sympathise with the poor young widow whose husband had died while working on a ship sailing overseas. But each time it was mentioned, she felt extremely guilt-ridden. No one who called into the shop knew Jimmy personally and so far the story had been kept from Nick and Dorrie, but Kathryn feared they'd eventually find out and believe that their brother really had passed away.

'Yer just going to have to tell them yer've created a little white lie and why yer've had to do so,' Ma suggested. 'It'd be a pity if they got the wrong end of the stick for nothing. I'll tell them if you like and explain it was all my idea.'

'No, Ma,' Kathryn said, patting her face with a handkerchief. She was feeling extremely hot for some reason. 'I'll tell them myself. I'll take them to Vicky Park on Saturday like Jimmy used to do and I'll tell them then. They need to hear the truth. I feel really sorry for them as they miss him so much. There's not been any word neither, they didn't so much as get a letter or card from him while they were still at the house.'

'But it might have taken weeks for a letter to arrive and by then they would have been living at the shop, and after that with Georgina. How would any letter or card have got to them anyhow?'

Ma spoke sense as usual.

'Yes, and maybe if it had arrived, O'Shay would have got his filthy mitts on it, and knowing him, disposed of it.'

'Have you seen him around lately?'

'No, thank goodness. Blossom reckons he hasn't been into the pub for weeks, it's like he's dropped off the side of the earth.'

'Maybe he's been slung into the slammer for a spell,' Ma suggested.

'Possibly. And it would be the best place for him an' all. Ma . . .' Kathryn began. 'Would you help me make some Christmas presents?'

'Yes, of course. What did you have in mind?'

'Well, Georgina says we can borrow her Singer treadle sewing machine. We'll ask Stanley Morgan if he can load it on the back of his cart for us.'

'Good idea,' Ma said as Kathryn noticed a faint blush to her mother's cheeks.

'I thought maybe we could make a new rag doll for Rosie as her old one, Jemmy, has almost fallen apart! Georgina has got plenty of scrap material we can use. Stan is good at making wooden toys, I was thinking maybe he'd make a wooden fort for Damon. Dorrie and Mags could do with a new dress each and maybe we could buy a book for Shaun. He's always asking about stories he'd like to read to Mr Bailey. That reminds me, I can make Mr Bailey a felt case for his spectacles.'

'What about Georgina?' Ma asked.

'I think we should get her something really special as she's been so kind to us. I saw a lovely cameo brooch in the pawn shop. It won't be brand new, but it's affordable.'

'I'm sure she'd love it,' Ma said. 'Now then, I need to get back to me baking. I'm thinking of trying some pastry puffs packed with sausage meat and sage and onion stuffing, what do yer reckon?'

'I think that sounds a lovely idea, Ma.' It was good to see her mother so animated and full of life after all her suffering in the wake of Pa's death. Kathryn guessed that Stan had more than a little to do with it and it gladdened her heart.

Snow had fallen fast and furiously during the night, leaving the area down below quiet with the stillness that only comes following a fresh fall. The rooftops were crowned in a thick white glistening coating with long icicles hanging from the eaves and windowsills. Kathryn drew back the drapes further to gaze in wonder at the pure virgin white brilliance of it all. There was no rumble of cartwheels or the usual costermonger cries this morning; indeed, would anyone bother to set up their stalls today? But an honest crust needed to be earned by most folk in the area, so she guessed they'd at least try. Would anyone even venture out to the shop? But people needed feeding and Kathryn decided that by hook or by crook she would have the shop up and running today. Shaun could use a shovel to clear a path to the front door of the shop, and he could scatter a pail of old ashes from the fire grates on to it to stop people from slipping and sliding on the icy pavement beneath.

It took longer than usual for the shop to open up but few people called as many could not get out of their homes that day, and Kathryn wondered if Georgina would make it in for her shift. But she did, though she arrived a little later than usual, her skirts covered in melting snow where she had fallen several times on the way. Kathryn immediately sent her to thaw herself by the fire in the back room while Mags put on the kettle so they could all warm up with a cup of tea and some hot buttered muffins.

As the shop was quiet they sat in the back room with their beverages, chatting away amicably. Then, after a few minutes, a smile appeared on Georgina's face and a gleam came to her eyes; she was obviously bursting to tell them something. 'I received this when I got home last night . . .' She drew an envelope from her skirt pocket and held it up for them to see.

'Such elegant copperplate handwriting!' Kathryn marvelled.

'What is it?' Mags asked eagerly, as Ma entered the room to join them – she'd been up early, baking her wares for the day, and she rubbed her floured hands on her pinny.

'It's a letter to say that the children's adoption is to proceed. It won't be much longer now, then Josiah and I can say Nick and Dorrie are legally ours. I think it was pushed through quickly as Jimmy can't be traced, though enquiries were made at the docks. I think either his name wasn't added to any ships' crew lists, or he gave a false one.'

Hearing that, a severe sadness tore at Kathryn's heart. Her

old friend Jimmy was kindness itself, someone trustworthy and loyal, unlike slippery Squire. She might never set eyes on him again. 'That's wonderful, Georgina,' she said. 'I had promised to take all the children to Vicky Park at the weekend, but don't suppose that will happen as no doubt there will be more snow on the way.'

'You mustn't worry about that,' Georgina said brightly. 'I think Nick and Dorrie are so excited about the adoption they've forgotten all about the park.'

But Kathryn severely doubted that. How could Georgina know about the regular jaunts they all took to the park on weekends, where Jimmy would buy the children ices in summer or hot chestnuts or a jacket potato in winter to warm their freezing fingers? She could never make up for his loss. Never. No matter how hard she tried.

When she looked back on it, it was never the big gestures that counted with Jimmy, it was the little ones, demonstrating his love for her – the way he took care of the whole family, like that night at the pie shop where he'd insisted that she ate her meal to keep up her strength instead of her saving some for the kids.

There were no flashy grand gestures or flowery words. He showed his love in the things he did for her and others. Why had she never seen this before? There was a lump in her throat and she swallowed down her sadness as she realised how much she loved him too.

Returning to the present, she said, 'When you go back

home, take them a poke of peppermint from me. I'll put the money in the till later, it's the least I can do to make up for things.'

Georgina nodded and smiled. 'You already do a lot of things for everyone,' she said.

The truth was though that Kathryn felt guilty. If it hadn't been for Jimmy falling in love with her, and one rejection too many, he would never have gone away from home in the first place. Why hadn't she realised how much she really loved him back then? When Squire came along with his sophisticated ways he had turned her head, and she hadn't been able to see the wood for the trees.

Why hadn't she said yes that night at the pie-and-mash shop? They could have been married by now and having a baby of their own. Only, now that was never going to happen.

The jangling of the shop door caught her attention and she went out to find Stan stood there huffing and puffing, his face blue from the cold. 'I came to see if you need any help today as the weather's so bad. I can take some orders out for you or pick up anything you need,' he offered, as he stood there with his cap in his hand.

'Oh Stan,' she said gratefully, 'you came all this way for us. Take the horse and cart around to the stable at the back and come in through the back door. I'll send Shaun to help you now. Meanwhile, I'll make you a cup of tea. You can have one of Ma's mince pies too.'

'I'd love that,' he said, smiling. It was so cold his breath puffed out in small clouds of steam.

He got back on his cart to ride it around to the back of the building and into the cobbled yard. They hadn't needed Stan's services for a while as they couldn't always afford to pay him in leftover goods, but in this weather his help would prove invaluable.

After warming up by the fire and supping a hot cup of tea and nibbling one of Ma's mouth-watering mince pies, Stan set about loading up his cart to take out deliveries that were already booked. Then Kathryn had an idea.

'As some can't make it to the shop today, Stan, would you take a little extra with you?'

He nodded. 'Sure thing.'

'There's Mrs Jefferson who calls in here every day. I know what she's likely to need, also a few others. They all live within a few streets of one another. I'll scribble down the addresses for you. Please tell them they can settle up next time they call in.' She turned to Georgina. 'If that's all right with you, of course?'

'Yes,' Georgina said excitedly. 'I think that's a splendid idea. We're so grateful to you, Stan. We can manage to pay you a little something extra and I'll give you plenty of good food to go home with.'

Stan blushed beet red as he gazed at Ma. 'If you don't mind, Enid?' he said, using her Christian name.

'No, I don't mind at all,' she replied good-naturedly. It was the first time Kathryn realised the depth of Stan's feeling for her mother. After all, he had implied that Ma had helped him out tremendously after his wife died by cooking for him.

'What are you smiling about?' Mags asked.

'I'll tell you later,' Kathryn whispered.

There was only one more customer in all day and when the man arrived he was covered from head to toe in snow. Mags took pity on him and allowed him to warm his coat on the boiler while she made him a cup of tea. He explained he had to get some food in as his parents were elderly and sick. Her heart went out to him.

'I think,' Kathryn said later, 'we'll need to keep these extra deliveries going for a few days, but soon we'll run out of stock ourselves as some of our delivery men won't be able to get through.'

'It is so exciting though!' Mags exclaimed. 'Us all being snowed in here.'

Kathryn frowned. 'Not for Georgina if she can't get back to her husband and the kids. Though I expect Stan will try to take her on his horse and cart when he returns. I'm going to tell her to knock off early, just in case.'

'Good idea,' Ma said, as she brought down some pies she'd baked. There were no hordes waiting to purchase them today. They'd have to be sent out with the deliveries to see if anyone wanted them, and of course, any left over they'd eat themselves. 'Where's Stan? I thought he'd be back by now?'

'No, no sign yet, Ma,' Kathryn said. She wasn't unduly concerned as he had a fair few customers to deal with. But as darkness fell, he still hadn't returned and her mother was looking increasingly worried.

'Stuff this!' Ma said, wrapping her shawl around her shoulders. 'I'm going out to find him!'

'Not on your own, you're not!' Kathryn said firmly. 'I'll come with you.'

'No, not in your condition.' Georgina shook her head. 'We wouldn't want anything to happen to the baby, now would we?'

As they began to argue amongst themselves who would go in search of Stan, the doorbell jangled and Stan came staggering into the shop, his forehead bleeding. He fell to the floor. 'I've been robbed . . .' is all he managed to say before passing out.

As Ma and Georgina fussed over him and Mags went to fetch a blanket to cover his cold body, Kathryn went outside to see if the horse and cart were there. She heaved a sigh of relief to find out they were. Stan's horse whinnied loudly and she realised he was distressed, maybe because he realised what had happened to his master. She went into the shop and called for Shaun to help her take the horse around the back, and to unhook the cart and stable him for the night. Stan would be devastated if anything happened to that horse.

By the time they came back into the shop, Stan was beginning to come round. 'Take him to the back room by the fire,'

Kathryn commanded. Shaun and Mags helped the man to his feet and they walked him slowly to the back room.

'I'll make him a cup of beef tea,' Ma offered, her face ashen.

'Good idea, Ma. The fire will help to thaw him out.'

After Stan had got over the shock of it all and sipped his warming beef tea, Ma used a clean wet cloth to clean his head wound. 'It's only on the surface, thankfully. So tell us what 'appened to you?'

The others gathered around to listen. 'I had taken out the last of the orders and was about to set off back here when two men rushed out of an alleyway and pulled me off the cart. The horse were right upset. I tried to get back on the cart as I didn't want anyone stealing him, when one man coshed me on the head. Then I heard a door open in the street and a woman called out, "Police!" Anyroad, the men got off the cart and ran off. They only made away with a sack of potatoes and I'm sorry about that.' He shook his head sadly.

'That was hardly your fault,' Georgina said. 'Can you remember what the men looked like?'

'One wore a battered top hat, he were the worst and most vicious of the pair – it were him that hit me over the head. Seeing stars I was. The other was a lot younger, hardly spoke but seemed to be under the orders of the first man.'

'Was the one in the top hat wearing a long tailcoat, very scruffy, by any chance?' Kathryn asked.

Stan blinked. 'Yes, he were, as a matter of fact.'

'It sounds like the same man who was watching the shop the other day and who tried to break into Georgina's house. He must be working for O'Shay.'

'If I get me 'ands on O'Shay I'll throttle him!' Ma said angrily, raising a fist.

'Keep calm, Ma,' Kathryn said soothingly, 'he's not worth getting yourself worked up about. But I do think we need to keep our wits about us.' She turned to Georgina. 'Well obviously Stan can't take you 'ome tonight on his cart, you'd better stay put 'ere. You can have my bed, I'll sleep on the settee upstairs, and Stan can sleep on the settee down here in front of the fire.'

Georgina nodded. 'Yes, but I won't turf you out of your bed in your condition, Kathryn. I'll sleep on the settee upstairs and you can have your own bed. If the weather lets up tomorrow, I'm reporting all of this to the police.'

'Sounds a good idea,' Ma said. 'Who knows what O'Shay will do next?'

The following day, the leaden skies had cleared to reveal a bright-blue one with a golden-yellow sun. It had finally stopped snowing but the recent fall had been deep. As soon as Shaun was up and dressed, Kathryn sent him to check on the horse. Thankfully, all was well in the stable, there were still several bales of hay, and Shaun topped up the trough with fresh water.

Stan was looking a lot better too. The cut to his head was only superficial, but nevertheless, the whole experience had shaken him up. Ma took him a cup of tea and a couple of rounds of buttered toast. She sat with him for a while and they enjoyed a friendly chat.

Georgina, though, was fretting about Nick and Dorrie. 'I need to get back to the house to check on them,' she said, chewing her bottom lip.

'Surely your husband can keep an eye on them?' Kathryn asked.

'Yes, he's very good but he has to leave for business today,' she said.

'I doubt if he'll get out in this weather,' Mags said.

'I don't know, it's within walking distance and he needs to speak to the fellow he works for. I don't want those children left alone with O'Shay and his cronies on the prowl.'

'I'll ask Shaun to walk you home,' Kathryn offered. 'If your husband has to go to that meeting, he can sit with Nick and Dorrie while you get on with whatever you need to do.' Kathryn realised how much Shaun liked Dorrie; she was a bit older but they got on well enough.

With Shaun accompanying her, Georgina set off for home, trudging through the thick white snow as Kathryn watched from the shop doorway.

They'll be all right, if they take their time.

Then she began to set up the shop for the day as she guessed there would be more people out and about, now it had stopped snowing. Within the hour though, Shaun had returned out of breath as if he had been rushing. 'It's Dorrie!' he cried. 'Someone got into the house and took her away while Georgina's husband was at that meeting. Georgina and Nick are beside themselves. They won't stop crying.'

Kathryn could see her brother's eyes were welling with tears as if he might start bawling at any moment. 'All right, calm yourself down, Shaun. We are going to do something about this. We know who is behind it an' all and after what happened to Stan yesterday, we need to go to the police. Come on, we'll get over there now, Mags and Ma can mind the shop and Rosie and Damon will be fine with Mr Bailey for an hour or so.'

Shaun nodded. He looked relieved that something was going to be done about the situation, but Kathryn's biggest fear was that Dorrie had been taken to be forced on to the streets to work. She didn't deserve such a fate, and it seemed so much more cruel now, just when she'd found herself a permanent home and was about to be adopted. How scared she must be feeling at the moment, away from the people who loved her and powerless to do anything about it.

The desk sergeant at the police station jotted down all the information and took Kathryn's claims seriously, especially when he saw the injury to Stan's forehead. 'I think I know the man Mr O'Shay has working for him, it's Donald Keates.

He's a rum character. And I've no doubt he was after young Dorrie more than the boy. The boy will grow too old to go up chimneys soon enough, but they could get good use out of the girl for many a year. She's highly profitable.'

Kathryn shook her head and glanced at Shaun, who looked so sad, she wished now she hadn't brought him along.

'Any idea where this Keates person lives?' Stan asked, as he wrung his flat cap between both hands as if he was wringing the man's neck.

'On Dorset Street, in one of those doss houses there. We've had him in here several times on charges of gambling and handling stolen goods, but lately he's got into the prostitution lark as he realises there's more money in it for him.'

For a moment, Kathryn wondered if Jess had any involvement with the man as her last place had been on Dorset Street.

The sergeant drew a breath before putting down his fountain pen. 'The best we can do is keep an eye out for him and bring him in for questioning. That's if we can find the fellow, he's a slippery eel that one . . .' He rubbed his bearded chin. 'I think though we might have more luck getting a hold of him if we bring in O'Shay himself, he's easier to locate.'

Kathryn nodded. 'Well, if yer manage to question either of them we'd be grateful to find out about any developments. I'm living at Bailey's Stores, a stone's throw away from here. Yer can't miss it!'

'I know of it, miss. Best pies in the area!' he said, with a huge beaming smile on his face.

Kathryn returned the smile and nodded. 'You have my mother to thank for the recipes,' she said, and smiled. 'Good day to you, Sergeant, and thank you for your time.'

He nodded and the trio left the police station. 'I hope they catch the brutes!' Shaun said fiercely. 'I feel really sorry for Dorrie.'

'Me too, Shaun,' Kathryn said sadly.

Everyone's spirits were at an all-time low, so they closed the shop early. Then as Kathryn went to shut the street door she heard in the distance the sounds of a brass band striking up a carol she recognised so well, 'God Rest Ye Merry Gentlemen', and her heart flooded with memories of years gone by with her dear father when they all attended church together. The sound grew louder, until she saw it was the Salvation Army who came marching right past the shop, all dressed in black, the women in their distinctive bonnets and the men with their brass instruments. Someone shook a metal bucket of coins in front of her and she dropped in a few pennies.

'Kathryn!' a voice exclaimed. She turned to see it was one of the women from the Salvation Army addressing her. How did she know her name though? Then she took a closer look under the gaslight and realised it was a face she recognised, but her appearance was vastly different; her hair was no longer loose on her shoulders but neatly pinned back, and now she no longer had garish rouge on her cheeks or painted lips.

'Jess? But how . . .? When . . .?' She had so many questions to ask but her heart felt gladdened to see the girl.

Jess smiled back happily. 'This is all down to you, Kathryn!' she said enthusiastically. 'The last time you called to see me I'd been drinking gin and was in no mood to come with you. I'm sorry. I remembered that place you told me I could go to as a refuge, the Hanbury Street shelter, so with the last shilling I had to my name, I took a cab from the West End to there. I realised the error of my ways and now I am so grateful. My God takes care of my every need . . .' She wiped away a tear with her white-gloved hand. 'The Army, bless 'em, 'ave been kindness itself to a poor girl down on 'er luck . . .'

Kathryn took her hand. 'Jess, I am so pleased for you. You have now got to keep away from your old friends. They're trouble.'

'I will do, Mary's death really made me think. It was days after when I found out . . .'

'I bet it did. That was right tragic.' A shiver coursed down Kathryn's spine as she thought of what had happened to the poor woman. 'Can you do me a favour please, Jess?'

'Anything, Kathryn, after how you've tried to help me.'

'It's young Dorrie, we think she's been kidnapped by someone with a view to getting her to work on the streets. If you hear anything, will you let me know?' Kathryn didn't mention O'Shay's name so as not to upset Jess in front of everyone.

'I will indeed, darlin'. A lot of the working girls call in to the shelter. I'll keep my ear to the ground. I have to go now as we have to cover a lot of streets tonight to raise money for the shelter.'

'God bless you, Jess!' Kathryn hugged her warmly and watched as the band marched off down the road to find another pitch.

She returned inside the shop, taking care to lock and bolt the door behind her. Later, as she looked down from the upstairs living room on to the street below, she wondered where Dorrie might be right now and hoped she was somewhere safe and warm. It broke her heart to think of the little mite lost and Jimmy not even here to help.

Chapter Twenty

A policeman called the following day to inform them O'Shay had gone into hiding and there was no sign of Keates or his accomplice. And if Mrs O'Shay knew where Dorrie was, then she was denying all knowledge of even knowing her.

'But she does know her,' Kathryn persisted. 'They kidnapped the kids once before. They worked Dorrie like a slave and sent her little brother, Nick, up chimneys. They're evil, the pair of them!'

'I see, miss,' the young constable said, his grey-blue eyes showing great compassion. 'I can well understand how you feel, I have a sister of that age myself. We shall do all we can to find the girl. Meanwhile, perhaps you can assist us by telling us of any places you know of that Mr O'Shay frequents?'

'There is one pub called The Horse and Harness. The landlady, Blossom, knows him but last time I was there she said she hadn't seen him for a few weeks.'

'I was just thinking, see, miss, that often these criminals do their dealings in the pub. Maybe that Keates goes there too.'

'It might be worth following up. You'd make a great detective constable.'

His face flushed bright red. 'Just doing my job, miss.' He smiled, obviously pleased that she thought so highly of him. 'Well, I'll be on my way. I'm Constable Hargreaves by the way.'

'And I'm Kathryn Flynn. What's your Christian name, Constable?'

'Joseph, miss . . .' He glanced at her for a moment as if only just realising she was pregnant. 'Mr Flynn is a lucky man.'

'There is no Mr Flynn, I'm widowed,' she said.

'Oh.' Suddenly, he looked flustered as he almost collided with a small Christmas tree that was stood near the wooden counter. He tipped his helmet to her before putting it back on his head. 'Anyhow, I'll be back if there is any news.'

After he'd departed, Mags came rushing out of the back room. 'I heard all of that,' she said, her eyes shining with mischief. 'You've got an admirer there, I reckon.'

'Oh, go on with you!' Kathryn smiled but she had to admit, she did like the young constable.

Dorrie sat shivering in the corner of the flagstone-floored scullery. It was a place she was totally familiar with. A place she'd been before. And in front of her with hands on hips stood a middle-aged woman she'd encountered previously – Mrs O'Shay. 'You silly little madam!' she shouted at the girl. 'It's your fault me Fergus is locked up by the rozzers!'

Dorrie drew her knees up to her chin and buried her head in her lap. She was trying to make herself as small and insignificant as possible, but it was too late. The wooden spoon came down crack on her skull, once, twice, three times. It hurt so much that she burst into tears. She tried to hold them back in case she angered the woman even more. How could it be her fault that Mr O'Shay had been arrested? She'd been dragged from her new home when she and Nick had been left alone for just one hour.

'Are you mad, woman?' A gruff voice, which wasn't Mr O'Shay's, boomed out. Before her stood the man who had kidnapped her – in his battered top hat and tailcoat, staggering and smelling heavily of alcohol.

Mrs O'Shay sniffed. 'The girl has to be punished, Donald. She's impudent and feisty. She had the cheek to plan an escape from here once before. Her and that skinny brother of hers could 'ave made us a packet an' all. Fergus said he could have used him up chimneys for a year or more as he was small for his age, then he'd have worked his hide off helping him in other ways. And the girl, she was skivvying for me . . .'

'Aye, I know that. But you know what your old man has planned for her now, don't you?' His eyes widened.

'I think he's going to sell her on to someone else when we've finished with her, someone in the gentry so we can make some good money.' She rubbed the palms of her hands together as if she was counting on it.

'Well, if that's what yer want to think!' He belched loudly.

Mrs O'Shay dropped the wooden spoon with a clatter on to the pine table beside her. Her mouth popped open. 'What do you mean by that, Don?'

'He's got high aspirations for that one, likes to start 'em young. She'll be a good earner all right.'

Mrs O'Shay shook her head savagely. 'Stop telling your lies, you're only jealous.'

A shiver skittered down Dorrie's spine. Whatever could the man mean? He was the one who had pulled her from her loving home. What did O'Shay have in mind for her if it wasn't skivvying for rich folk?

The man drew near to Mrs O'Shay. 'Look Sybil, yer know how your husband runs a team of unfortunates, makes a good livin' from 'em and all?'

She nodded, but the way she stuck her chin in the air, Dorrie could tell she didn't want to admit what her husband was doing. What were those unfortunates?

'In any case,' Mrs O'Shay said, 'I wouldn't allow it, the girl is far too young. She's flat-chested anyhow.'

What did her chest have to do with this?

'I'm telling you the truth. I don't really like it meself. I'll rob people blind, but the girl is a child. I reckon we should let 'er go while Fergus is in the slammer. We can pretend she's escaped again.'

Dorrie peeped through slitted eyes to see what the woman's reaction might be.

'M . . . maybe you're right, Donald, but Fergus will beat me if I lose her again.'

'I'm sorry I brought 'er here now. I didn't realise until he told me what he had in mind for her. I find it hard to go along with this as she looks so young and reminds me of me little sister.'

So the man really had a heart.

'I'll think about it,' she said. Then she cut off a piece of stale bread from the loaf on the table and put it in the dog's tin bowl, poured some slops from the teapot onto it and flung it in Dorrie's direction. 'Eat that!' she commanded.

Realising she might not get another meal for a long time, Dorrie forced the food down her gullet. She was scared and she wished Jimmy was here right now.

Jimmy was finally back on dry land. It was now mid-December and he hoped to surprise Nick and Dorrie. When he'd recuperated, he had been able to work and barter on the streets of Morocco for spices, exotic materials and other items that would sell well back home. And of course, he now had his wages paid by the captain.

He'd put on a little weight following his dreadful illness and his sunbronzed skin gave him a healthy glow. He rapped on his aunt and uncle's door, and when his Aunt Maisie answered she stared at him for the longest time. 'Well if it ain't our Jimmy, I didn't recognise you. Home from the seas, then?'

'Yes, and I can't wait to see Nick and Dorrie. I wanted to get home

in time for Christmas. I could have gone back out on another ship but changed my mind. I've made enough money to keep us for a couple of months, meanwhile I'm going to look for a new job.' He peered past her in the passageway as if expecting to see them. 'Where are they, then?'

'I . . . I haven't seen them for a long while . . .' He noticed she was avoiding his eyes. 'Took off they did without so much as a word to me and yer uncle!'

'But I paid you good money so they could lodge at your house! Dorrie had her cleaning job with Blossom at the pub, so she could even pay for their food. What's going on?'

'A lady came looking for them some time ago. She was worried they might have been taken to the workhouse by that O'Shay, the rent man. Dunno what happened after that.'

Jimmy felt so angry he could have shaken his aunt until the few teeth she had in her head rattled. He had placed his trust in her and his uncle and they had let him down.

'Well then,' he said quietly, 'seeing as they are no longer here, perhaps you'd better return the money I gave you for their keep.'

His aunt's mouth popped open. 'I would if I could, but I can't, your Uncle Tom has spent it all . . .'

'That's how it is, is it? No doubt he peed away the money in The Horse and Harness! Don't worry, neither myself nor my brother and sister shall ever darken your doorstep again.' He paused a moment, needing time to collect his thoughts. 'The woman who called here, what did she look like?'

'Dark hair, pretty, very ladylike, I think she called herself Kate.'

'Do you mean Kathryn?' he asked hopefully.

'Yes.' Her eyes lit up. 'That was the name.'

He turned and walked away, never wanting to see *Auntie Maisie* or *Uncle Tom* ever again. Where could he go now to find out where the kids were? He'd tried knocking at their old home but there was no answer. He still had a key but for some reason it wouldn't turn in the lock. He'd try *The Horse and Harness* pub, where Dorrie had her cleaning job. Maybe Blossom would be able to shed some light on the children's whereabouts.

Chapter Twenty-One

Dorrie ended up snuggling into the dogs under the table in the scullery to find a bit of warmth. In Mrs O'Shay's eyes she was no higher than an animal and so was treated as such.

When she finally managed to doze off, she suddenly felt herself being yanked to her feet with the strong smell of ale around her. In the dark, she tried to focus on who it was as her heart hammered a tattoo.

'Can't have yer sleeping with the hounds, you might get fleas, young lady!' It was the man who had abducted her. 'Come on, I'll get you out of here, darlin'!'

Relief flooded through her, she was going to be set free at last.

'Thank you, sir.'

'Sssh,' he slurred as he wrapped a thick blanket around her before slinging her over his shoulder like a sack of spuds and carting her out the back door and down the road.

'Where are you taking me? I can walk now,' she pleaded.

'Yer ain't going home yet, young lady. I've got plans for yer!' he grunted as he hurried along the street.

Oh no, she was in just as bad a position as ever. The journey seemed never ending as he carried her through alleyways and courts lit by dim street lighting, all viewed from upside down, until finally she found herself outside an old dilapidated building. Then he set her on her feet. 'Don't you dare move a muscle!' he growled. He knocked at the door in front of him. It was drawn open a fraction. A young boy not much older than Nick stood there, and another male voice from inside shouted, 'Who's there, Tinker?'

'It's Mr Keates, Mr Flook, sir.'

'Let him in then!' the voice bellowed.

'He's got a young girl with him wrapped in a blanket!' Tinker shouted.

Within moments an elderly man sporting white mutton chop whiskers stood there. 'Come in, Keates, what have you brought for me?'

Keates removed the blanket and pushed her into the building. 'This here is a fine filly called Dorrie. She's nimble and fast on 'er feet, I reckon she'd make a great dipper!'

Dipper? Whatever did he mean?

The elderly man inspected her with his big beaky nose and dark beady eyes. He pinched the flesh on her forearm so that she winced in pain. 'Hmm, looks well fed enough I reckon. She might do. Better than that one you brought me the other day from the Hanbury Street shelter, at least. How much do you want for her?'

Keates stroked his stubbled chin, seeming to have sobered

up quite quickly now he was discussing his favourite topic – money. 'I would say I'd be happy with a couple of sovs, boss.'

'I'll give you one sovereign for her, tops.'

'Come on now, Mr Flook, she's worth more than that, she'd make that the first day she worked for you. I reckon she's worth three sovs at least.'

Worked for him? What did he want her to do for a sovereign?

'Hmm, you drive a hard bargain, Keates. All right, three shiny sovereigns it is, then!' He dipped into his pocket and brought out a black velvet pouch and handed Keates the payment. Flook wore fingerless gloves and licked his lips a lot as he spoke. Dorrie thought him very odd indeed.

When Keates had been paid, he asked, 'Any chance of a dram o' rum?'

'Aye, go on then. Not only are you fleecing me of my hard-earned money, but you want to get a drink out of me too. Just the one, mind!'

Keates roughly pushed Dorrie in front of him into a room which took her breath away: it was packed full of young boys and girls. They looked well fed enough and seemed to be in good spirits, but their faces were etched with grime and their clothing was tattered and torn.

'Would you like a tot of rum, m'dear?' Flook asked.

She shook her head and the old man laughed. 'You'll get used to it. It'll warm you up on a night like this.'

He poured a tot into a small tin mug for Dorrie and rather a lot more for Keates, which Keates knocked back in one go, rasping and wiping his lips with the back of his hand. Both men watched as, gingerly, Dorrie took a sip, then coughed. The old gent was right, it was warming but very strong, so she decided to take her time drinking it.

"Ere . . . who are you?' a freckle-faced lad asked as he smoked a long-stemmed clay pipe. Her eyes widened as she'd never seen a lad smoke a pipe before. He stood waiting for her answer as he puffed out clouds of steam as if he'd been doing it all his life.

'I'm Dorrie Dawkins, and I've no idea what I'm doing here!' she replied indignantly. All she knew was she might be better off here than with the O'Shays, so that was a relief at least.

'Yer in a den of thieves, me dear!' the lad replied with a flourish of the hand.

'But I ain't no thief!' Dorrie protested.

'Not yet, but yer'll soon learn the fine art of picking pockets, dipping into those of the gentry. A silk handkerchief 'ere and a thick wallet there . . .'

'Oh. And what if I don't want to do that like the rest of you?' She lifted her chin in defiance.

'You don't have much choice, darlin',' Keates whispered in her ear. 'Beggars most certainly cannot be choosers!'

Dorrie stiffened, realising he was right. For now she must bide her time and do whatever was asked of her. It would be better than sleeping on the cold floor with the dogs and being beaten around the bonce with a wooden spoon, that was for sure.

*

When Jimmy arrived at The Horse and Harness, it was quite busy for an early afternoon. Blossom was in the midst of serving a man at the bar, and her husband, Arnold, was chatting to a group of men in the corner. He waited for her to finish serving her customer and then approached.

'Any chance of a pint?' he asked, pleased to see a friendly face.

'Jimmy!' she yelled, blinking in astonishment. 'I never thought I'd see you again. Come here, me darling.' She was around the other side of the bar like a whippet, hugging him and kissing his cheek. 'My, my, but you look so well and tanned too, as brown as a nut yer are. Are yer back for good?'

'Yes. It's good to see you too, Blossom, but I can't find my brother and sister.'

Her face clouded over and her good nature seemed to vanish like the sun behind a heavy grey rain cloud. 'Well, what do yer expect? You left those kids to their own devices while you sailed the high seas to find yer fortune!'

'It wasn't like that, Blossom. I had paid my auntie and uncle to take care of them. It was them what left the kids to their own devices.'

She shook her head and then her smile returned. 'Sorry, it's just what yer friend Kathryn told me.'

He let out a long sigh. 'Is that what she thought? I'd just abandoned my own flesh and blood without a care?'

'I'm afraid so, ducks. That girl is to be commended for

saving your brother and sister though. She got them away from that 'orrible O'Shay after he kidnapped them.'

'What?' Jimmy could hardly believe his ears.

'Yes, she managed to get them back and Georgina is taking care of them. Her dad owns Bailey's Stores, where Kathryn and her family now live.'

'I've never heard of that place. So they're with this Georgina now as we speak?' he asked enthusiastically.

She shook her head. 'Not exactly, ducks. Nick is still with Georgina and her husband, but Dorrie has since gone missing. The police have been informed and it's thought one of O'Shay's heavies took her . . .'

Jimmy almost collapsed from shock. 'How could I have been so foolish? I only went to sea to try to make some decent money for their future. Now you're saying I might have lost my sister forever?'

Blossom smiled sympathetically and touched his hand. 'Don't take on so, pet. I'll pour you a pint now to settle yer nerves and then we'll decide what you can do. At least you can see Nick. But there's something else . . .'

What now?

'Georgina and her husband have been making plans to become their legal guardians . . .'

He shook his head. How he'd let those children down. No wonder someone wanted to adopt them.

And Kathryn . . . What must she think of him?

*

The following day, out of the blue, a letter arrived for Kathryn.

My dearest Kathryn,

This is a hard letter for me to write as I guess you are wondering why I lost contact with you. My wife, Constance, sadly took her own life unexpectedly. It was nothing to do with me and you, I mean our relationship. I was about to tell her the circumstances of the impending birth and how it was you I really loved when it happened.

I have subsequently discovered that she tried to end her own life once before without my knowledge. It was an incident that was covered up by her father who found her after she'd consumed a strong dosage of laudanum.

I have been grieving, as although I wasn't happy living with Constance, she is all I have known these past ten years, until you came along and changed my life.

We need to discuss things. I intend to call around to the shop to see you soon.

All my love as always,
Squire

A feeling of uncertainty swept over Kathryn. She didn't know if she wanted to be with the man any more. Blossom was right, he hadn't even told his wife he intended to leave her, and indeed would he ever have done so at all?

It wasn't just that; for all his promises, he hadn't taken

care of Jess properly either. No, she told herself firmly, she didn't want or need him in her life, though she realised she needed to speak to him face to face. The man lacked integrity in her book, and he'd broken her trust so many times. She couldn't carry on forgiving him forever. It would be far better to be alone without any man in her life than have a father for her baby who kept letting herself and their child down.

He arrived at the shop as she was closing up the following night. It hadn't snowed for a couple of days and now people were able to get out and about with relative ease.

When she opened the shop door, she was astonished to see how gaunt and thin he appeared, no longer the same robust man with wit and good humour. That was guilt, she assured herself. He hadn't treated his wife with the love and respect she'd deserved while she was alive. He stepped towards her as if he was about to take her into his embrace.

'No,' she said firmly, taking a step back. 'I think we can no longer have that type of relationship!'

He frowned as if puzzled by her reaction, the hurt apparent in his eyes. 'But I thought you loved me, Kathryn?'

'I did, I still do, but not in the way you'd like me to love you. I know you've been through a lot lately, but why did you allow Jess to end up selling herself at the apartment when she was recovering from a severe beating from O'Shay?'

He blinked. 'But I didn't.'

'You left her to her own devices, didn't you? You didn't

keep an eye on her like you promised. She was drunk when I paid her a visit and she was obviously entertaining someone.'

His face clouded over and his eyes became guarded. 'I didn't mean it to happen that way. I was so busy, then when Connie passed away I was so shocked and needed someone to speak to, some comfort if you like . . .'

A sense of revulsion filled her, squeezing her gut and making her want to heave. Was she hearing him correctly? Surely not! 'Y . . . you mean you had sexual relations with Jess when she'd been badly beaten up?' She swallowed hard.

He nodded slowly. 'Believe me, I'm not proud of it! I found myself at the apartment with a bottle of brandy in my hand. We drowned our sorrows together, then it just sort of happened. The truth is it didn't mean anything to either of us . . .'

What a pathetic excuse for a man he was, why had she been so blind to all of this? He'd put his own needs before Jess's need for safety and security.

'I think you'd better leave before I say something I might regret,' she said, turning away as she blinked back the tears. It was all too much to take in right now.

It was evident he could tell by the tone of her voice she meant what she said.

'If that's the way you want it to be,' he said, handing her a small velvet drawstring bag.

She loosened the strings and peered in to see several sovereigns inside.

'Please do not treat me like another of your whores!' She

threw the bag back at him, the coins scattering on the floor at his feet. 'I don't need your thirty pieces of silver!'

'The money's for the baby . . .' he said.

'*We* do not need your money. Now please take it with you. Goodbye, Squire!' There was a note of finality in her tone and she watched as he scrabbled on the floor to retrieve the coins and return them to the pouch. He stood, then placed it in the top inside pocket of his jacket and stared at her through misted eyes.

Slowly, and hunched over, as if all the stuffing had been knocked out of him, he turned and left the shop, just as she broke down in tears.

Standing on the corner with his eyes on Bailey's Store was Jimmy. He'd just summoned up the courage to go to see Kathryn, but who was that man leaving the shop? He looked familiar. Recognition suddenly dawned. It was that Squire! He looked thinner than he last remembered. She was still seeing him, obviously. Didn't she have any self-respect? Furiously, he turned on his heel and strode back to the pub, gritting his teeth in anger.

'There's one – there!' Tinker nudged Dorrie with his elbow. 'Look, he's got a silk handkerchief sticking out o' 'is pocket. Yer can bet he's got a nice fat juicy wallet in there as well!'

The boy's eyes had widened like two saucers, he was positively drooling at the mouth.

'I . . . I . . . don't know if I can do it,' she said, petrified in front of the rest of the ragged gang of boys and girls who were looking at her with expectation in their eyes. Her stomach flipped over. She realised she had to do this. If she didn't, they'd tell Flook and he'd tell Keates . . . and then Keates might drag her to the workhouse or even worse, back into the clutches of the O'Shays. Oh heck!

They were in the middle of Petticoat Lane open market and the fellow in front of her looked very well-to-do in his long dark-grey tailcoat, silk cravat and top hat. Under his left arm he held a silver-tipped walking cane as he browsed a second-hand book stall. It was perishing cold, though most of the snow had been shovelled out of the way for shoppers to pass by.

'I'm looking for a first edition . . .' she heard the man say to the stall holder, whose face broke out into a smile as if he had just the right book for this customer. Dorrie edged closer and closer until she was just inches away from the man, who hadn't even noticed her approach as he was in heavily animated conversation with the stall holder. Her hand slipped gingerly forwards and slowly she drew the length of handkerchief from the man's jacket pocket with her thumb and forefinger. She could hardly believe how easy it was. She quickly shoved it into her dress pocket and ran off towards the others, who were all waiting to pat her on the back.

'Yer a natural,' one young girl called Ebony said. Ebony

had eyes as dark as two shiny pieces of coal and Dorrie wondered if that was how she'd got her name in the first place.

Tinker, though, was scowling. 'Yer should have done better than that. That was a game opportunity there. That man didn't even notice you, he'd have had a wallet in one of his other pockets too, I just told you that.' He was just about to kick her on the shin when Ebony intervened.

'Leave 'er alone, Tinker. She did well for a first-timer!' She wrapped her arm around Dorrie's shoulders.

Tinker made a noise akin to a harrumph and held out his grubby palm. 'Well hand it over then, I've got to take stuff back to show old Flook or he won't be best pleased.'

She did as instructed, drawing the handkerchief from her pocket and placing it in his outstretched hand.

'Do you want me to go back and try for his wallet?' she asked, trying to please the boy.

He shook his head. 'Nah, you never know, someone might be watching now. You can try again later. There'll be another opportunity, lot of toffs 'ere today!'

The kids had a profitable morning as three wallets and two silk scarves were acquired by sleight of hand and Ebony even managed to snatch a silver neck chain from one of the stalls. As they walked back to the den, she grabbed an orange from one of the stalls and ran off with Dorrie in pursuit over the slippery cobbled ground. 'We'll share this later,' she said. 'Don't tell the others, I ain't sharing with any of those.'

*

The following day when the shop's business had quietened down and the lunchtime pie trade had fallen away, the door opened. Mags was upstairs taking her break so Kathryn was all alone in the back room.

'I'll be with you in a moment!' she called out. Then tidying up her hair and putting on a clean pinafore as the other was full of grubby stains from the old sacks she'd been unpacking in the back room, she made for the shop floor.

There was a man in front of the counter, with his back towards her. He appeared to be staring out of the window. His shoulders were broad and filled his jacket well, but his hair was a little longer than she'd have considered usual for most men she knew, and when he turned to face her and met her eyes, she could see it was her oldest friend. He now had a beard and moustache too and seemed a good couple of years older. His swarthy sun-kissed skin gave him an almost Mediterranean appearance, and she gasped at how handsome he really was.

'Jimmy!' she exclaimed, ready to run into his arms just like the old days, but there was something in his eyes that was creating a barrier between them.

'Kathryn,' he said curtly. 'I hear that you have been taking care of Nick and Dorrie and I'd like to thank you for that. It wasn't what you'd imagined; that I'd run off to sea and forgotten all about them.'

The memory of it caused her to go on the offensive. 'But you didn't make adequate provision for those kids, they were left to their own devices!'

'No, I had paid my aunt and uncle to take care of them. They were supposed to be staying at their house, but I was saddened to discover that wasn't the case and O'Shay had got hold of them. I've been awake all night long worrying about my sister as I hear she was taken by one of his men. Is this true?'

She nodded slowly. 'Blossom told you?'

'Yes. I need to know where Georgina lives so at least I can check on Nick.'

'I'll take you there now, Jimmy, he'll be so pleased to see you.'

He smiled a smile that did not quite reach his eyes. He seemed no longer the Jimmy she had known. This seemed to be a stranger before her and it broke her heart. 'Just give me the address and I'll find it myself,' he replied curtly.

'Have I done something to offend you?' She stared at him. What had changed so much?

'If you must know, I don't approve of your relationship with that Squire fellow. I saw him leave the shop yesterday.'

'I can assure you there is nothing going on between me and *that gentleman*!' She pursed her lips in annoyance.

He walked towards her as a slow smile played upon his lips, but then his expression turned to one of horror as she stepped from behind the counter and she realised he had noticed her small stomach bump. There was no covering up the fact she was pregnant.

'I can explain . . .'

His eyes flashed dangerously. 'Believe me, there is no explanation that you can offer me that will explain why you have had relations with another man when you turned me down when I offered marriage! I wasn't good enough for you! And if you are no longer in a relationship with that man, then whose baby are you carrying? I dare to hazard a guess!'

She stepped forward and sent a stinging blow to his cheek with the flat palm of her hand. 'Yes, it is Squire's baby, but things aren't quite as clear cut as you might imagine. Ma was ill and I needed money to support the family. I'm not proud of myself for what I did, believe you me! I did wrong as he was married, but now his wife has passed away and I could marry him if I so wished . . .' She was trying to recoup her battered pride, with little success.

He rubbed his reddened cheek. 'For a woman, you pack a powerful punch, my dear.'

Feeling the sting of humiliation and wanting rid of him, she returned behind the counter and scribbled down Georgina's address. 'Turn right when you get as far as the church on the corner,' she said, holding out the note for him.

He snatched it from her grasp. 'And to think only a few months ago, I was begging you to marry me, Kathryn.' He had a look of disdain on his face.

She nodded in agreement. 'You deserve far better than me, Jimmy,' she said, as she opened the shop door allowing him to leave. Yet there was sadness in his eyes as she watched him go.

She turned the sign on the door around to 'Closed'. If only

she could turn back the hands of the clock! But she knew she couldn't do that, all she had was here right now in the moment. Realising she needed to go after Jimmy, she dashed to get her bonnet and shawl from the back room and made after him.

Georgina would be shocked if he just showed up at her door; after all, she didn't even know him and had the misconception he'd just abandoned Nick and Dorrie.

'Jimmy!' she cried out after him in the freezing night air. It was so cold it made her throat sore and a puff of steam emerged. She coughed.

He stopped in his tracks and as if realising how difficult it was for her in her condition, walked to her side and took her arm. 'You shouldn't have come after me, not in your . . .'

'Condition? Go on, you can say it, Jimmy. I am with child. And yes, this child inside me will be a bastard!'

'Sssh,' he said, 'someone might overhear.' He glanced around but the streets were empty save for a man driving a cart in the distance. 'Is that why you're wearing black? So people believe you are widowed?'

She nodded. 'Yes, it was Ma's idea.'

'And who is the unfortunate fellow who is supposedly the father of this child?'

'You!' she said forcefully, causing his chin to drop.

'Me? What made you choose me?'

'Because I thought you were never coming back home. Oh Jimmy, I thought I'd never see you again . . .' She began to sob.

'Is that what Nick and Dorrie have believed too?'

'No, they were more hopeful. They were insistent you'd be home to see them again soon.' He took her in his arms and allowed her to cry her heart out.

For the first time she saw compassion in his eyes for the plight she now found herself in. 'There might be a way out of this for all of us, a simple solution, but the first thing I need to do is find Dorrie.'

She nodded through glistening tears. 'I'll do all I can to help you, Jimmy. I've been to the police, so they are keeping their eyes peeled for Keates and O'Shay. But my fear is that Dorrie might be forced on to the street to sell herself.'

'Over my dead body!' Jimmy said, fiercely. 'Take me to Georgina's house so I might see my brother, then I'm going to the police station.'

She nodded. Jimmy was a man on a mission and if anyone could find Dorrie, it would be him.

After Jimmy had been reunited with his younger brother, where there were many tears, but this time of joy, he set off to the police station with Kathryn at his side. The same sergeant was at the desk and she asked to speak to Constable Hargreaves.

'I'm afraid he's out on his beat, ma'am,' the sergeant said. 'What did you want him for?'

'He called to see me at the shop the other day and said he'd let me know if anything turned up about Dorrie's disappearance.'

The sergeant cleared his throat. 'Nothing has transpired so far, we've tried our best.'

'Then obviously your best isn't good enough!' Jimmy spat out the words in fury. 'My sister has been missing for days and you know the men who might be responsible.'

'It's all this Whitechapel Murderer business, son. People are petrified and all sorts of suspects are being brought in for questioning. A lot of it is nonsense and all. A gentleman was frogmarched here only last night by a group of men just because he looked suspicious, loitering on the street corner. It's taking up a lot of our manpower . . .'

Jimmy shook his head. 'Meanwhile, who knows what will happen to a young girl on the streets of Whitechapel! Maybe there'll be another laid to rest at the workhouse morgue. One less for you to trouble yourself about, eh, Sergeant?'

Kathryn laid a restraining hand on Jimmy's arm, before he said something that might really get him into trouble. She feared he might get arrested himself. 'Let's go and see Blossom,' she said gently. 'Maybe she'll have heard something. She keeps her ear to the ground.'

Jimmy nodded. 'I spoke to her only yesterday, but you never know.'

At that point a crowd of people rushed into the station protesting. 'Oh no, they're back again!' the sergeant said, shaking his head.

'Who are they?' Kathryn frowned.

'It's the Whitechapel Vigilante Committee and it looks as if they've brought another one in as a suspect!'

'Pity they don't round up O'Shay and his henchmen!' Jimmy shouted, raising a fist. 'There have been no other Ripper murders, Blossom told me it's all gone quiet, yet a young girl on the street gets ignored.'

'Jimmy, Dorrie isn't the only young girl wandering the East End each day . . .' She laid a gentle hand on his shoulder. 'There are thousands of them. The police don't have the manpower to look out for them all. You must see that?'

He nodded. 'It's just that she's my sister.'

She looked in his eyes and she could see he was holding back the tears. Kathryn understood only too well. At least Jess was now off the streets and safe in the care of the Salvation Army, which gave her an idea. 'I think we should head off for the women's shelter at Hanbury Street. Jess, a woman I know, helps out there and she has contacts on the street. She might know something.'

Jimmy nodded as a couple of men jostled past him with shouts of, 'String this bastard up!' and 'Justice for all!'

Kathryn was beginning to feel desperately sorry for the desk sergeant.

Chapter Twenty-Two

From outside the night shelter at Hanbury Street, Kathryn and Jimmy watched a long line of women queue at the door for a bed for the night, hugging themselves and stamping their feet to keep warm. Kathryn realised some were street-walkers who would have recently sold their bodies for the chance of a bed and a hot cup of tea or coffee. It was a way of life for them; sometimes all they earned was enough for bare essentials and sometimes, if really unlucky, they earned nothing at all.

On admittance to the shelter, Kathryn and Jimmy passed down a long narrow passageway where several women were huddled on benches around a long table sipping hot drinks and nibbling dry hunks of bread, their faces full of despair and lined with the ravages of time. At the end of the room a blazing fire roared. The walls of the room were whitewashed and clean-looking.

At that point, Jess entered wearing her Salvation Army uniform and carrying what appeared to be a tray of currant buns. 'Kathryn!' she exclaimed, her violet eyes shining brightly in recognition. 'The Lord has brought you 'ere. What can we do for yer?'

'It's lovely to see you again, Jess,' Kathryn said, smiling. 'This is my friend, Jimmy. His young sister is in trouble. Is there anywhere we can speak in private for a moment?' She realised that walls had ears and there was the likelihood that one of the women might be acquainted with O'Shay or Keates.

'Yes. I'll sort something now. I just have to ensure everyone gets a bun as if I leave them here on the table there'll be ructions as a fight will break out.'

Kathryn watched as one bun per person was carefully allocated. Then Jess tucked the tray under her arm and followed them to the corridor where she led them into a small room with just a desk and chair. She laid the tray down on the desk and shut the door behind them. 'Now what can I do for yer both?'

Jimmy spoke. 'We believe my sister Dorrie was taken away by a man called O'Shay, or if not him then a man called Keates . . .'

Jess's face paled and she steadied herself by placing the palms of her hands on the desk.

'I'm sorry,' Kathryn said. 'I know you've had dealings with O'Shay yourself, that's why I didn't mention his name to you when I said she was missing. I didn't want to bring it all back for you.' She glared at Jimmy for butting in; she had intended breaking the news gently to Jess, but of course Jimmy wouldn't realise the woman had been beaten by O'Shay.

Finding her breath, Jess said, 'If that man has her then I don't much fancy 'er chances. You know what he did to me!'

'What did he do?' Jimmy wanted to know.

'He beat Jess, she was in a bad way,' Kathryn explained, then turned back to Jess. 'Can you think where Keates or O'Shay might be hiding out?'

Jess shook her head slowly, but after a moment she said, 'I have just thought of somewhere. There's a place where a gent by the name of Flook keeps stolen goods. He runs a gang of thieves to pinch handkerchiefs and wallets from local marketplaces. O'Shay and Keates have dealings with him. It might be worth you trying there. I'd wager she could be there!'

Kathryn smiled. 'Thank you, Jess. Where is this place?'

'It's near to Flower and Dean Street. There's an alleyway leading to it, but it's very dangerous crossing there as the old building is nearly tumbling down. It's a slum, all rickety and ramshackle. Only good enough for the rats, if yer ask me.'

She sketched a rough map for them using a piece of paper and pencil that were on the table. 'It's not a great map but it will give you some idea.'

'Thank you,' Jimmy said, as she slid the piece of paper in his direction.

Kathryn gave Jess a big hug. 'We are indebted to yer,' she said with tears in her eyes.

Jess shook her head. 'No, it's me what needs to repay you for how you picked me up off the pavement and took me in that night. It was so cold, I could have been dead by morning otherwise.'

Kathryn had no doubts in her mind that O'Shay had left her for dead, all of which made her realise they urgently needed to find Dorrie.

Flower and Dean Street was just off Commercial Street and not too far to walk. The building Jess spoke of was down an alleyway and Kathryn would never have guessed that such a place existed. A series of wooden planks had been placed on top of old bricks, which she guessed had been there previously to stop people stepping in puddles, but now that the ground was slushy from the snow, it seemed more perilous as the planks were slippery. 'Take care here, Kathryn,' Jimmy warned, 'perhaps you'd better wait in the street until I come back.'

'No, I'm coming with you,' she said firmly. 'It might soften the old man if I speak to him first.'

Jimmy nodded as if he could see the sense of that suggestion. 'There's a doorway here,' he said, holding out his hand to help her to stand on the plank. 'Watch your step, it's treacherous . . .' He was back to his old self, taking care of her once more, and it warmed her heart to hear him talk that way.

Finally, when they arrived at the door, Jimmy hammered on it. There had been a lot of noise coming from inside, then all fell quiet as if the occupants were pretending they weren't in. So he hammered again and pushed at the door, which opened a fraction. 'I haven't come to harm anyone and I'm not the police! My name is Jimmy Dawkins!' he shouted inside. They heard a lot of rustling and footsteps, then an elderly man stood at the door, his back hunched over. 'What is it you want then? To do business?'

Kathryn stepped forward, holding up the hem of her dress as the slush had turned to pools of water near the doorway. 'We're seeking a young girl who goes by the name of Dorrie. She's Jimmy's young sister who was taken away,' she said softly. 'He would love to see her again as he's been overseas.'

The man rubbed his chin and narrowed his eyes. 'There's no girl of that name here,' he said.

'Please, sir,' Kathryn pleaded. 'You won't get into any trouble.'

'How about I give you something for your time then?' Jimmy asked hopefully.

'How much have you got?' Flook's eyes widened.

'I can give you a sovereign and a special jewel I brought from overseas.' Jimmy held the pink crystal object up in front of him.

The man was about to take it but Jimmy snatched it away from beneath his nose. 'Not so fast. Is my sister here or not?'

'She may be.'

'Then I want to see evidence she is safe and well!' he declared.

'Tinker!' Flook shouted behind him, 'Go and fetch Dorrie to the door!'

There were sounds of scuffling and then there she was, thinner than Kathryn last remembered and a lot dirtier too in her rags, standing barefoot inside the doorway. A moment later she was in Kathryn's arms and weeping and then Jimmy swept her up into a fierce embrace. 'I thought I'd never see you again, poppet,' he said, with tears streaming down his face.

Flook stood there salivating, with his hand outstretched. 'Payment, please!'

Jimmy dropped a shilling into his palm.

'What's this?' Flook wanted to know.

'Sorry, I thought I had a sovereign but it's a shilling. Still, this pink jewel is worth far more anyhow.' Flook grabbed it from him and slammed the door behind himself, leaving the trio outside.

'My goodness Jimmy, I'm sorry you had to part with a precious jewel,' Kathryn said.

Jimmy laughed. 'Precious jewel indeed, it's just a pretty pink piece of glass I got from Morocco on me travels. We'll be far away from here before the greedy so-and-so realises it.'

Gingerly, they made their way out from the area. Jimmy got Dorrie to climb on his back as she was shoeless and as they got to the main street, Kathryn recognised someone walking towards them, staggering on the pavement. 'Quick, this way,' she hissed. 'It's Keates and he might recognise Dorrie.' They turned away just in time as it was obvious Keates, with an old sack slung over his back, was on his way to see Flook. What a lucky escape.

The police were informed that Keates had gone to see Flook, so it looked likely that both men might be arrested in due course.

'Those poor children living in that den of vice!' Kathryn related the whole sorry tale to the family later. Jimmy had taken Dorrie back to Georgina's where after a grand reunion and a good slap-up meal, she was bathed and put to sleep safely in her own bed.

'Sounds like Jimmy came back at the right time,' Mags said, watching Kathryn as if to gauge her response.

'Maybe,' Kathryn said wistfully.

'So, what's going to happen now then?' Ma sat forward in her armchair beside the fire.

'I really don't know. For the time being, Jimmy is delighted to be reunited with Nick and Dorrie.'

'At least the police will have the chance to get the rest of those kids away from that old crook!' Ma said, forcefully and with feeling. 'Poor children, going on the rob to line his pockets!'

'That may be as such,' Kathryn said, 'but from what Dorrie was able to tell us, he was keeping them well-fed and at least he provided some sort of a roof over their heads. Who knows, maybe some of them were better off with old Flook than begging on the streets or being lambasted by drunken parents.'

'Maybe,' Ma said thoughtfully. 'I suppose those they find now will end up in the workhouse. Dorrie is one of the lucky ones to get rescued by people who love and care for her.'

Kathryn stared into the flames of the fire as they licked up the chimney. Would the impending adoption of Nick and Dorrie go ahead now Jimmy was home? Might he demand that Georgina and her husband hand them back to him?

Chapter Twenty-Three

The following Sunday before Christmas was the 23rd of December, and the entire family including Georgina, her husband, and Nick and Dorrie, attended the church. Even Mr Bailey was there in his best suit and bowler hat, his old customers looking generally pleased to see him. The aisles were decorated with wreaths of holly and ivy and a large white Advent candle burned brightly from every windowsill.

The message of the service was 'God's precious gift to mankind'.

As the final hymn 'O Come, O Come, Emmanuel' was sung, leaving behind a haunting final chord that echoed around the church, a tear trickled down Kathryn's cheek at the thought of her own new-born babe to come.

There had been so much going on that she hadn't given too much thought to whether it would be a boy or a girl, or even how they'd all cope with the extra mouth to feed, and the extra demands and stress a young baby might put upon them all. But as she touched her stomach, she felt a swift kick from inside as if he or she were reminding her she needed to get a grip.

'Soon Christmas will be here,' Ma said cheerfully, as everyone formed an orderly queue to shake hands with the minister in the porch. His wife, who was a portly woman, stood beside him, rosy-cheeked and smiling. 'Welcome to the parish. Hope to see you again over the Christmas season,' the minister said heartily, as he pumped their hands with a firm grip.

Ma nodded and wished the pair the compliments of the season.

Mags, though, who was stood at the back of the line-up holding Rosie's hand, had a big scowl on her face. Once outside, Kathryn nudged her mother. 'What's eating her?'

'Aw, it's because Stan's interested in me and I want to invite him for Christmas dinner with the family. She told me she thought he was getting his feet under the table!' Ma chuckled.

'She's probably concerned you'll remarry, I suppose. I know she likes Stan well enough.'

Ma nodded. 'Yes, I understand all of that, but no one could take the place of your father and I wouldn't want them to either. But if Stan were to ask . . .'

Kathryn had suspected it might have something to do with Mags thinking someone had come along to replace their father, but she could never allow her mother to give up on a chance of happiness with someone as loyal and caring as Stan.

'Just take it a day at a time, Ma,' she advised. She was sure her sister would come round eventually.

'Aye, you're probably right, gal. You usually are,' Ma said wistfully.

Kathryn noticed a little smile crease the sides of her mother's mouth. She tucked her arm into the crook of her mother's. 'Come on, we best get home, there's so much to do and so little time . . .' she said merrily. It was going to be a great Christmas, she could feel it in her bones.

Tonight she was going to need Ma's help to finish making those festive gifts and to plan the menu for Christmas Day. This year she quite fancied cooking a turkey for a change; usually the family had goose and apple sauce, but this year there would be so many sitting around the table that a turkey would be easiest. And Ma would make one of her mouth-watering Christmas puds in brandy sauce. This was going to be the best Christmas ever and she hoped Jimmy would join them. He'd been very evasive about his plans for that particular day so far, although she knew he'd definitely want to see his brother and sister. But he hadn't even told her where he was staying; he could of course no longer go back to his old home to sleep as the rent hadn't been paid and that was why O'Shay had captured the children in the first place.

Later, she took a walk over to Blossom at the pub to bring her a basketful of goodies for Christmas.

Blossom was pleased to see her. ''Ere, ducks!' she said, wrapping her arms around Kathryn and hugging her so tightly she felt there wasn't any room to breathe, 'you are so good to me but you shouldn't be out walking in your condition.' She released Kathryn from her embrace and held her at arm's length. 'My, you do look well an' all. You've got that bloom about you. Come into the back room and I'll send me home 'elp to make us a nice sweet brew.'

Kathryn nodded gratefully as the weather was bitter cold outside. Once safely ensconced in Blossom's living quarters with the roaring fire and cosy comfortable armchairs, she removed her bonnet and cape. A young girl, all flustered and clumsy, rushed into the room to take the garments, glancing at her mistress for confirmation of what was required of her.

'Kathryn, I'd like you to meet Becky. She's me new 'elp and a good and willing worker an' all. Becks, please fetch us a nice pot of tea and me best china cups and saucers . . . and a couple of matching plates as well . . .' She took a peek inside the covered wicker basket Kathryn had brought with her. 'Hmmm mince pies and a loaf of Christmas cake. We'll 'ave a slice of cake each with it, thank you, Becks. Have a slice yerself!'

The girl bobbed a curtsey before leaving the room: 'Thank you, ma'am.' This amused Kathryn as you'd have thought Blossom was royalty, not a landlady in a backstreet East End pub.

As they sat sipping their cups of tea in front of the fire and nibbling on the cake, Kathryn felt her legs, which previously had been like two blocks of ice, begin to thaw as she stared into the flames.

'A penny for them, darlin'?' Blossom asked, setting her cup and saucer down on the small table beside her.

'I was just thinking about Jimmy and wondering where he's staying the night. I wanted to invite him over on Christmas Day for dinner.'

Blossom's eyes widened and then twinkled like candle lights on a Christmas tree. 'Why, he's staying 'ere of course. I've been putting him up 'ere as long as he likes. I can tell him he's invited if yer like?'

She nodded gratefully. 'If you would. We'll be dining about one o'clock as we'd like to go to church first. We have a lot to be thankful for now Ma is back in good health . . .'

'Yes, you 'ave an' all and then there's the new life inside you. Does Squire know about the baby?'

'Yes, he does, Blossom.'

She frowned. 'And? He doesn't want to know?'

'Oh, he does, he'd do anything for me, but it's the deceit I can no longer live with. I wish now that . . .'

'You wish what, luvvie?'

She felt a large lump rise in her throat, threatening to choke her as she thought about it all. 'I wish I'd accepted Jimmy's proposal and then he would never have gone to sea. I never realised until now it was him I really loved.' She stared down into her lap as she twisted her handkerchief. Now it was all too late.

'I'll tell you what I think, shall I?'

Kathryn was sure that even if she said no, Blossom would tell her anyhow. 'Yes, go on . . .'

'I think you should remain friends with him and see what 'appens. Love often finds a way anyhow. It was obviously not to be, with you and Squire, but be thankful for your relationship with him as you wouldn't be where you are now and realising you love Jimmy . . .' She let out a long breath. 'And for all his faults Squire can be very benevolent.'

'Oh, you're right there, without him I'd never have scraped up enough money to put Ma in that rest home.' She squirmed as the memory of what she'd intended to do for that money came rushing full force at her. She'd somehow managed to block it from her mind until now and apart from Jess, no one else knew what she had done to get it.

'There's something you're not telling me,' Blossom said, looking deep into her eyes.

Kathryn swallowed. 'Oh, Blossom, you must swear never to tell another soul of this, it's a secret I've kept to myself.'

'Yes, go on . . .' She sat forward in her seat.

'I first met Squire as I wanted to earn money for Ma to go into that rest home. He sold my virginity to the highest bidder . . .'

Blossom just sat there, her face a blank canvas apart from her ingrained wrinkles, which showed her years of life experience. She nodded.

'It was awful, all those men were leering at me and some were quite old.'

'It 'appens dearie, we do these things because we think it's our only option at the time.'

Kathryn couldn't believe how understanding the woman was. 'But I feel so guilty now about it all. It was like it wasn't me doing it. But luckily the man who was to take my honour couldn't perform the act. But then . . . Squire . . . Well, he . . .'

'He took you anyway?' Blossom shook her head. 'He took advantage of a vulnerable young woman?'

Kathryn nodded. 'I wasn't the first either. I discovered sometime later there were two other women he'd set up and he'd given them rings too, identical to the one he gave to me, so we believed we were engaged to him. When I discovered that, I was mortified. Even worse was the fact he had a wife, but he'd made out it was a loveless marriage . . . Yet, he was heartbroken when she passed away and then he cut off contact with me for a long while.'

'That's men for you, dear. They say one thing and mean another. I suspect The Squire did really love his wife, or at least to begin with. But his gambling debts probably got in the way. You know, there are men who view their wives at home as being like their mothers so they seek excitement elsewhere . . . I hear it all the time in the pub. "Me wife doesn't understand me . . ." If I had a sovereign for every time I've heard that one, I'd be a very rich woman by now!' She threw back her head and chuckled, causing Kathryn to smile through her tears. It was wonderful to be with someone so wise, with so much life experience she could put it all into perspective.

'Thank you, Blossom.'

'What for? I ain't done nothing!'

'You have, believe me.'

'Listen Kathryn, doll, don't beat yourself up about what's gone. Look to the future now. 1889 is just around the corner. And, thankfully, there's been no more Ripper murders since the Kelly girl, God rest her soul. Yer Ma is in fine health now, you have a roof over your head and a good job and a lovely baby on the way. Yer old life has gone forever. And who is going to tell anyone what you did? No one knows around here, as it all happened up West.'

Kathryn nodded, thankful too that things had improved for Jess. Now all she wanted to know was how things stood between herself and Jimmy.

On Christmas Eve, Kathryn awoke with a spirit of optimism. She had a lot to be thankful for, she realised, as she drew back the living room curtains and gazed down at the street below. She heard Ma pottering around in the kitchen; when Kathryn entered, she announced, 'I thought we'd all have pancakes as a treat! It's going to be a busy day ahead.' She clanked around getting a couple of frying pans and a glass jug out of the cupboard, then went in search of a bag of flour and a few eggs.

'Yes, it'll be busy in the shop that's for sure as people buy last-minute provisions. I've nearly finished that rag doll for Rosie.'

'That's good,' Ma said, rubbing her chin as if in deep contemplation.

'What's wrong, Ma?'

'Oh nothing wrong at all, just trying to ensure I have everything I need to cook for the big day tomorrow.'

'Well I'll be helping, yer won't have to do it all alone.'

'And I'll help too,' Mags chipped in as she entered the kitchen. 'What yer making, Ma?'

'Pancakes for a change. I thought we could have them with a little lemon and sugar, or there's some honey in the pantry.'

'Grand!' You should have invited Stan over, he'd have enjoyed some of those!' Mags said, causing Ma and Kathryn to look at one another in wonder. Maybe Mags finally realised that Ma had a life of her own to live and she'd been silly and selfish yesterday by wanting to keep her all to herself. Pa had gone forever and there was no bringing him back.

Ma hugged Mags to her bosom. 'What 'ave I done to deserve this?' she asked, looking puzzled.

'Nothing, you're just being you,' Kathryn smiled as she winked at their mother. She was almost drooling at the mere thought of the breakfast that awaited them. Lately, she was definitely eating for two, her appetite was that good. She'd got over the initial morning sickness and now found herself starving all day long and fancying all manner of things to eat. Some she wouldn't normally fancy, like liver and onions. But Ma had told her that was her body's way of telling her what was missing from her diet.

By the time they'd all eaten breakfast, with Damon and Shaun asking for second helpings, Kathryn and Mags made their way downstairs to the shop where already a small queue had formed outside. As Mags unbolted the door, she almost got knocked over as Mrs Jefferson barged in. 'Sorry, ducks. Me old fella wants his bacon for breakfast.'

'I'll see to you now,' Kathryn said, as she sent Mags to serve another customer who looked as if she had a very large order indeed, judging by the length of the shopping list in her hand and the two large wicker baskets in the crooks of her arms.

They hardly had time to draw a breath all morning, but when the trade began to quieten down and Mags announced she'd make a cup of tea, Kathryn sighed as she heard the front door bell jangle once again.

'Oh, no, are we ever to have any peace and quiet?' She felt angry now as she was so tired, but it turned out to be not a customer but Constable Joseph Hargreaves. His cheeks were ruddy and pinched from the cold and his nose was pink.

'Hello, Constable, anything we can do for you?' she asked composedly, letting out a long breath as her anger slowly dissipated.

'I have some news,' he puffed.

'Hang on a moment.' She turned the sign on the door to 'Closed' and turned the key in the lock. 'We're just about to have a cup of tea and yer look like yer in need of one, am I right?'

He smiled and nodded, then followed her to the back room.

Mags startled when she saw the handsome constable.

'Mags, you can close your mouth and pour an extra cup of tea. P.C. Hargreaves has some news for us.'

The constable placed his helmet on the table. 'It's about O'Shay and Keates. They've been captured and are now in police custody. They're going to be put away for a long time on the charges of abduction of young children, soliciting women as prostitutes, grievous bodily harm, gambling, thieving – the list goes on and on . . .' He smiled.

'That's wonderful!' Kathryn exclaimed. 'How about old man Flook?'

'He's been brought in as well but on a lesser charge. He didn't harm the kids and from what I can see, apart from encouraging them to steal to order, he kept them clothed and fed, so some of that will go in his favour. I think he'll serve a far shorter sentence given his ripe age, if he serves one at all.'

Kathryn nodded, then watched as the policeman's face clouded over. 'What's wrong? There's something else, isn't there?'

He nodded slowly. 'I'm afraid there is. We're holding some-one else at the station who you know.'

Kathryn frowned to think who that person might be. 'Not Jimmy?'

'I'm afraid so. He took matters into his own hands and made threats to O'Shay and punched him in the jaw. O'Shay is threatening to press charges. He has made a bit of a mess of his face.'

'Well I think the old devil deserves it!' Mags said sharply.

'Sssh Mags, the law is the law,' Kathryn said sadly. 'We know what he did to Nick and Dorrie, and I saw what he did to Jess, he almost killed her.'

'Who's Jess when she's at home?' the constable asked.

'She's a former lady of the night who has reformed her ways. She now helps out at the Hanbury Street shelter.'

The constable's eyes widened. 'If she'd agree to speak out that would help to put that evil man and his accomplice away.'

'Oh yes, Keates was involved in all of this,' Kathryn said. 'I didn't know him back then but I caught him watching this shop early one morning. He must have been looking for Nick and Dorrie and then Georgina moved them to her house for safety, but he managed to track them down and got away with Dorrie.'

Joseph Hargreaves nodded and took a sip of his tea. 'Would you like a mince pie, Constable?' Mags asked as she batted her eyelashes, causing Kathryn to smile.

'I would indeed, miss. I've been on a shift since six o'clock this morning and won't be getting to my bed until late tonight. Haven't had time for a break up until now.'

Mags went to fetch the mince pies, leaving Kathryn alone with him. 'What about Jimmy though, he'll have to go to court, won't he?'

'I'm afraid so, miss, and there's a chance he might get a short prison sentence for his behaviour. He'll appear before the judge this afternoon.'

'I have to go to him,' Kathryn said. 'Yer see this is all my fault.'

'Fault, miss? How can that be?'

She was about to tell the constable how Jimmy had made a decision to go off to sea, leaving his brother and sister in the incapable hands of his aunt and uncle, when Mags burst into the room with a selection of mince pies on a china plate. 'Ma says we can have these few as they're not quite up to standard for the customers. One's a bit burnt and the others are broken or odd shapes.'

Good old Ma. 'Thank you, Mags,' Kathryn said, taking the plate from her grasp and offering it to Joseph. 'Take a couple, they're not very big,' she said. He nodded and smiled as he took two.

'I can't see how the whole thing is your fault, miss,' Joseph said, taking a bite and pausing to savour the mouth-watering sweet concoction. 'It wasn't you who punched O'Shay in the face knocking his front teeth out!'

Mags began to giggle. 'Good enough for that old letch! He was 'orrible to us when he called for the rent money, threatening all sorts. And I don't like what he done to those kids neither, making Dorrie little more than a slave and sending Nick up chimneys.'

'I can see why Jimmy did what he did,' the constable said,

'but the law demands that he has to go in front of the judge at two o'clock today.' He took another bite from the pie and closed his eyes as if it was other-worldly.

'Then I shall be there to support him. I think, too, you should contact Jess at the mission.'

Joseph opened his eyes and nodded. 'We will now you've told us, miss.'

'What a carry-on for Christmas Eve though!' Mags exclaimed.

Kathryn was inclined to agree with her.

The court was bustling as Kathryn arrived and took her place in the gallery. The mood was one of gaiety from the people around her, as if watching this spectacle was entertainment for them. First of all, Keates was brought into the dock, looking more dishevelled than usual. He glared at the spectators as his name and the charges were read out.

'How do you plead, guilty or not guilty?' asked the judge.

'Not guilty!' he growled, causing several boos and hisses from the crowd. Something whizzed past Kathryn's head and she realised that folk were throwing rotting fruit and vegetables at him.

'Silence in court!' the judge intervened. 'Anyone else shouting or throwing things will be led away and charged with contempt of court.'

The crowd fell silent as Keates was led away to be dealt with at a later date.

Then O'Shay was led to the dock to address the court. His jaw looked severely swollen and bruised and he winced several times during the proceedings. Kathryn glanced to her right and noticed Jess was there, staring at him. No doubt if he pleaded not guilty she'd be required to give evidence against him at a future hearing, but to Kathryn's astonishment he pleaded guilty. The judge peered at O'Shay over his gold-rimmed spectacles.

'Fergus O'Shay, you shall remain in custody and be brought back to this court at a later date for sentencing for your crimes of child stealing, under section 56 of the Offences Against the Person Act of 1861, soliciting of prostitutes, illegal gambling and various acts of theft depriving good upstanding members of the public of their honest, hard-earned property.' He glanced at the two police constables who were flanking the prisoner. 'Take him down!'

There was a huge cheer from the crowd, but it was not over yet as Flook was led into the dock, looking very sheepish and much older than Kathryn remembered.

'Thomas Archibald Flook,' the judge said, 'you have been caught in the act of running a gang of young thieves from an unoccupied property just off Commercial and Flower and Dean Streets. From my understanding your dealings have been going on for at least one year, and all this shall be taken into account. However, several of the young children have spoken up for you with regards to your kindness towards them when they were otherwise destitute, so all of this shall be taken into consideration. How do you plead?'

Flook, who had been twisting his hands with apprehension, looked up at the judge with trepidation in his eyes as he answered, 'Guilty, Your Honour.'

'Is there anything you'd like to say in your defence, Mr Flook?'

'Only that I never sought to harm any of the children in my care, Your Honour. The thieving kind of happened by accident when I run out of food one day and carried on from there. It was my aim to help those young kids . . .'

'Let old Flook go home!' a woman shouted from the crowd.

'I can't do that, madam!' the judge explained. 'What this man has done is illegal no matter how good his intentions were. You shall be brought back at a later date after Christmas for sentencing. Meanwhile you shall be held in the cells. The fact that so many people, including the children themselves, speak highly of you, shall surely shorten your sentence. Take him away!' he instructed the two constables who had by now returned.

Finally, Jimmy was brought to the dock, looking nervous. He glanced over and locked eyes with Kathryn, causing her heartbeat to quicken. She smiled at him and hoped that would reassure him.

'James Dawkins . . .' the judge began. 'It has come to my

attention that on the afternoon of December the 23rd last, you entered the property of one Fergus O'Shay and a fracas began, ending up with you throwing a punch at Mr O'Shay and knocking out two of his front teeth . . .' There were ripples of laughter from the court. The judge turned to the crowd and shouted, 'Silence in court! You have all been warned!' Turning back to Jimmy, he carried on: 'However, your intentions in leading the police to Mr O'Shay were good insomuch as your younger brother and sister had been abducted by the man, so there was, in my opinion, good grounds for provocation, though you should have left everything to the police and not taken matters into your own hands. As I am in a good mood today, I have decided not to take this matter further and you are free to go, but I am warning you, if anything else like that happens again then next time I won't be so benevolent.' There was a huge cheer around the court room which caused the judge to smile and this time he didn't even bother to silence the crowd as he stood and walked away.

Kathryn could hardly believe her ears as she rushed towards Jimmy, jostling through the crowds that stood in her way.

'Oh, Jimmy!' she said, falling into his arms. 'I'm so glad you're a free man!' Tears streamed down her cheeks as he embraced her and by the wracking of his shoulders she realised he was crying too.

Chapter Twenty-Four

There was much merriment back at the store when Kathryn walked in with Jimmy. Georgina and her Josiah stood in the corner as Nick and Dorrie rushed out to greet him.

'Jimmy, are you going back to sea?' Nick asked, not realising his elder sibling had just escaped a short jail sentence.

'No, Nick. I'm afraid you're saddled with me for a long time yet.' He glanced at Georgina and Josiah. 'You will see me regular every day but I want you to continue living with these good people. You like living with them, don't you?' He knelt down so he was at eye level with Nick.

'Oh yes, they're the best. Aunt Georgina makes us cups of hot chocolate when it's cold at night and Uncle Josiah takes us to the park. And the house is the best I've ever lived in!'

Georgina and Josiah glanced at one another and smiled.

'Well I don't like living there!' Dorrie shouted, causing the room to fall silent. Mags and Ma stood there, mouths agape, and Kathryn could hardly believe her ears as Dorrie went on to say, 'I don't like living there – I love it, silly!' That caused everyone to laugh as Jimmy hugged her.

Then going over to Georgina and Josiah he said, 'If it's all right then, I'd be more than happy for you to adopt my brother and sister, they deserve a good home.'

They both nodded with tears in their eyes.

Ma suddenly clapped her hands. 'Time to shut up shop then and get on with the festivities! Mags, go and bolt the door, but stay there to check as Stanley is due at any moment. We don't want a crowd suddenly surging through the door, they've all had more than enough time to buy their Christmas provisions.'

'Yes, Ma!' Mags shouted, as she ran to the front door.

They all followed Ma upstairs where the smell of cinnamon and orange permeated their senses. 'I've just sliced up some Christmas cake and made a rum punch for the adults and egg nog for the children,' she said brightly. 'I'm roasting a ham for later. Then we'll all go to Midnight Mass.'

Mr Bailey, who was dressed in his best suit, stood near the punch bowl with a cup ready in his hand.

'My, my, you're keen, Mr Bailey,' Ma said, with a twinkle in her eye.

The old man chuckled. 'Yes, first in line when I can be. Now where's Shaun? He promised he'd read to me later. We're on the final chapter of *A Christmas Carol*.'

'I'm not sure where he is,' Ma said.

Kathryn looked out the kitchen window and saw Shaun

on the cobbled yard below, helping Stan in with his horse and cart. 'He's outside, Ma, helping Stan stable his horse. It's just started snowing, too.'

'At least we're all together, cosy and warm,' Ma said. 'Hope the snow doesn't get too thick though as I want to get to church tonight.'

'If we can't go, we can always try the Christmas Day service tomorrow,' Kathryn reassured her. She turned suddenly to find Jimmy behind her. The sight robbed her of her breath. It was the way he was looking at her, with such intensity. He closed the kitchen door behind them, leaving the others outside.

'I need to see you alone, Kathryn,' he said, with a gleam in his eyes.

'Well, here we are . . .'

He moved closer and for a moment she thought he'd kiss her. But then Damon and Rosie burst into the room. 'Me want egg nog!' Rosie said.

'Me too!' Damon shouted behind her.

'Ma's serving some up out there, you two.' She smiled at them.

She shooed them out and was about to turn back when Shaun entered the kitchen. 'This is hopeless, we'll have to speak later, maybe on the way to church,' she whispered in Jimmy's ear.

'Very well,' he winked. 'Later then . . .'

Kathryn's heart hammered all evening every time she

looked at Jimmy, but she tried to get into the spirit of things by singing Christmas songs with the others. Mags read a couple of ghost stories and Mr Bailey spoke about the old days at the shop.

The snow was now falling thick and fast and people could be seen scurrying home on the pavements outside, some slip sliding away. A policeman walked past the store and looked up at the window; Kathryn wondered if it was Constable Hargreaves, but she couldn't tell as it was now dark and he was only a silhouette beneath the lamplight.

The ham was sliced up by Stan and dished on to the plates by Ma and passed around the table, everyone helping themselves to boiled potatoes, peas and shredded cabbage. There was even a sweet pickle delicacy from the shop that went down well as an accompaniment. And when they were all full to bursting and thought they could eat no more, Ma brought out one of her infamous sherry trifles causing Stan to rub his tummy with delight.

'This baby is going to be a right bruiser if I carry on scoffing so much,' Kathryn laughed.

'Aw well, if you can't eat well when you're pregnant, when can you at all?' Ma reasoned.

They completed their grand meal with a cup of tea and a small slice of chocolate Yule log, then donned their warm coats, hats and mufflers for church. It had stopped snowing. Mags offered to stay behind with Rosie and Damon as it was well past their bedtimes, and Nick and Dorrie remained too, while the rest trooped to church. The children and Mags would go in the morning.

Ma and Stan strode out of the shop first, arm in arm, with Mr Bailey and Shaun not far behind them, and Georgina and Josiah behind those, while Jimmy and Kathryn took their time. Every so often Shaun scooped up a snowball to throw at some unsuspecting statue or building. Everything was so magical and glistening white, it was almost as if night had become day, but so cold on their feet and legs.

And in the distance, there was the church with its spire calling all to worship.

'I need to ask you that something now,' Jimmy said, taking Kathryn to one side and leaning against the church railings.

She looked into his glittering eyes, holding his gaze for a long while, and in that moment she saw in the way he was looking at her so tenderly the immense love he had for her.

'Kathryn, I know this isn't the best start in life for you, but I promise if you'll take me as your husband I will be the best one I can possibly be for you. I admit I was angry with you when I returned, especially when I found out you were having another man's child, but I know I'll be a good father for your child and love him or her as much as I love you . . . If I can't have you then I don't want anyone else, you are and have always been the only woman for me. Please, will you marry me?'

He knelt in the snow as a few flakes fluttered down, and produced a small velvet box from his pocket. He opened it to display a ruby ring surrounded by several small diamonds. 'I bought this on my travels in Morocco. It cost me a month's wages, but you're worth it. Please tell me you'll marry me?'

She looked down at the man who wanted to make her his wife and knew without a shadow of a doubt he would be a good husband and father. 'Yes, yes, Jimmy. I'd be very happy to be your wife,' she answered breathlessly, through her tears.

He stood and embraced her tightly. 'You don't know how happy you've made me. I've waited so long. I better not kiss you here in case someone sees!'

'Oh, go ahead and kiss me anyway . . .' she said, throwing caution to the wind. 'Make an honest woman out of me!' Then his lips were on hers, and though a sprinkle of snowflakes fell on their heads, they were too busy to notice it . . .

The Matchgirl

A heartwarming saga, from the eBook bestselling author of *The Workhouse Waif*

Sixteen-year-old Lottie Perkins has an important decision to make . . .

Conditions at the match factory she works at are dire. The girls get treated badly by the management and there is a severe risk to their health. But then a young journalist, Annie Besant, begins asking questions.

Will Lottie and the other girls welcome her help, even when it could cost them their jobs – and their livelihoods . . .

Available now in paperback, eBook and audio.

Quercus

The Workhouse Waif

**Destined to a life of poverty, this little girl
has bigger plans in life . . .**

After the death of her father in a mining accident, Megan
and her family had no choice but to move to the local
workhouse. Separated from her mother and five siblings,
young Megan must learn how to stand on her own two feet.

But one day she meets a young boy who's stealing apples
from the local market, and together they set out on a path
to find a better life for themselves . . .

**Perfect for fans of Dilly Court, Katie Flynn and
Nadine Dorries.**

Available now in paperback, eBook and audio.

Quercus